one big happy family

BOOKS BY SAM VICKERY

One Last Second
My Only Child
Save My Daughter
Her Silent Husband
The Guilty Mother
The Child at My Door
The Perfect Baby

The Promise
One More Tomorrow
Keep It Secret
The Things You Cannot See
Where There's Smoke

NOVELLAS
What You Never Knew

one big happy family

SAM VICKERY

bookouture

Published by Bookouture in 2025

An imprint of Storyfire Ltd.
Carmelite House
50 Victoria Embankment
London EC4Y 0DZ

www.bookouture.com

The authorised representative in the EEA is Hachette Ireland
8 Castlecourt Centre
Dublin 15 D15 XTP3
Ireland
(email: info@hbgi.ie)

ISBN: 978-1-83525-860-6
eBook ISBN: 978-1-83525-859-0

For my stepdad, Smudge, whose support and kindness are never-ending.

ONE

CARRIE

The smell of the sea air has always brought me comfort. Reminded me of a time in my childhood when life was simpler. When I was free from the worries and obligations of being an adult. I stood on the shoreline, breathing in the scent of salt and seaweed, goosepimples prickling my bare calves as the chilly tide rushed over my feet. I'd kicked off my shoes, dipping my toes into the icy water, desperate to pretend that it was summer – to put an end to the darkness that this past six months had brought with it. I longed for some hope, something brighter to focus on.

When I'd picked up the kids from school and driven here, I'd expected the beach to be deserted, but we'd arrived to a half-full car park, finding several other families spread out on blankets, eating sandwiches and chocolate bars and taking advantage of the promise of spring on this first warm day of March, and I'd wondered if perhaps I wasn't the only one who needed this. Who was ready to turn my back on a nightmarish winter.

I sighed, shuffling my feet uncomfortably, the pretence now becoming painful. My toes were turning numb as the sea splashed over them, and I stepped back onto the warm pebbles, feeling instant relief as I rubbed my mottled skin against them. I watched the sun glinting on the surface of the water, which was quickly changing from a pretty green-blue to a choppier grey as the sky morphed from clear to cloudy. Tension radiated through my body, ruining the peace that should have come.

To my left, Maisy and Ava were playing contentedly, Maisy encouraging Ava to fill the blue plastic bucket with sand, smiling at her little sister's clumsy attempts to scoop some up on her pink spade. Maisy caught me looking and smiled conspiratorially as we watched Ava toddle a few steps, then bend down low to tip the almost empty spade into the bucket. I gave a watery smile, turning to look behind me to where Tommy was sitting, wishing he'd come and join us. He was sitting amongst a family camped out in a spot twenty or so metres up the beach, his back turned towards me in what I was sure was a conscious gesture – a message intended for me. I watched his friend lean in and say something, and heard the familiar laughter of my twelve-year-old son, the sound triggering emotions in me I had to fight to suppress. When had he last laughed so freely with me?

I bit my lip, feeling my eyes sting with tears I refused to acknowledge. My gaze burned into his back, as if he might feel it, might turn and see me, remember the way things had once been between us. That he might realise how hard I was trying to show him how much I cared – how I would do anything for him. It broke my heart that he couldn't see it.

He'd been moody when I said we were coming here after school, too cool to want to join me and his little sisters to come and make sandcastles and paddle in the gentle waves. He'd brought a book with him and slumped down, refusing to help, even when I told him he could use the hammer to whack the poles of the windbreak in – a job he usually loved.

I'd hoped he might open up and tell me what was bothering him once the girls were occupied in their play. It wasn't easy carving out these moments for the two of us – not with his sisters to take care of, my work, the mountain of tasks and worries that filled my mind – but I tried. I did my best. But when I'd set Maisy and Ava up with their buckets and spades and come to sit next to him, he'd acted like I was carrying some contagious disease, like my proximity was repulsive, and my hopes of getting anywhere with him had vanished. I'd been on the verge of snapping, shouting at him that I wasn't a fucking mind-reader, I couldn't make this better if he wouldn't talk to me, when the other family arrived and he'd recognised his friend from school. It had been the first time he'd cracked a smile all day, and despite my desire to tell him to stay with me, *talk* to me, I'd relented and let him go and join them.

I tried to smile now, though it was hard when I felt everything slipping out of my grasp. But I had worked too hard to let that happen. I wasn't finished fighting yet. Watching him laughing and joking, I wondered if I should try again. Invite him to come and join in with his sisters. To spend some time with us – his *family*. I sighed, already knowing what his response would be if I dared to go over there, how he would accuse me of embarrassing him again. Or worse.

Maybe if Maisy went to ask him? The two of them had a bond like no other. Perhaps he'd say yes if *she* were the one to approach him. It had to be worth a try, or today would have been a wasted effort. The thought of heading home with him still not speaking to me was intolerable. Grasping on to the idea, I turned back to the girls with a smile.

Maisy was sitting staring out to sea, the blue bucket lying abandoned on its side.

'Maisy,' I said, frowning as I looked from left to right. 'Where's Ava? Where's your sister, darling?' My heartbeat sped up as I moved towards her, scanning the beach.

Maisy bowed her head, and I rushed barefoot across the sharp stones, bending down low and grabbing her shoulder.

'Maisy!' I repeated, giving her a little shake. 'Where's Ava? She was just here! Where did she go?' I cried.

Maisy's face was blank, and I couldn't understand why she wasn't speaking, why she wouldn't answer me. I had barely turned away for more than a few moments. I'd been less than twenty feet away. Ava couldn't have gone far. I stood up, casting my gaze up and down the beach, panic igniting in my chest, instant and visceral.

'Ava!' I shouted, turning in a circle, searching, seeing nothing. '*Ava!*' I snapped my head back to where Tommy sat, hungrily searching, hoping she had toddled up the beach to be with her brother, but he was still laughing with his friend, and there was no sign of her.

All around me were people reading, talking, laughing. Children playing noisily. I rushed up the beach in the opposite direction from where I'd been watching Tommy, desperate to catch a glimpse of her but finding no sign. 'My baby!' I tried to scream, but the words were barely a whisper.

I ran back to Maisy, adrenaline pounding through me. 'Maisy, *please*! Your sister is two years old! She can't be alone on the beach. Where did she go? You must have seen something.'

Wordlessly, she continued to stare out to sea. My gaze followed hers, a trickle of ice running down my spine.

'No,' I whispered, watching the water as if I might see Ava's curly hair bobbing on the surface. 'No!' I screamed, and this time I saw people starting to stare, to realise what was happening.

'Help me! Please, help me find my baby! Oh God! Maisy, don't move... don't...' I couldn't finish the sentence.

My heart was pounding so hard it felt as if it might explode as I ran full pelt into the water, diving under, the salt burning my eyes, my hands grasping at pebbles and rocks as I silently prayed to make contact with Ava's tiny body. The image of her cherubic little face burned into my mind, her shining gold ringlets, her bright blue eyes.

Her sweet voice seemed to call to me from somewhere deep and dark, and I kicked hard, the pressure in my ears building as I flailed desperately, needing to find her. Running out of air, I surfaced, screaming her name, choking on the brine, gasping, then diving again. I couldn't lose her. I *had* to do this. I couldn't stop, would never, *never* stop. Anything to protect her, to keep her safe.

Ignoring the burning in my lungs, I kicked my legs out, the cold like knives jabbing into my skin, my hands grasping nothing but water.

I stood, my head barely scraping the surface now, and looked back to the beach, shocked at how much distance I'd covered. A crowd had gathered on the shoreline. Someone had their arm wrapped tight around Maisy, and though I couldn't make out the face from so far away, I suddenly felt afraid that it might be *her*... Leah. The words the last time we'd spoken had made my instincts flash up on high alert. She'd made it clear what she wanted... what she had planned for my family.

I blinked away the salt water, turning away from them all, seeing nothing but the grey sky building overhead, the sea turning rough and unwelcoming, and as I dived again, stretching out my fingers into the dark, empty ocean, I wondered how I could have let this happen.

TWO

My body was convulsing, the shivering out of my control, my muscles ineffective against the crashing waves as the wind whipped around my frozen head, and yet I couldn't bear to stop my search, my eyes raw and stinging as I dipped my head once more beneath the surface of the water, diving low until I felt the seabed with the palms of my outstretched hands. It was so murky, the building storm churning up the sand and seaweed, filling my vision with grit, a dull impenetrable brown that was impossible to navigate. She could be there, just out of reach, and I'd never know. She *must* be in the sea. How long had it been? Three minutes? Five? It felt like for ever, and yet no time at all. Would she even be alive if I reached her now? I didn't want to think of it.

My lungs burned with the need to take a breath, and I battled against them, determined to use every last second, kicking harder as I grasped at the nothingness ahead. I felt the sudden warmth of something – a hand against my leg – and let out a bubble of a scream, leaving me with nothing in my lungs as my heart swelled with a hope born of delirium. She had found me! My sweet, clever girl! But the grip was too strong, too wide, and I felt an arm grasp my waist, forcefully dragging me upwards, away from where I most needed to be.

As we broke the surface, the rain pelting in tiny stinging bullets against my face, I saw who had grabbed me, who had given me such hope only to steal it out from under me. The man – in his thirties, fit and muscular, with glistening black skin and even darker eyes – was breathing hard, one arm still clamped around my sodden T-shirt as he began towing me towards the crowd on the beach.

'You hold on to me, darlin',' he instructed. 'Everyone's searching for your little one. But you need to come back now.'

'No!' I spluttered and found my voice was raspy, the word painful. How much water had I swallowed? 'I can't stop—' I broke off, coughing, shaking my head violently as I tried to prise him off of me. 'I can't!'

Ignoring me, he continued to swim towards the tiny silhouettes in the distance, and despite my protests, I found I didn't have the energy to fight him. My body seemed to give in, betraying me. *Her.*

I felt the hot sting of tears clouding my vision and through them saw the crowds of people in the water, on the beach, the blue flashing lights on the road beyond. I had known the police would come, but I didn't want to see them, to talk to them. It would make it too real somehow. And, I thought, instinctively leaning into the warmth of the stranger as my body shook with violent shivers, I was afraid I might say the wrong thing. That they would find out the secrets I'd been keeping, and somehow the blame would fall on me.

The stranger who'd had her arm around my daughter – a much older woman than Leah, as it turned out – was talking to a police officer nearby. Listening to her relaying what she'd seen was setting my nerves on edge. I knew I should go over and thank her, but I couldn't move, my body convulsing as I sat on the wooden bench.

The paramedic adjusted the foil blanket tighter around me.
'Slow, steady breaths,' he said, his voice gentle as he tried to get
me to look him in the eye.

I couldn't stop staring out at the water. Above the horizon,
the sky was turning darker with frustrating speed. It would be
night soon. The thought of Ava out there was agony.
Unbearable.

'Carrie! Oh my God, what's happened?'

I looked up at the panicked voice to find Shannon, the
receptionist who worked at the A&E desk at my hospital,
rushing towards me. What was she doing here?

She was dressed immaculately as usual, her blonde shoul-
der-length bob smooth and shiny, her pink lipstick applied to
perfection. At the best of times while I was rushing around the
hospital ward with my hair in a messy bun, make-up the last
thing on my mind, she made me look scruffy, but sitting here
with my wet hair tangled and stringy, my eyes swollen and red
from the salt water, the contrast between us was no doubt startling. She'd been a good friend to me since she'd taken the position six months ago, and her kindness made me forgive the fact
that she always made me look like a bag lady.

'It's Ava,' I whispered, gripping her hand, grateful to see a
familiar face. 'She... she's *missing*. She was playing, and then
she was just gone.'

Shannon's eyes widened. 'Oh, Carrie, no!' She glanced
down at me, taking in my appearance. 'You're soaked! You don't
think...' She gasped. 'She can't have gone in the water?'

I pressed my lips together, unable to answer, to say there
was a strong possibility that she could have drowned. Wordlessly, she slumped down beside me, and I felt her hand
tighten around my own as if I'd spoken the awful words out
loud.

'Mrs Gold?'

I looked up to see a female police constable standing above

me. She'd tried to talk to me a few minutes earlier, but the paramedic had told her firmly to back off while he saw to me first.

Shannon shook her head. 'She goes by Dr Gold,' she corrected quietly.

'Are you sending boats out?' I asked, panic filling my voice as I leaned forward. 'She might have drifted. She could be miles away by now!' Shannon's hand anchored me, and I held on to her, fighting against my urge to run straight back to the ocean.

'Dr Gold, I'm PC Mayville. I just need to ask you some questions,' the officer said. 'Your daughter is two, is that right?'

'Yes.' I nodded. 'Her birthday was in December. She can't swim, but she can float on her back. We taught her last year when we went to Spain. She could still be okay – she could be out there waiting to be found!' I cried, though I knew the reality was that floating in a calm swimming pool with a parent by her side was a completely different ballgame to remembering what to do in a freezing-cold ocean with waves and fear to contend with. I shook away the image of my baby being buffeted around like a ragdoll out there.

PC Mayville gave a sombre nod, and I got the awful feeling she was humouring me. 'The coastguard is already out there, and several more boats are en route. Can you tell me when you last saw Ava?'

Her words seemed to echo around my brain as I stared past her to the water, unable to see the coastguard. I looked from left to right, watching the hordes of police shepherding the public off the beach. Several of them seemed to be arguing that they wanted to keep helping with the search, and I wondered why they couldn't.

Shannon jiggled my arm. 'Carrie, the lady asked when you last saw Ava. Do you remember?'

'I... I don't know. We got to the beach just before four, and then they were playing for a while, maybe an hour or so. She and Maisy were on the sand...' I said, looking down to where

Maisy was sitting now on the pebbles nearby. I frowned, realising she was wearing an unfamiliar blue fleece, and I wondered who it belonged to. I shook my head. 'They weren't right next to the water – probably twenty feet back from the shore. More even. I was distracted just for a moment, looking at Tommy—' I broke off. 'Where *is* Tommy?' I whispered, numbness creeping over me.

PC Mayville gave a reassuring smile. 'Oh, your son? He's gone home with his friend from school. The mum said he's welcome to spend the night; she's given me a phone number for you to let them know later. Don't worry – she didn't tell Tommy anything; said she'd keep him busy until Ava was found.'

I nodded, knowing the mother was only trying to help but feeling irritated that she'd taken over without bothering to ask my opinion. I didn't even know the woman! Didn't she realise I needed my children close right now, needed to see that they were safe?

Shannon nodded. 'That sounds like it's for the best. You don't want him being caught up in this – it will scare the life out of him. He's a sensitive boy,' she added, looking at the policewoman.

I held my tongue, though I wanted to argue that if anyone knew what was best for Tommy, it was *me*, not some random woman, not the police and *not* Shannon. I didn't want him to hear about this and be frightened. Shannon's wide eyes met mine, and I had to remind myself that she didn't have children of her own. She couldn't possibly put herself in my shoes right now. She broke her gaze, looking back to the policewoman.

'So,' PC Mayville continued, 'how long was Ava out of your sight?'

I shrugged, wishing I could remember the details. It all felt so cloudy now, and I wasn't sure of anything. 'She could only have been gone half a minute at most when I turned around and noticed her missing,' I said, though I wasn't certain that was true.

'You didn't hear anything? Screaming? Splashing?'

'No,' I whispered.

'You seem pretty certain she went into the water. Did you see anything suspicious? Anyone hanging around who made you uneasy?'

I shook my head, looking down at my lap.

The officer nodded and wrote something on her clipboard. 'Do you have a photograph of Ava you can show me? A recent one?'

I nodded blankly, then frowned. 'Oh... my phone – it was in my bag... I don't know where it went. I left it on the beach...' I scanned the pebbles, then spotted the burgundy leather satchel where I'd abandoned it.

The policewoman called to a colleague, and he jogged down to retrieve it. He came back up and handed it to me with a sad little smile.

I rummaged inside, pulling the phone out and flicking to the photographs. The image of my daughter's face filling the screen made a wave of nausea hit me, and I let out a moan, pressing my hands to my face. 'I can't...' I whispered through my fingers.

Shannon leaned closer. 'Shall I, Carrie?'

I felt her reach to take the phone clamped in my hand, pressed to my cheek, and shook my head. *I* was Ava's mother. I needed to be stronger than this. I had to do better – for her.

Swallowing, I lowered my hands, turning the phone to show PC Mayville. 'This was taken last week,' I said, my voice shaking. 'She's wearing the same light pink dress today, but with a navy cardigan, and her hair was in bunches with pink plastic heart-shaped ties. She had red-and-white trainers on... Velcro ones. She refused to let me take them off – she hates the feel of sand between her toes,' I explained, remembering the argument that had almost erupted when I suggested it. 'And she has a little cut above her right eye.'

'Oh?'

'From tripping into the corner of the coffee table,' I explained, wishing I hadn't admitted the detail.

'Right.' The policewoman gave a short nod. 'Can you send that picture to me now and I'll circulate it, along with Ava's description, to everyone who needs to see it.'

She gave me the phone number, and I followed her instructions robotically, then watched as she typed out a message.

'I've sent that to my supervisor, DCI Farrows. He's back at the station getting hold of the CCTV as we speak, so he'll be waiting on this information.'

She put her phone back in her pocket.

'We're covering all bases,' she said, her voice soft, as if she didn't want to send me into a panic, though that horse had clearly already bolted. 'I want to reassure you that no stone will be left unturned. Like I said, the coastguard is out now, and support is on the way to continue searching... out there.' She spoke as if her words had conjured the lifeless image of my toddler's body being dragged from the ocean to the forefront of her mind. 'And we've already started combing the area looking for anywhere Ava might have wandered off to.' She gave a deep sigh. 'Then' – she hesitated, looking from me to Shannon, as if I couldn't handle what she might say next and would need my friend's support – 'there's the possibility that someone has taken her – either believing her to be lost or...'

'Kidnapped her,' Shannon finished flatly, her lips pressing together in a white line.

'Well, it's one avenue we need to rule out,' the PC answered, her voice tight and uncomfortable. 'Is there a chance someone you know could have taken her? Is her father around?'

I was silent as I thought of Jimmy, how he would react when

he heard what had happened. I needed to call him. To hear his voice.

'He's in the picture, but he's away with work, isn't he, Carrie?' Shannon said, though she didn't wait for me to correct her. 'He works on the oil rigs, so Carrie does the lion's share of parenting, but you're expecting him home in six weeks, right?'

I wished she would stop talking. I could see that she thought she was helping, but she was only making it all the more complicated. I didn't want to have to discuss this now, not with her lingering, *listening*. Not when I knew she was about to realise I'd only told her a selection of the story since we became friends six months ago.

I cleared my throat, aware that I had to say something before PC Mayville left and discovered that Shannon's version of events wasn't quite true. I couldn't imagine that would shine a good light on me.

'Shannon's mistaken,' I said, my voice clear and strong now, leaving no room for argument. 'The children's father and I are separated, going through a divorce. I haven't been in contact with him for a few days. And I don't know who you're thinking of, Shannon, but Jimmy's a lawyer. He doesn't work on oil rigs.' I studiously avoided glancing in her direction as I wrapped the foil blanket tighter around my shoulders, looking solely at the police officer.

'Do you have a number we can contact him on?' she asked.

I recited it from memory, then looked up his new landline number on my phone, reading it out to her along with the address of his new house.

She gave a nod, then glanced over her shoulder to where a man was giving instructions to a group of people in rescue boats. She looked back to me. 'Thanks for this. I think the best thing you can do right now is head home and wait by the phone. Any updates and you'll be the first to know.'

'I can't do that.' I shook my head, my eyes drifting back to the dark sea, the sliver of muted orange sun almost completely sunk below the horizon now, distorted by the haze of rain that was being blown to the east. It would be dark in twenty minutes. Maybe less.

'I understand.' She bowed her head as if she was sorry for my loss, and I wanted to scream at her not to give up, not to think it was over. I couldn't bear the finality of the gesture.

'Please excuse me,' she said. She turned, walking over to the man in charge of the boats, and I felt Shannon, silent beside me, release my hand and turn in her seat to scrutinise me.

'Carrie,' she began. 'I think you might be in shock... I think you might have told the policewoman the wrong thing just then... You're not separated, not getting divorced. You were telling me only yesterday about how Jimmy sent you that sweet love letter from the rig. You said you couldn't wait to see him.'

I shook my head. 'No, I didn't.'

'You *did*. I think we should get the paramedics to take you in to be checked. Did you hit your head out there?'

I met her eyes, seeing confusion, *fear*. For six months, I'd made sure every meet-up had been just the two of us. I'd kept her at arm's length, never quite ready to introduce her to my children, bring her fully into my world – not when I had so much to deal with in my personal life. Instead, I'd let myself enjoy having something that was just mine; a friendship that had blossomed in the rare quiet moments in the staff room. Our girls' nights, drinking wine, talking about nonsense that held no meaning. Me sharing only the details I was comfortable with her knowing about the children, my life with their father, my own feelings, without complicating it with all the parts she didn't need to know. It had been exactly the escape I needed.

I pressed my lips together, turning to where Maisy was sitting silently a few feet away, her scrawny arms wrapped tightly around her knees as she looked down at her pink jelly shoes.

Shannon followed my gaze. 'Let me take her home,' she said softly. 'She can't stay out here; it's getting cold, and she's had a shock too. I'll make her some dinner.'

I watched as my daughter dug her fingers through the rubber holes in the pattern of her shoes, feeling the rain trickling down the back of my neck, making me shudder. 'She should be with me,' I said, reaching to lift Maisy into my arms. I hitched her onto my hip, though at nine years old, she was far too big to be carried.

Shannon stood up. 'Please, Carrie, let me help you.'

I shook my head. 'You can't,' I whispered. '*Nobody* can.'

I turned, leaving Shannon to stare after me, and walked back down to the shore as the next group of boats fanned out.

They would never find my baby out there.

THREE

LEAH

I lifted the sweet-smelling apple-and-cinnamon muffins from the oven, then set them down on the cooling rack I'd placed ready on the new oak counter we'd had fitted just last month. My mouth watered, but I turned away, picking up my mug of peppermint tea and taking a sip, reminding myself that these weren't for me – they were for the children.

I was enjoying the role of stepmother far more than the fairy tales I'd grown up on would have led me to believe possible. Not that we were married yet, but the weight of the princess-cut diamond on my finger was a pleasant reminder that a wedding wasn't far off. But as much as domestic bliss seemed to suit me, I didn't want to become the type of woman who picked at the kids' leftovers, steadily losing my waist along with my self-respect. I wanted to keep my man's eyes firmly trained on me, never giving them a reason to wander, to imagine the grass might be greener elsewhere. If his ex had made that commitment, who knows what might have happened between them. Men were fickle creatures, and the key to success in a relationship was remembering that.

I took another swig of my tea to dissipate my craving for the delicious-smelling baked goods and glanced at the clock on the kitchen wall, wondering why Jimmy wasn't back yet. It was getting late, and we had to leave to go and pick up the children soon. I didn't want to turn up late and have Carrie make out we didn't care, or that we'd forgotten them. I knew she'd love the opportunity to point the finger at me, to make not-so-subtle digs, comparing herself to me in Jimmy's earshot, pathetically letting him know the door was still open – he only had to come to his senses and she'd be there to welcome him back. She didn't seem to realise he was so much happier with me than he'd ever been with her.

Leaving the muffins to cool, I pushed open the back door, stepping over a puddle on the patio, taking the paving-stone path over the lawn to check that the new trampoline was ready for their arrival. It was almost dark now and they'd be here too late to enjoy it tonight, but first thing tomorrow, I planned to bring them out here and let them go wild, let off the steam they built up at school all week, not to mention living up to the high expectations of their unpleasant mother when they got home.

While I'd been baking, the skies had opened, drenching the black fabric, leaving it glossy beneath the twinkling fairy lights I'd wound round the trunk of the oak tree, but there were no more storms predicted, and tomorrow looked set to be warm with a much-needed breeze – my ideal kind of day. I planned to picnic on the lawn and make paper kites with Maisy. I'd asked Jimmy to get the sand table out ready for little Ava. And Tommy was going to love the *Star Wars* Lego set I'd bought for him – borrowing Jimmy's credit card, of course.

I'd already prepared myself for the awkward handover. It never got easier. If I went with Jimmy to pick up the kids, Carrie would pretend I didn't exist, but on the occasions I had to go to get them in his stead, she was visibly livid. There had been a couple of times I'd worried she might not even let me take them, but if Jimmy didn't get home soon, I'd have no choice but to go alone. Maybe his meeting had dragged on longer than anticipated, I thought, picking a few dead heads off the winter jasmine bush that was nearing the end of its bloom, the pretty yellow flowers turning brown, carpeting the lawn beneath it. Sometimes it was well into the evening before he made it home, but I tried not to resent him working hard, and I relished the time I got to spend with his children, who were quickly beginning to feel like my own. I loved having one-on-one time to bond with them, and I didn't want to miss these opportunities. I looked up at the sky, the clouds still too thick to see any stars, and smiled as I pictured how they'd react when they saw all the treats I'd prepared for them.

Heading back inside, I glanced again at the clock, knowing barely any time had passed since I'd last looked at it. I'd never imagined when I'd been working extra shifts at the bar, having every man who walked through the door ask me out, or at the very least let their eyes roam over my body, that I would ever feel insecure when it came to a man. And yet, I was shocked to realise how fragile I'd become since moving in with Jimmy six months ago. I'd been confident – no, cocky, in fact – a twenty-four-year-old with the world at my feet, and I'd enjoyed the power I had. Not that I'd slept around. But I *could* have. I had seen it written on the expressions of too many men to ignore the knowledge that I was exactly what they wanted. I thought I was what Jimmy wanted too.

My gaze drifted up to the clock again and I snapped my head away, picking up a cloth to wipe the counter down, irritated that this was what he'd done to me. That I'd become the type of girl who waited around for a man. He should have stepped out to send a message if he was going to be late, at the very least.

As if in answer to my prayers, the landline began to ring out in the hallway, making me jump. I'd forgotten we even *had* a landline – couldn't remember the last time anyone had called on it. Maybe Jimmy had lost his phone and needed help. I wouldn't swallow his excuses easily – and yet I longed to hear his voice.

Dropping the cloth, I darted out to answer it. 'Hello?'

'Is he there? Is he back yet?'

I tensed, recognising Carrie's voice, hating the implication that she knew he'd been out – perhaps even with her.

'Jimmy isn't available right now,' I replied, annoyed that rather than sounding commanding and clipped as I'd intended, my voice only emerged as juvenile and high-pitched. Carrie never failed to deliver a condescending, withering remark, but then she did have nearly twenty years on me – plenty of time to hone those skills.

'Leah, for fuck's sake! I need to speak to him *now!*' she yelled.

Something about the way she'd lost her composure in an instant, the panic she was doing nothing to conceal, despite always holding herself so stiffly in my presence, made the hairs rise on my arms.

'What's going on?' I asked quietly. 'Has something happened?'

'I don't have time to explain this to *you*,' she spat, the emphasis falling heavily, trying to make me feel small and inconsequential as she always did. 'Is he there or not?'

I bit back a retort, too worried about what could have happened to rise to her bait. 'He's working late.'

She made a scoffing noise. 'Of *course* he is. Got a new secretary, has he? Well, the minute he gets back, have him call me. Do you understand?'

I didn't appreciate being ordered around, nor the way she implied that he would play away with his secretary when he had me waiting at home. Carrie had worked long hours during their relationship, always putting her career first. She'd made it clear that her patients were her priority, and if that meant letting down her husband, cancelling plans she'd made with the children because she felt she couldn't walk away from the hospital, couldn't bear to leave her colleagues to deal with the never-ending hordes of people arriving in ambulances, then so be it.

I understood the pull she must have felt, the inability to just go home at the end of her shift when there was still so much to get through, but that was exactly the reason she should have made a choice a long time ago. Medicine, especially the unpredictable nature of life as an accident and emergency doctor, wasn't a suitable career for a mother. It wasn't fair on the children to always have to come second to her work. And poor Jimmy had taken up a place so low in her priorities he barely even registered. It was inevitable that their marriage had fallen apart. She'd spent years neglecting him, but I was different. I was here the moment he walked through the door. I never let him down. He had no reason to stay late with some girl to get the attention he craved. He had me.

I glanced at the door, unable to stop myself from questioning why he was back so late, hoping he'd have a good excuse. 'I'm sure he'll be home any minute. We're coming to pick the kids up in half an hour anyway. That's still the plan, right? You can talk to him then,' I added firmly, trying to regain control of the situation.

I waited for her to agree, wondering what on earth Jimmy could have done to offend her so deeply. Perhaps she'd found out about the Nintendo DS he'd gifted Tommy, despite Carrie saying he couldn't have one, claiming she was worried about how reliant he was becoming on screens. Jimmy was far more laid-back as a parent, and I thought it unfair that Carrie got the final say on what we bought for the children. I'd made no secret to Jimmy that I thought he was right to do what he wanted with his own son.

'Carrie?' I said, waiting impatiently for her to confirm this evening's plans.

There was no answer.

I listened to the static, pressing the handset hard against my ear, and realised she'd hung up on me. I placed the phone back down, seething. She'd always been like this. Trying to keep me out of the loop, exclude me from her discussions with Jimmy as if I had no right to know what was being said.

What she needed to come to terms with was the fact that I was going nowhere. And whether she liked it or not, *I* would soon be Jimmy's wife and the official stepmother to their children. And I intended to be a very involved one indeed. I couldn't wait to disprove her assumptions that I was just another distraction to her wayward ex. Jimmy and I would be a proper family, last the distance. He would never betray me.

I turned to head back to the kitchen, then froze, replaying the conversation. Carrie had said 'Is he back *yet*?' *Had* he seen her earlier? Had he been keeping secrets from me? Jimmy wasn't a man who liked to explain himself. He was used to getting what he wanted in life. There had been a time I'd felt the same about myself.

The phone rang from the little table beside me, and I stared at it incredulously before reaching slowly to answer it. 'Yes?' I said, my patience waning now.

'Good evening. This is Detective Chief Inspector Farrows. Is it possible to speak with a Mr James Gold, please?' His tone was polite but expectant, and I pictured a man with large pores and a thick, greying moustache.

'Who?' I asked, feeling slow and stupid. I always froze when faced with the police, as if they would find something I hadn't known I needed to hide. I was the type of person who couldn't relax if a squad car was behind me in traffic, always waiting for the blue lights to flash – to be taken away and locked up with no chance of escape. I knew the reason for my fears was valid, but I'd never shared it with anybody. Not even Jimmy. Why the hell were the police calling here? Could it have anything to do with Carrie's call? My thoughts went to Jimmy and the children. Tommy, Maisy... sweet little Ava. She was the one who was proving hardest to win over, but I was determined to get there. This family meant everything to me.

'Oh, you mean Jimmy!' I exclaimed, my voice trembly to my own ears, though I hoped he hadn't picked up on it. 'He isn't home. What's this about?'

DCI Farrows cleared his throat. 'Do you have a pen?'

'Oh, um, yes,' I said, scrambling to open the pristine notepad that was sitting unused on the phone table. It was the same set-up my nan had once had in her dusty council bungalow, and I'd never understood the need to replicate it here when we all had perfectly good phones in our pockets. Just one of the compromises that came with being in a relationship with a much older man. Jimmy liked things to be traditional. Just so.

'Write down this number,' the detective instructed. He recited the digits and had me read them back to him. 'Good, have Mr Gold call me the moment you hear from him. It's imperative we speak as soon as possible.'

'Yes, but—'

The line went dead for the second time that evening, and I folded my arms tight across my chest, wondering what the hell my fiancé had done. And how on earth I was going to get him out of it.

FOUR

CARRIE

Then

I would have forgiven him the affair. It would hardly have been his first. I knew that made me sound pitiful, like a doormat who was happy to turn a blind eye, but that wasn't it. I'd known we'd never last after Tommy was born twelve years ago. That Jimmy wasn't the man he'd led me to believe he was. When Maisy came along three years later, it only cemented that certainty. I should never have had a third child with him, but perhaps there'd been a part of me that had hoped, after so long, he might finally step up. Change.

And, I thought, staring out of the kitchen window at the pink and orange stripes that lit up the powder-soft clouds, if I was honest, perhaps my desire to have another baby had been stronger than my disappointment in my marriage. My disdain for his inability to turn away from the slightest scrap of female attention. I wasn't even shocked by that point. But I'd have forgiven him, if only to keep my children by my side. Not to have to endure the sound of his car pulling up outside every

Friday evening, the tears as he prised my baby – *our* baby – from my arms and handed her to another woman. It took everything I had to smile, to hug Tommy and Maisy, to release my grip on Ava and pretend I wasn't boiling with rage, breaking apart inside as he drove away time and again.

My pale pink shirt was folded on top of the laundry basket ready for tonight's shift, and I reached for it, a rust-coloured speck catching my eye as I shook it out, sighing as I ran my nail over the bloodstain the sixty-degree wash had failed to remove. I tossed it on the kitchen floor near the washing machine, then rooted around in the basket to see if I had another clean top smart enough for work, playing back the injury that had caused the stain, propelling me to excuse myself to go and clean my arms with Clinell wipes before heading back to the craziness of the A&E ward.

The patient, a man in his sixties, had strolled into the bay from the waiting room with no sense of urgency, casually unwrapping his bandaged hand to display the cut he'd given himself when he'd slipped with his craft knife. As he'd pulled back the bandage, brandishing the wound with a flick of his hand, I'd been showered in droplets of claret – something he hadn't seemed to notice. Once I'd given it a good clean, the wound hadn't looked nearly so dramatic, though I'd put in a couple of stitches to be on the safe side. Not that I'd been worried. If he'd nicked an artery, there would have been a hell of a lot more blood than that, and I doubted he'd have been nearly so casual. I was used to blood. Used to acting quickly, staying calm where others might panic. And after so long in the job, it was rare that anything fazed me.

And yet, three days on from my last shift, I still couldn't stop thinking about the woman who'd been blue-lighted in at 11 p.m., unresponsive and barely breathing. She'd been accompanied by her terrified husband, a good-looking man who wore too much aftershave, his greying hair styled and manipulated into a quiff, his brown eyes locked on the lifeless form on the trolley. He'd asked me over and over if he was too late, if I could save her, but I'd been too focused on what needed doing to give him a response. He'd held on to the stretcher as we tried to wheel her through to the cubicle, and I'd seen Malcom, one of the paramedics I'd met a handful of times, gently but firmly prise his fingers from the rails and hold him back as, like a plague of locusts, we swarmed the woman he loved.

A thirty-six-year-old mother of four, she had put a rope round her neck and stepped off the dining-room table. Her husband had come home unexpectedly early from a night out and found her swinging from the wooden beams in their country cottage, cutting her down and finding her alive, but barely. I'd been nothing but professional as I'd treated her – did everything I was supposed to do – but I couldn't seem to suppress the fury I felt at her decision to not only abandon her children but to end her life while she was supposed to be taking care of them. What if one of them had awoken from a bad dream and found her before her husband had?

But even though I struggled with the selfishness of her actions, I couldn't deny that there was a time in my own life when I'd considered that my children might be better off without me. That I had never been so far along my tether, that I'd felt as if I had nothing left to grip hold of. When the tension and stress and to-do list mounted, and I could barely focus on the task ahead of me. When the horrors of my past reared up and refused to be ignored... But long as I might have lingered over those thoughts, I had never brought them into my home. Never given up on the hope that things would one day be easier.

The paradox of motherhood was how you could be so exhausted, so desperate for a shred of time to yourself, and yet when your wish was finally granted, all you could think about was getting back to your babies. A year ago, having been worn down by the pattern of surviving on twenty-minute bursts of sleep, of never getting to eat a meal while it was still hot, of putting myself at the bottom of the list of priorities – so far down I never reached my name, in fact – I would have done anything for a break from my children. For my husband to announce he was bringing our baby on the school run and then taking all three of them to the park so I could do whatever the hell I wanted with one of my precious days off. I'd fantasised about it. *Craved* it. I'd envied the other mothers I knew, who hadn't married men who'd reverted to their own boyhoods the moment they were faced with a shred of responsibility. But now, the saying *be careful what you wish for* had never felt more true.

Through the open kitchen window, I heard Jerry next door start up his lawnmower, and Ava dropped the crayon she'd been peeling the paper casing from, her mouth forming an O as she began to cry. She'd been so nervy about loud noises recently. I'd forgotten this stage.

I put down the top I was holding, careful to keep it flat to save me from having to get the iron out, and bent low to scoop her up, kissing her pink cheeks, smelling her head, the weight of her reassuring in my arms. My phone vibrated on the counter, and I frowned, not wanting to reach for it, to see the time and know how little I had left before the inevitable moment came, but knowing there was no point avoiding reality.

Meet me for an early dinner at the Dolphin before your shift? We can drive in together. I'm working tonight too.

I smiled, looking forward to it already. I didn't make a habit of socialising with my colleagues, but Shannon was different. She'd started as a receptionist last month, and so far, she seemed oblivious to my strictly professional relationship with the rest of the doctors and nurses, never mentioning the fact that I always found an excuse not to go to the pub with *them*. She was aware that I had the kids to think of, and as far as she knew, my mother was at home babysitting while Jimmy was working away. I'd had to come up with a few white lies to explain why I had an abundance of free time on the weekends, why she so often saw me without my children, but to make up for the things I couldn't share, I'd tried to be open about other stuff. I'd told her I was going through a tough time, making out I was missing Jimmy.

The reality was more complicated, but I'd been ashamed to tell her the truth. As much as I appreciated the 'me time' after waiting years for such a luxury, three months on from my separation, I was still struggling with sharing custody with my cheating ex and his twenty-four-year-old girlfriend, who'd stepped into my shoes as if she was Cinder-fucking-ella. The hours between saying goodbye and getting them back were agony. Shannon didn't have kids of her own, and I didn't feel ready to tell her all my secrets yet, but we'd clicked and I was grateful for the friendship – probably more grateful than she'd ever know. And a part of me felt there was no need to rush into telling her something that might be fixed soon. If Jimmy came home, there would be no need to air our previous troubles. And I was certain that he *would* come back sooner or later.

I kissed Ava again, then bent down, lowering her to the carpet, where she toddled off towards the box of toys Tommy had left on the coffee table, delving inside to pull out a blue-and-grey robot that lit up when you pressed on its head. I smiled as she turned it upside down, mashing it hard against the rug, squealing in delight as the echoey voice threatened to blast her to smithereens. Having older siblings had given her access to toys I'd never dreamed of buying when *they* were this age.

Leaving her to play for a moment, I walked out to the hallway and called up the stairs. 'Kids, come down now.' Glancing in the mirror above the little upcycled table where we – I – kept the keys and post, I bit my lower lip and pinched at

my cheeks, then pasted on the smile I was becoming so practised at. I'd always prided myself on being open with my children, showing them real and raw emotions, but not now. Not
like this.

Tommy and Maisy clattered down the stairs, both holding
plastic dinosaur figurines, still deep in conversation about the
game they'd been absorbed in. '*You* didn't see, but the professor
left the gate unlatched, and when he came to check, the raptors
had escaped!' Tommy declared, brandishing his dinosaurs
before him and giving a growl.

'Yes, but what *you* didn't realise was that he did it on
purpose to cause a distraction!' Maisy retorted. 'And the trained
oviraptor will sneak in to steal the raptors' eggs so the professor
can experiment on them!' She waved her toy dramatically in
Tommy's face.

I followed them into the living room, looking them up and
down to make sure they didn't have dried food on their faces or
stains on their T-shirts. 'Daddy will be here in a minute,' I
reminded them.

Tommy gave a groan – still so loyal, such a mama's boy who
loved being here at home more than anything – but Maisy
looked more conflicted. I knew she hated leaving, but she and
that woman seemed to be bonding lately, and as much as it
stung to hear her coming back with stories about the cakes
they'd baked together, the movie she'd been allowed to stay up
and watch, I didn't want to react in a way that might make her
try and hide things from me in an attempt to protect my feelings. I was prepared for the pain, but I couldn't bear being
shut out.

As if on cue, the sound of a horn beeping outside made my
heart sink. I never stopped hoping they would call and say
something had come up and they couldn't make it. Instinctively,
I reached for Ava, wanting to lock the door, close the curtains,
hide until it was just us again, but Maisy was already on her

feet, rushing over to the window and waving a little too enthusiastically for my liking.

'Leah's out there! Where's Daddy?' she said, grinning at the woman who'd stolen my life from me.

I followed her and Tommy as they ran down the hall and opened the front door, Ava held firmly against my hip. I stared at the woman on the path, unwilling to make anything easy for her.

'Carrie, hi!' She smiled before bending down to kiss Tommy and Maisy on their cheeks. 'Did you get Jimmy's message?'

'No, he hasn't sent anything,' I replied, unsmiling.

'Held up at work and now he's run out of petrol on the way home. He's had to walk to the garage, but I didn't want to keep you waiting around all evening, so I thought I'd come and get these guys at our usual time.'

'Right,' I answered, unable to return her smile. By rights, I didn't have to hand them over to her. She wasn't their parent. Wasn't married to their father. She was just some girl he'd walked out of a perfectly good marriage for. My arrangement was with *him*, and even that hadn't been through the courts. I considered saying as much, but then caught Maisy's expression and checked myself, nodding as I forced myself to meet Leah's eyes. 'That was kind of you, but you didn't have to. I'm never in a rush to pass them off, you know.'

'Oh, but it's an awkward time, what with dinner and all, and you have your work, don't you? No rest for the doctor, right?'

'Right.'

'And no need for you to cook a big meal when you've already got so much to do. I've made spag bol. Your favourite, Tommy.' She grinned at him and I felt my insides squirm, hating the way she looked at him, waiting in expectation for him to smile back, almost as if she were giving him no choice. She knew how polite he was. Because *I* had raised him well.

There was no decision to be made, but that didn't make it any easier. It never did. After hugging them both, I watched as they ran round the car, climbing in and resuming their dinosaur game loud enough for me to hear through the closed windows.

Their bags were piled just inside the door, and Leah pointed to them. 'I'll pop those in the boot, shall I?' She took them without waiting for a reply, then returned, an expectant look on her face.

Ava clung to me and I did nothing to ease her away, feeling secretly smug that at least I was still *her* favourite.

But Leah dug into her jeans pocket, pulling out a Thomas the Tank Engine toy, and Ava gave a delighted squeal. Leah reached out, taking her from me, and pressed the toy into her chubby palm. 'Don't worry, Carrie. She's always fine as soon as you're out of sight. She never even asks for you – you've no need to worry.' She gave a saccharine smile, then turned away.

'Say bye-bye, sweetie,' she said, though she didn't wait for Ava to catch my eye. 'Let's go and find your daddy, shall we?'

I waved dumbly as she put my baby into her car, then closed the door. What reason could she have to say something so cruel, if not purely to hurt me? To make me feel as if I could be replaced... as if the process had already begun. Did she think she could push me out? That they could ever love her as much as they loved me?

'I think *he'll* be bringing them back,' Leah said. 'You got a nice weekend planned?'

I dug my fingernails into the door frame, shaking with the effort to maintain my frozen smile, though I didn't reply. She dipped her head, as if she'd been expecting my silence, then gave a tiny shrug and walked around the car, climbing in and starting the engine. I stepped out onto the driveway, waving as she drove away, but the children were too busy laughing at something I couldn't hear to notice me standing there.

This couldn't go on. I had to find a way to keep my children close. To make sure they didn't fall for her little tricks – the spoiling them with gifts, embodying the role of the fun mother I could never be. I had to protect them from whatever sick game she was trying to play because watching them disappear, knowing I had no other choice, was killing me. And I was certain Leah knew that.

FIVE

Now

I walked into the kitchen, standing in the dark, unable to bring myself to flick the light switch on, to go through the normal rituals of coming home after a busy day. The moon was barely more than a sliver and I was glad of the darkness, concealing the evidence of the gaping hole that had opened up, the person who was no longer here. The clock on the oven told me it was after midnight, and I shivered, realising that Ava had been gone for almost seven hours. Feeling my throat tighten, the urge to scream building inside me, I swayed on the spot, unsure what to even do now that I was here.

I hadn't wanted to come home from the beach, the idea of leaving the place where my daughter had last been seen completely outlandish and terrifying. I'd wanted to stay rooted to the spot, the tide lapping at my raw, salt-burned ankles, shivering and unable to turn my head from the sea, but some do-gooder, some woman I'd never met before, had bundled me into her car, insisting I come home to get some rest. As if such a thing were possible in these circumstances. I hadn't had the strength to argue, and somehow, despite my silence, someone must have given her my address, as she'd known where to bring me... no, not me, *us*.

Turning in panic, I pressed my hands to my mouth as I saw Maisy standing in the porch, the front door still wide open behind her. I'd been so wrapped up in looking for Ava that I'd neglected to consider my nine-year-old, how late it was, how scared she must be. I'd put her into the car myself, though my thoughts had been elsewhere as I went through the motions of strapping her in, but now, seeing the way her tiny body seemed to curve in on itself, her narrow shoulders hunched, her lips blue with the cold, her teeth chattering, I felt terrible.

Shannon had offered – practically insisted – to take her home, but when I'd refused, she had left, saying that she would go and search the surrounding streets herself, but to call her if I changed my mind. I'd been consumed with finding Ava, hounding every police officer on the beach for information, waiting on the boats that came back and forth, each one frustratingly empty, offering no hope. But seeing Maisy now, I realised I hadn't been thinking straight. I never should have made her wait on the beach for so long. I should have snapped out of my shock and taken care of my daughter. I'd let her down.

'Oh, Maisy!' I gasped, rushing back down the hall. I slammed the front door closed behind her, the air cold and biting against my skin, and squatted down in front of her, pulling her into a hug. 'I'm so sorry, darling – you must be exhausted.'

Her body trembled against my chest, and a hot stab of self-hatred pierced my belly, the guilt overwhelming.

I'd always wanted to be the kind of mother that people admired, the kind that were written about in Enid Blyton stories – warm, sweet, always baking and darning socks – but the reality was, being a working mother, and lately, a *single* working mother, had taken a toll on my patience, my time, and most days I barely scraped by with the minimum connection and quality time. I wanted so much for my children, and yet I repeatedly let them down, and each time I did, I blamed myself all the more.

I hugged Maisy closer, rubbing her back as I lifted her into my arms, carrying her upstairs. Her body was rigid, filled with tension, and it was hard not to drop her as I took the steps one by one, my own muscles screaming in agony after swimming so hard earlier.

I pushed open the door to her bedroom and set her down, stripping off her rain-soaked clothes and pulling a fleece onesie over her skinny ankles, choosing the thickest pair of socks in her drawer and rolling them over her ice-cold feet. I suddenly remembered she hadn't had dinner.

I bit my lip, trying not to cry as I put myself in her shoes: a little girl, hearing her mother scream for her baby sister before disappearing into the ocean, followed by hours of police interviews, flashing lights and nobody explaining what was happening, all the while freezing cold and starving. I *should* have let Shannon take her home, though I wasn't sure how well she would have coped with the task of babysitting – she had no experience taking care of children and seemed oblivious when it came to the amount of work involved in meeting their needs. She'd made comments in the past referencing my concerns about Tommy, saying that *her* mother had never worried about stuff like that and she'd turned out fine. She didn't seem to realise how much had changed since the eighties. How monumental the expectations on modern mothers were, the burden of it suffocating at times.

I'd let down my walls a little recently, and Shannon had met the children a handful of times in the past month, albeit briefly, but she still didn't know them well. In any case, if anyone was going to take care of Maisy, it should have been her father. If only Jimmy could have been there to step up when he was needed, but that was too much to ask for. His phone had been switched off, nobody was answering his office number, and Leah had said he was out. I'd tried several times without success. I'd needed him tonight. I couldn't be to blame for everything.

I settled Maisy under her quilt and kissed her cheek. Her eyes wouldn't meet mine and her hands made fists around the covers, the tension still radiating from her. I tucked her old teddy, Buster, in beside her and whispered, 'I'll go and get you something to eat and drink, sweetheart. And a hot-water bottle.'

I straightened, then headed out of the room, determined to make it right. I jogged back to the kitchen, ignoring the rumbling in my own stomach as I poured milk into a pan and stuck a bagel in the toaster, letting it turn golden brown before smothering it in jam and butter. I knew I should call to check on Tommy too, but it was late now – I couldn't wake the whole household – and besides, he wouldn't want to talk to me anyway. When his dad had left, he'd been almost protective over me. He'd made me feel like he was on my side, that I had nothing to worry about with this new woman he so clearly resented.

But in the past few months, that had begun to change. He'd been less concerned about hiding his growing affections for the girl who could have practically been a big sister to him. And on a couple of occasions, he'd asked questions that had made me wonder how much he'd overheard when Jimmy and I had lived under the same roof; if it was possible that he knew more than he let on, had heard something he shouldn't have. I'd brushed off his questions, changing the subject, reasoning that he couldn't possibly know the secrets Jimmy and I had kept. He was too young to understand the way the world worked. The choices we had to make as adults. I wanted to protect him from all that. It would only bring more confusion... more questions that should remain unanswered.

I put the milk and bagel onto the tray with the pretty pattern of bees and flowers, Maisy's favourite, then carried it back up to her room, pushing open the door. I'd forgotten the hot-water bottle, I realised. In the glow of the unicorn night light on her bedside table, I could see she was fast asleep. I set down the tray, wondering if I should wake her and encourage her to eat, or just let her rest. In the end, I tiptoed out, leaving the food behind. It was best she slept. I had things I needed to do.

'Carrie?'

The voice at the other end of the phone was sleepy, and I felt bad for having called so late, and yet not so bad that I was about to change my mind.

'Shannon, I'm sorry to wake you.' I didn't want to admit that when it came down to it, I'd come to the horrible realisation that she was my only option. How humiliating to get to my age and have nobody aside from a casual work friend to call in an emergency.

'No, don't be silly.' I heard movement and pictured her sitting up in bed. 'Have you heard anything? Have they found Ava?'

I shook my head, my eyes filling with tears. 'Nothing at all. It feels so wrong to be here, looking at her toys, her high chair, and knowing she's not asleep upstairs. It's so quiet. I can't just sit around, go to bed like it's a normal night. I need to be out there. What if she wandered off from the beach and she's hiding somewhere? She won't come out for a stranger – she needs me to find her. She'll be so frightened. I know I was rude to you on the beach, Shannon, but please, will you come? I can't get hold of Jimmy, and I need someone to be with Maisy in case she wakes up. She's had such a shock and—'

'Say no more,' she interrupted. 'I'll come right away. Will you text me your address?'

'I'll do it now. Thanks. I really appreciate it.'

I hung up, wishing I could force time to move faster, my hands shaking with the need to get outside and start moving, start looking for my daughter. If there was the slightest scrap of hope, I had to chase it. I *would* keep hoping. It was the only way to stay sane.

I paced back and forth across the kitchen floor, already wearing a raincoat and woolly hat, ready to leave the moment Shannon arrived. I had changed into my most comfortable jeans and a thick fleecy jumper, and pulled on well-worn trainers, prepared for the long night of walking I had ahead of me. I'd not wasted time showering, though, and now my skin itched, and I wished I'd made the effort to have a quick rinse-off at the very least. The moon was still high, and I attempted to make some sort of plan for where I should go first. The beach would hopefully still be full of police searching, but I wondered if I should try nearby. The little alleyways, paths running behind shops and flats... it made sense to check those places, but the stronger pull was that I couldn't bear to look at the sea again. Not yet, at least.

I pictured my tiny daughter hiding behind a wheelie bin down a dark alley and shivered, wishing Shannon would hurry up so I could get going. I'd tried Jimmy's phone a dozen more times, longing to hear his voice, to tell him everything, but every time it went straight to voicemail, and I knew there was no point trying again now.

I turned to the sink, grabbing a glass from the draining board and filling it with water, gulping it back in three mouthfuls, then refilling it. As I was finishing the second glass, there was a gentle tap on the front door. Hurriedly, I put down the glass, then went to answer it. Shannon stood on the front step, her hair in a bun, and it took me a minute to realise what was different about her. She wasn't wearing a scrap of make-up. Seeing her bare-faced, though she was still remarkably pretty, was like seeing a completely different person, and it took me by surprise to realise how long she must spend on her make-up routine every morning.

I shook away the thought and stood back to let her in, already picking up the backpack I'd left beside the door, stuffed with warm clothes for Ava, along with snacks and a drink. If I found her, she'd be so hungry. 'Thank you for coming over,' I said. 'I know it's the middle of the night, but—'

'Honestly, it's fine, Carrie,' she interrupted. 'I'd only just got into bed, and it wasn't as if I was going to sleep anyway.' She touched my arm. 'I've been sick with worry for you and poor Ava. I'm so glad you asked me to help. Where are you going to go?'

'I don't really know.' I shrugged, glancing at the drive with a frown. 'Is that my car?'

She nodded. 'I went back to the beach earlier – I wanted to bring you and Maisy some food, but the police said someone had taken you home. You left your car parked there. And this,' she added, holding up my red leather satchel. I recalled dropping it on the bench after I'd shown PC Mayville the photo of Ava. 'Your keys were in it, and I thought you might need the car,' she said, looking sheepish. 'I hope you don't mind that I took it upon myself to bring it over? The parking is extortionate there! I'd taken it back to mine and was planning to drop it here first thing and Uber back home, but then you called and...' She flushed, meeting my eyes. 'I wasn't overstepping, was I?'

I shook my head. 'I'd completely forgotten about it,' I admitted. 'Thank you. You're being so kind...' I swallowed against the solid lump that had wedged itself in my throat, Shannon's sympathetic gaze making me feel like falling apart. But I couldn't. I had to be strong. To get out there and find my baby. I blinked back the tears and turned for the door. 'Maisy's fast asleep in her room. I can't imagine she'll wake up, but if she does...'

'I'll tell her you just had to pop out. I know she doesn't know me very well, but I'm sure we'll manage just fine. And you can't be everywhere at once, can you?'

'Thanks, Shannon.' I stepped outside, then froze as an unfamiliar silver car pulled up on the road, blocking me in. A man got out, dressed smartly in blue chinos and a navy shirt and tie. He was stocky and not much taller than me, but as he strode across the driveway towards me, I could instantly detect an air of confidence about him. He stopped in front of me, unsmiling, and I felt Shannon step out to stand beside me in a show of solidarity. I felt suddenly terrified of what I was about to hear.

'Carrie Gold?' the man said, looking from me to Shannon with a questioning eyebrow.

'That's me,' I replied, my voice sounding stronger than I'd expected. 'Who are you?'

'DCI Farrows,' he said, his grey eyes travelling over my face as if he were trying to read my thoughts.

'You've found her?' I whispered. 'Is she—'

He held up a hand, cutting me off before I could finish the question. 'We haven't found Ava yet,' he said, his voice gravelly and devoid of apology. He eyed the backpack in my hand, his gaze running over me from top to bottom, and I wondered why I felt under scrutiny. Suspicion seemed to ooze from his every pore. Wasn't he supposed to be on my side? 'Going somewhere?' he asked, looking pointedly back to the bag.

I nodded, gripping the backpack tighter. 'I'm going out to look for her.'

He raised an eyebrow. 'Do you know something we don't? Where are you planning to search?'

I shook my head. 'I can't just stay here. I have to do something.'

He appraised me silently for a moment, then gave a short nod, and I felt a jolt of dislike for the man. He seemed oblivious to the emotional distress I was going through right now. Shouldn't he be kinder? More empathetic? Shouldn't he be making an effort to reassure me? I stared into his cold eyes and felt sure that he could be standing an inch from Ava and she still wouldn't come out from hiding into his waiting arms. She'd be terrified of a man like him.

'Let's step inside,' he said finally. 'I have something I want to show you.'

I glanced down as he patted a laptop case I hadn't noticed he was holding. 'What is it?' I asked. 'What have you found?'

He twisted his mouth as if he was unimpressed that I'd asked a question rather than jumping to follow his orders. I felt suddenly frozen to the spot, as if going inside with him would bring nothing good. Whatever he had to show me was something I didn't know if I could bear to see.

'Come on, Carrie,' Shannon said softly, linking her arm through mine and guiding me back into the house.

I let myself be led into the kitchen, where Farrows unzipped the laptop case and settled himself down at the table, in the chair that had once been Jimmy's.

'We're still working on obtaining the CCTV footage from the beach car park, but we *have* found this,' he said, pointing to the screen.

I peered over his shoulder, hardly daring to breathe as he clicked on the video he'd enlarged, Shannon's hand slipping into mine, squeezing tight.

'You said you last saw your daughter at just after five p.m. This footage was captured on a bus heading away from the beach at ten past five. I want you to look closely – the image is very brief.

I leaned in and watched. He pressed play, and I recognised the inside of a bus. DCI Farrows tapped a face on the screen: an elderly lady making her way slowly up the aisle. Shannon's hand tightened even further around my own as she too leaned closer. The old woman took a seat, and I frowned, not understanding. Then she bent forward and lifted a child I hadn't seen onto her lap, cradling her against her chest, obscuring her face. I gasped, my hand flying out of Shannon's to cover my mouth. The curly hair, though her bunches had come out, the red-and-white trainers... She was wearing a jacket I didn't recognise, but it was her. I was sure of it.

'Ava!' I cried. 'It's her! It's my baby! Oh, thank God!' Relief flooded through me as I pressed my hand to the paused image. 'Where did they get off?' I asked breathlessly. 'Have you found the woman?'

DCI Farrows turned in Jimmy's seat to look at me. 'You think it's her?'

'Yes!' I nodded. 'It has to be!'

Beside me, Shannon was shaking her head. 'I'm not so sure, Carrie. Her hair looks longer. And it makes no sense. Why would she be so calm with a total stranger? Didn't you say she has separation anxiety? She'd be screaming...'

'No, it's *her!*' I insisted.

Shannon looked at Farrows. 'Is there more? Can we see when she gets off the bus? Can we look at the child's face?'

He gave a heavy sigh. 'Afraid not. This lot here,' he said, indicating a group of very tall men in the aisle, 'moved to stand in front of the camera and blocked it for several stops. When they finally got off, the woman and child were gone. We're not sure where she got off, but obviously we're checking all along the route.'

'Oh,' I whispered, the hope that had been filling me with adrenaline suddenly bursting into a cloud of vapour. 'How many stops were missed?'

'Seven.'

'Fuck!'

He frowned, making an expression of distaste at my language, then leaned back, folding his arms. 'Do you recognise the woman?'

I peered at the screen. 'No... wait, maybe...' I looked again, feeling sure there *was* something familiar about her but unable to place her. 'I don't know,' I admitted. 'But you'll find her, won't you? You'll find my daughter?'

He flipped the laptop closed. 'We're doing everything we can,' he said, pushing back the chair. 'In the meantime, if you remember anything that could help, anything at all, give me a call.' He handed me a card and I took it without looking at it.

'I will,' I said, nodding. 'Can you tell me the bus route she was on? And which stop did you notice they'd got off?'

He fixed me with a hard stare, as if he was about to warn me not to make a nuisance of myself and get in their way, then sniffed. 'It was the eighty-six, northbound. And she got off somewhere before the community centre on Green Lane.'

'Thank you.' I wrapped my arms tight around my body, picturing the route. I'd been stuck behind that bus numerous times on the way to the hospital. It went right through the centre of town. So many buildings she could have ducked into. So many narrow paths hidden from view, not to mention that huge council estate just a few minutes' walk from the community centre, the monumental tower blocks sprawling out like a concrete jungle. The thought of combing through each flat to find my baby felt both daunting and terrifying.

Shannon walked Farrows to the door, then returned to the kitchen and pulled me into a hug. 'It's going to be okay, Carrie. It has to be.'

I nodded, desperately needing to believe she was right. 'I just want my family back,' I whispered. 'It's all I ever wanted.'

She pulled back, and I saw a frown pucker between her

eyebrows in a silent question, but then it was gone. 'Shall I make some tea?' she offered.

'No.' I shook my head, picking up the backpack and slinging it over my shoulder. 'I can't... I have to go.'

She nodded silently, and I walked through the quiet house and out into the night, wishing Jimmy was by my side. Like he'd sworn to be. *For better, for worse. In sickness and in health. Forsaking all others. Till death us do part...*

SIX

LEAH

The house was eerily quiet as I climbed the stairs, unsure what else I could do now. After those unsettling calls from both Carrie and the police, I'd sent countless messages and left a dozen voicemails for Jimmy, demanding that he call me back.

I knotted my fingers together, fidgeting. It wasn't unlike him to be late home; in fact, it was a source of contention between us on a regular basis – my wondering where he'd gone and who he'd been with, him barely acknowledging my questions. I had to remind myself he'd never done anything to break my trust.

Apart from walking out on his wife for me, that is.

We'd only been seeing each other three months when Carrie had caught us in their marital bed, and Jimmy subsequently decided it was time we brought our relationship out into the open. It had felt wonderful at first, but he couldn't seem to understand that his actions, his poor contact and inability to stick to his own schedule, made me feel insecure.

But, I thought – my stomach tensing as I listened at the small window on the landing for the sound of his car pulling up outside and hearing nothing – even when he planned to arrive home late, he always managed to send a quick text in an attempt to stop me from worrying. Tonight, though, there had been no response. I'd wondered if maybe I'd got it all wrong. Jumped to conclusions because a part of me had been waiting for this moment. The not knowing was making my head spin, and with Jimmy unable to confirm my suspicions, I'd felt my only option was to summon my courage and find out for myself what exactly the police wanted with him. The more I could ascertain, the more prepared I could be when the inevitable questions came my way.

I'd called the station back, explaining who I was and how unsettled DCI Farrows' call had made me, and a junior officer had taken pity on me and told me that as far as she knew, they just wanted to ask Jimmy some questions about something. She'd sounded as if she was going to tell me more, but then, after asking about my relationship and discovering I was only the fiancée, she had backtracked, giving nothing away. It rankled that I was still seen as secondary to his wife. The fact they'd been separated for almost seven months didn't seem to matter. *She* was still his next of kin whilst I was left to worry in silence, and until Carrie agreed to the divorce, we would all continue to live in this frustrating state of limbo.

I'd hung up and found myself with nothing to do but anxiously pace the floors of the big house we'd rented – with Jimmy footing the bill, of course. I was only just out of uni and had yet to find a position, though Jimmy had promised he would put a word in for me at his law firm. I'd considered it, weighing up the pros and cons. I would like being there, under the same roof as him. Getting to know all the secretaries and staff he worked with, and making sure his eyes didn't wander too far from me. I'd given up the bar work that had kept me fed over the past four years, mainly because Jimmy hated the idea of me going out in the evenings to serve drinks to anyone other than him.

He'd mentioned on a handful of occasions how comforting

he found it to have me at home, not working. How much he enjoyed coming back to a warm house that smelled like delicious food, rather than the empty place he'd had to endure during his marriage to Carrie, her cold, bossy texts sent way after her shift should have finished, telling him she couldn't leave the hospital yet and demanding he cook a meal for the children after his long day at the office. I knew he preferred the more traditional set-up, and to be honest, I liked it too. Perhaps I wouldn't work outside the home at all. I enjoyed cooking, taking care of the house, making up games with the children on our weekends with them. I just didn't want to do it all by myself. Evenings and weekends should be our time. He should be here too.

As darkness had begun to set in and I'd still heard nothing, I'd made up my mind to stick to the normal schedule, and had got in my car and driven over to Carrie's place to collect the children. They always came at 6 p.m., and it wasn't the first time Jimmy had been late, prompting me to go alone to pick them up. I didn't know what was going on, but I wanted to show them I hadn't forgotten. I'd spent the whole day preparing for them.

But when I'd arrived, the house had been dark and silent, and there had been no answer when I'd pressed my finger down on the bell, letting it chime again and again. I'd called Carrie's mobile, though I hadn't expected her to answer. She never had in the past, preferring to pretend I didn't exist. Eventually, after half an hour waiting on the doorstep, hoping to see little Maisy running along the pavement, excitement in her eyes at the surprises I'd have in store, I'd given up, and gone back home feeling disappointed and annoyed.

I paused at the top of the stairs now, looking through the empty doorway to Tommy's room. He'd tucked his great white shark teddy under his duvet when he'd left for school Monday morning, its nose propped up on the pillow, and a wave of sadness washed over me as I thought of his handsome face, how I wouldn't get to see him tonight.

I turned away, but instead of heading into my bedroom, I unlocked the door that led up the narrow staircase to the loft. There was a small skylight in the tiny landing above, but it was too dark to make a difference now, and I flicked on the light. The stairs creaked, and the light gave a dusky, orange glow. I made a note to change it for a brighter one. It felt a little creepy, and if I was going to be coming up here more often now, I wanted to make it less of an unappealing prospect.

I turned the smooth round brass handle on the only door, and, hearing it click, pushed it open, listening. Stepping inside, I closed the door behind me and with gentle footsteps padded across the thick, cushioning carpet to the little white cabinet on the far side of the room, turning the key in the lock and pulling out the white wicker basket I'd stored inside.

SEVEN

CARRIE

I'd had long nights in my life, but nothing compared to the one I'd just endured. Every inch of my being had compelled me to keep walking, keep searching, keep fighting for my daughter. The relentless call of the ocean had driven me half mad, the longing to run back to the beach and, beneath the moonlight, swim until I found her, but I'd ignored the desperate pull, instead concentrating on the bus route and the surrounding streets. I'd been surprised at how few people had opened their doors to me when I'd knocked, choosing to stay tucked up safe in their beds rather than come down and talk to me. Perhaps they were too desensitised to disturbance – drunks and teens banging on their doors at all hours – to bother coming to investigate, but the few people I *had* spoken to had been short and unhelpful. None had offered to step out and come and search with me. And for the most part, they'd seemed all too keen to shut the door and go back to their privacy, as if what had happened to me might be contagious somehow.

As I'd walked up and down the narrow dark alleyways, directing my torch behind mountains of rubbish, trying not to feel the fear that was pulsing through me as I passed homeless men sleeping on cardboard mattresses, I couldn't prevent the fantasies – and I knew they *were* fantasies – from chasing through my mind. How I would find myself back at the beach. I would step out onto the pebbles, hear the crunch of shells beneath my feet, and there would be a tiny cry in the distance. I would turn, and there, by some miracle, she would be, cowering by the breakers, cold and frightened but happy to see me. And most importantly, alive and unharmed, despite her ordeal. I would scoop her up against my chest and never let her go again. It felt so real, and a part of me knew it was the only way to cope – to disassociate from the cold reality of my situation and force this alternate ending to play on a loop in my mind.

I'd walked through the front door at dawn, my legs like hollowed-out jelly, my head pounding, the guilt at having come back empty-handed breaking me apart. Shannon had been half asleep on the sofa, her phone gripped in her palm, and had jumped up, instantly awake at my return, the hope in her eyes quickly replaced by sadness and sympathy. She'd offered to stay, to help with Maisy when she woke up so I could go to bed, but I'd known there was no point. I would never sleep. As exhausted as my body was, my mind was too busy to ever have a hope of switching off. She'd left reluctantly, and I'd felt relieved to have a moment of silence, to not have to see the pitying way she looked at me when she thought I couldn't see.

My lips felt tacky, my stomach empty and growling, and I realised I hadn't eaten anything since lunchtime yesterday. The thought of taking care of such basic needs under the circumstances felt indulgent somehow, the idea of food making my stomach recoil. I didn't think I could bear it. And yet I *had* to keep going, keep my strength up for Ava. She would come back to me. I knew it deep in my bones. She *had* to come back. I would keep searching. There was no choice.

I looked across at the living-room window, squinting as the weak sunshine filtered through the net curtains. The clock read

just after 7 a.m. There had been no calls all night long. No
updates. What did that mean? And where the fuck was Jimmy?
What kind of a parent just went off grid? I couldn't imagine
ever turning off my phone when he had the kids with him. I was
never fully at ease, always on duty, even on his nights.

Moving slowly, as if in a trance, I pushed myself up from
the low sofa where I'd slumped down for an indeterminate
amount of time after Shannon's taxi had arrived, stretching out
my back, hearing it crack and pop, the joints aching, my muscles
heavy and sore. There was no sound from Maisy's bedroom
above, and I was grateful that at least *she* had been able to sleep.
I'd expected Shannon to tell me she'd been up with nightmares
after all she'd been through, but she'd said she hadn't made a
peep, and that was a small mercy.

I picked up my phone from the coffee table and dialled the
police station, tapping my foot impatiently as I waited for the
automated response to finish and put me through to a real
person. I didn't want to have to 'press one' to report a fucking
crime; I shouldn't have had to be the one to call in the first
place. Where was Farrows with my update about the lady on
the bus?

Shannon had been not nearly as enthusiastic over the
footage as I was, and after he'd left last night, she'd made me
question myself, wonder if I was seeing what I wanted to see
because the alternative was too much to bear. Had I jumped at
the idea that the little girl on the bus could be Ava because I
needed it to be? I wished DCI Farrows had sent me a copy of
the footage so I could watch it back again.

I'd been angry when she'd softly asked why someone would
kidnap a child only to take them on a public bus with a hundred
witnesses to turn them in. Why this woman would have any
need to take my child.

'Hello, Dr Gold?' a voice said into the phone.

'Any updates?' I asked, not bothering to check who I was

talking to. It was a female voice that had answered, and I was annoyed that Farrows hadn't made the effort to speak to me himself. 'Did you find the lady from the bus?' I asked, my tone clipped and cold.

'I'm sorry, but we don't have an update for you yet. But I can assure you we're working on it. We haven't been able to get hold of Ava's father. Can I double-check the details we have for him?'

I recited them again, half relieved that at least Jimmy was ignoring the police too; that it wasn't just me he was ghosting. It would have hurt to discover he'd been taking their calls, fully aware of the situation, and yet hadn't bothered to get in touch and see how I was doing. I thought he'd have come here, searched with me. Where *was* he?

I hated the way Leah seemed able to get under his skin, change his mind about views he'd held for decades, make him think he was too good for me, that *she* could give him everything I couldn't. From the moment I'd met her, I'd seen through her. But beyond my hatred was a deeper emotion. One I'd never admit, even to Jimmy. Fear. Pure and undiluted terror at the idea that not only did Leah have the power to take everything that mattered to me but that she wanted just that. She longed to shove me out of the picture. Take my place in my children's lives. And if I dared to speak that truth to Jimmy, he would only hear the desperate pleas of a jealous ex. He would never believe me.

The policewoman made some empty promises to be in touch, and I hung up without bothering to say thank you. I was too angry, too disappointed that with all the resources at their disposal, they were doing such a pathetic job at finding one woman. One child. It was unacceptable. I gripped my phone hard, tempted to throw it at the wall but restrained myself, reminding myself that I'd need it later.

I walked over to the window, staring out at the dew-covered

grass, trying to breathe through the panic that was thrumming through my veins. I held on to the windowsill, swaying on my feet, the exhaustion hitting me hard. There was too much to keep straight in my mind, and this tiredness was making it all the more difficult to think clearly. A chill swept down my spine as I replayed the question Shannon had asked before she'd left.

'Carrie,' she'd said quietly, 'why didn't you tell me that you're going through a divorce?'

The question had taken me by surprise. 'It's not something I like to advertise,' I'd replied, not meeting her eye.

'I can understand that. And you're entitled to your privacy, of course. But I'm trying to understand why you'd feel the need to lie. We've been close, I thought. We've shared such a lot, haven't we? You know *everything* about me. Why would you keep such a huge part of your life from me?' Her tone had been gentle, her expression filled with hurt. 'And more than that, why would you fabricate a story about your husband being away on an oil rig when he's actually a lawyer? I can't understand it. Did you think I'd judge you? Do you really think so little of me? That I would care?' she'd asked, her voice cracking.

I'd folded my arms, unable to fathom why she would bring this up now of all times. Anger had surged through me as I'd finally met her wide, wet eyes. 'You know full well my parents were Catholic. Divorce wasn't an option growing up. The failure of my marriage is hardly something I'm going to share with the whole world, is it?'

'But I'm *not* the whole world, am I?' She'd shaken her head. 'I hadn't been aware there were such big secrets between us. It makes me feel like... like I don't know you.' She'd looked down at her feet. 'I would *never* have judged you, Carrie.'

I'd stared at her, wondering why any of this mattered. None of it meant anything, not any more. I'd muttered as much and been grateful when the sound of her taxi pulling up outside had put an end to the interrogation. I hoped it would be the last time we'd speak about it, but I had an uneasy feeling that it wouldn't. And I just hoped she wouldn't share my lies with the police. I needed them to trust me.

Shannon was correct in saying that we'd been close. I wasn't used to having friendships, and up until today, I hadn't been sure if she felt as close to me as I did to her. As far as I knew, it could have been just casual chat for her. But for me, it had meant so much more. I hated the fact that she'd found out I'd lied to her. I had sat still, listening to the engine as the taxi drove away, and felt terrified of what else might come out in the wake of Ava's disappearance. It didn't bear thinking about.

I leaned my forehead against the cold glass, my thoughts tumbling over each other, fighting to be heard. My stomach churned, bile rising in my throat, sour and burning, as my memory flashed back to the icy cold of the ocean, the waves that had almost swallowed me yesterday, the tang of salt and despair. I felt as though I had left a part of myself there, and I stumbled back, pressing my hands over my face, stifling the scream that bubbled unbidden from deep within my soul. Gasping, I forced myself to suck in a series of jagged breaths, composing myself, masking the emotion as best I could.

It was getting lighter now. I knew I should let Maisy sleep some more, but I couldn't stay here. I couldn't be inside these four walls while Ava was out there alone. Was she with that old lady? Was she hiding somewhere? Or, I thought, the sudden sound of the ocean deafening in my ears, was she gone for ever?

I bit my lip, then turned, striding up the stairs to Maisy's room. I caught sight of myself in the mirror and felt a jolt of shock at the sight of my red, splotchy skin, irritated by the seawater I'd neglected to rinse off, the tangled mess of my light brown hair matted above my shoulders in unruly clumps. Maisy would be afraid if I went in to her like this, but the thought of taking a shower, summoning the energy to brush through this mess was too much. Instead, I grabbed a silk scrunchie and wound the clumps into a messy bun, threw some cold water over my face, wiping away the black smears of mascara from beneath my eyes, and slapped a layer of thick moisturiser on my skin. It wasn't a great improvement, but it was all I could do right now.

I couldn't hear a sound from Maisy's room as I walked across the thick carpet towards it. I pushed open the door and was surprised to see her sitting on the edge of her mattress, fully dressed in a pair of black leggings and her favourite red-and-white striped T-shirt. Her head was bowed, her hands clasped in her lap, and the sight of her made me want to cry.

'Oh, love, how long have you been awake?' I asked, heading over to sit beside her on the bed.

Her shoulders stiffened, but she didn't reply, and I took one of her hands in my own, noting that it was cold and clammy. Maisy and I had always shared a special bond. And I had learned over the years to sit quietly and wait whenever she had something playing on her mind. After yesterday, I knew she'd need to talk – not that I had any answers, nor the strength to hold myself together and be the supportive ear she needed. But it was my job. And if I couldn't hold back the tears, I was only human.

I squeezed her hand, waiting for her to ask questions, share her devastation with me, steeling myself for the conversation I wasn't close to being ready to have. But nothing came. When, after a few minutes, she still hadn't spoken, hadn't even looked my way, her hand limp in my own, I lifted my finger, smoothing her hair out of her eyes.

'Maisy,' I said softly. 'Do you want to talk about yesterday?' A lump seemed to wedge itself in my throat, and when she didn't answer, I couldn't help but feel relieved. She obviously wasn't any more ready than me to go to those dark places yet.

'Come on,' I said, standing and leading her by the hand across the room. 'Let's get you some breakfast. And after that,

I'm going to give your daddy a call,' I said, praying that he would pick up. Because I couldn't do this alone. I was going to need him to step up. To be the man he'd let me believe he was all those years ago. It was time he stopped messing around with that woman and came back home. His family needed him.

EIGHT
LEAH

Then

The bar was packed, the bass thumping through my veins, making my hips sway involuntarily as I tilted the glass under the tap, pouring the cold pint of golden lager. I handed it to the waiting customer with a flirtatious smile, and he winked before taking it over to where his friends were seated. I loved this job. Loved getting out from behind my laptop after a long day of studying to see real people, watch couples on first dates, rooting for them to make it, or, more often, tallying red flags as I eavesdropped, silently cheering when 'the good guy' walked away without falling for any nonsense.

I loved the fact that the bar was a favourite with local bankers and lawyers coming to wind down after a day poring over dull files – or no doubt getting some poor assistant to do it for them. They always arrived in groups, mostly made up of men dressed in expensive suits and doused in delicious-smelling aftershaves, and with the kind of confidence that was hard to resist. They would flirt over the bar as I poured their drinks, catching my eye and asking to take my phone number, before heading home to their wives and children. They never called, but it was a boost to my confidence, and I enjoyed it nonetheless.

I wanted someone who was just as confident, just as successful. Someone who could offer a lifestyle where I'd be comfortable – spoiled even. Meeting these lawyers and bankers, learning how they operated, what their expectations were, was a good lesson to me that I'd never be able to drop the ball once I found the right match. I saw how easily their heads could be turned. I wouldn't be naïve to the fact that I'd have to work to keep the relationship strong. Though most of them were only flirting light-heartedly, I wouldn't put up with my man even glancing elsewhere. I wanted to have his full attention. Be the only woman he saw.

Tonight, though, the man who'd caught my eye wasn't giving me the same playful, harmless-fun vibes. There was something about the way he'd looked at me when he'd ordered his expensive glass of whisky that made me sure he was looking for more than a bit of banter, and he had me intrigued. I kept glancing over to the table beside the door, and each time, it seemed like he was looking right back at me, as if he'd been waiting for me. It sent a frisson of excitement through my body, and I couldn't help the blush that set my cheeks aflame. I bit my lip to keep from smiling as he stared at me now, those dark eyes brooding and sexy, then I turned away, serving another customer, focusing on pouring the drinks, keying in the digits to the card reader.

'Leah!'

I spun, seeing my manager, Liz, standing behind me, her bleached white hair in a frizzy halo surrounding her round face, plumped with filler in an attempt to make her look ten years younger. The reality was, she just looked like a blow-up doll, her lips shiny and taut, fit to burst. 'We're down to the last bottle of white,' she said, handing a glass over the counter to a woman in a red trouser suit with matching acrylic nails. 'Can you go downstairs and grab a couple? I'll get Blaize to bring up a crate once he's back from his break.'

'Sure.' I nodded.

The stairwell was painted black, but the spotlights overhead were bright, and the temperature was notably cooler out here. My ears were ringing from the music, and as I reached the basement, I perched on the edge of a crate, grateful for the momentary escape.

'You look hot.'

I jumped up, seeing the doorway filled with the frame of the man who'd been watching me upstairs.

'No need for that,' he said, smiling, his eyes twinkling mischievously. He glanced over his shoulder to the stairwell behind him, then back to me. 'You want me to go? Because I will.'

I bit the inside of my cheek, wondering if he meant it, and realised I felt no fear. I was sure if I told him I wasn't interested, he'd walk away. He probably had plenty of options when it came to women. I shook my head, a smile tugging at the corners of my lips.

He walked forward, his expensive-looking shoes echoing against the concrete floor. 'Jimmy Gold,' he said, extending a hand.

I took it, and when I did, he ran his thumb along the edge of my wrist, making it tingle. 'Leah,' I said. 'Leah Rigby…'

He still hadn't let go of my hand. 'What time do you finish, Leah Rigby?' he asked, his eyes locked on mine.

'In an hour.'

'Good. I'm taking you to dinner.'

'At midnight?'

'I know a place. You want to?' He leaned in, placing his free hand on the crate beside me, and smiled again, like he already knew my answer.

His face was inches from my own, but I broke his gaze, glancing down and seeing the unmistakable circle of paler skin on his third finger. I'd expected as much. I opened my mouth to make some acerbic comment, asking if his wife would mind, but he followed my gaze, then brazenly slid his hand up the length of my spine, cupping the back of my head and pulling me an inch from his lips.

My comment faded into nothing. This was an opportunity, a chance I shouldn't let slip through my fingers. I wanted him. And if I gave him just enough, then made him chase me for more, if I could resist until I had him hooked on winning the prize, maybe I could get everything I had ever wanted. The life that had always seemed so out of reach to me.

I nodded, feeling his breath hot on my lips. 'I'll go to dinner with you, Jimmy Gold. But I'm not spending the night with you.'

He raised an eyebrow, as if he was sure he could change my mind later, then pulled me into a kiss. I opened my mouth, letting him in. Men like Jimmy loved the thrill of the chase, the excitement and unpredictability of the games. And if his wife couldn't manage to hold on to him, that was *her* loss. Because I was an expert when it came to playing.

NINE

Now

I woke from a light sleep to the sound of a key turning in the
front door. Jimmy's side of the bed was still smooth and unwrin-
kled, and I sat up, listening to the familiar sounds he made
when he came home – his keys jingling as he hung them on the
hook, the thud as his briefcase hit the wooden floor. I jumped
up and rubbed the sleep from my eyes, yanked open the
curtains, then, trying to remind myself not to be the nagging
shrew I so desperately wanted to be right now, walked down the
stairs, following the sound of the kettle switching on. He was
standing with his back turned to me, his white shirt crumpled,
the smell of aftershave and cigarette smoke clinging to him.

'Where have you been?'

He turned, a frown marring his handsome features, and I
knew instantly that he didn't appreciate being greeted like this.

'What's the matter with *you?*' he asked, turning to push two
pieces of bread into the toaster and turning it up to high – he
always liked it overdone, practically burned.

'I asked where you've been. You never called, never sent a message. Do you know what's been going through my mind?'

He shrugged, pulling the butter dish from the larder and fishing around in the cutlery drawer for a knife. 'I had too much to do. I'm working on a big case and I lost track of time.'

'And you couldn't let me know?'

'My phone's not working.'

I stared at him, knowing as well as he did that if he was at work, he could have used any one of the hundreds of other phones to call me.

'Are the kids okay? Still upstairs asleep?' he asked as the toaster popped. He pinched the hot slices between his fingers, dropping them one by one onto the waiting plate.

'The kids aren't here! For Christ's sake, Jimmy! The police have been calling here for you! Carrie phoned last night and made some panicked demand that you call her back, and then she disappeared off the face of the bloody earth. I drove over there and the house was empty! I've been worried sick, and you stroll in and start making breakfast without a care in the world!'

He dropped the plate of toast on the counter, already striding towards the hall. 'What did the police say?' he demanded.

'They wouldn't tell me a thing. Here,' I said, handing him the pad with the number for DCI Farrows. My fingers were trembling as he dialled.

I folded my arms, listening as he asked to speak to the detective, unable to stop myself from looking at him, trying to spot some clue as to where he'd really been. Who he'd really been with.

'What?' he gasped, leaning back against the little wooden table. 'I don't understand. How can—' There was a long silence as he listened to an explanation I longed to be able to hear. 'Oh my God,' he finally whispered, the words hissing through his teeth like a prayer. 'But you're still... Oh, yes... Yes, okay, I will.' He hung up the phone, then picked it up again instantly.

'What is it?' I asked, tension forming a knot in my gut. 'Jimmy? What did the detective say?'

'I have to call Carrie...'

I wanted to demand he speak to me first, tell me what on earth was happening, not turn to his ex, but it was too late.

'Carrie,' he said, his voice urgent. 'I just spoke to the police – what the hell is going on? They said that Ava— What!' he cried as he was interrupted again. He shook his head. 'I don't believe you!'

My ears pricked as I heard Ava's name, my heart in my mouth. I wished I could hear Carrie's side of the conversation because the more Jimmy spoke, the more afraid I felt. I clasped my damp hands together, willing him to hang up, to look at me.

'No!' he cried. 'Drowned? Have they found a body? Then it's not true! I won't believe it! Not our baby!'

I leaned back against the wall, my ears ringing. *Our baby... drowned...* The words made me feel dizzy, unhinged. It *wasn't* true... it just wasn't...

I looked up, realising Jimmy had ended the call. 'They're saying Ava disappeared at the beach yesterday... that they think she might have drowned! Carrie thinks she's been taken by someone. She was rambling, not making any sense!'

He made a sound of despair, and I stepped forward, gripping his arm. 'What did the police say?'

'They want me to go to the station, answer some questions.'

'Answer questions about *what*? You weren't even there.'

'I... I don't know.'

I chewed my lip for a moment, making up my mind. 'You have to go and get Tommy and Maisy and bring them to me. Carrie won't be able to take care of them right now. I can look after them while you figure out what's going on.'

He stared at me blankly, then gave a nod. His eyes were

glassy, unfocused, and I felt like he was trying to process too much all at once. '*Jimmy*. Go, get the kids. Ava will be okay. She's going to turn up, I promise.'

He gave a slow nod, though I could see he was still on the verge of panic. 'Yeah,' he replied, his voice shaky. 'You're right. I'll text Carrie now – let her know I'm coming over.'

I watched as he pulled his phone – the phone he'd been so adamant was broken – from his trouser pocket and saw the screen flash up instantly as he sent the text. A moment later, it vibrated and he looked down. 'She says no,' he said, his head bowed over the phone as if he didn't know what to do next.

'Go anyway. I'm sure they'd rather be here.'

'Right... Yeah, I will. I need to see them.'

'Good.' I nodded, looking down at my pyjamas – red satin shorts and a camisole that did nothing to keep me warm but everything to keep Jimmy looking at me. 'I'll just get dressed. Give me two minutes.'

His head snapped up, his brow furrowed, and I saw how hard he was fighting against his panic. 'No,' he said, seeming to come to his senses. 'You should wait here, babe. I don't think Carrie will take too kindly to you coming with me... not today.'

I opened my mouth to argue, but then closed it, realising he was probably right. I didn't want to do anything to make her dig her heels in and refuse to let Tommy and Maisy come here.

'Fine. Okay. But, Jimmy, be careful, okay?'

'Careful?' he asked, his face blanching as he slipped his feet back into his loafers and pulled on his jacket.

'You know how unhinged she was when you left... how manipulative she became. This could all be some sick game to get you back, to bond as you search for Ava.'

He straightened. 'I can't believe you would say that. You know, when you talk like that, you sound like her... like you'd go to any lengths to get your way. The police have just told me my daughter is missing, presumed dead, and you're worried about who gets my fucking attention?' He shook his head, grabbing the keys from the hook. 'Get a roast or something on. The kids are going to need it when they get here.'

I nodded quietly, watching him go, picturing sweet little Ava, the baby I'd always wanted. And I knew Jimmy would come back to me. Because I held the key to his heart.

TEN

CARRIE

I paced back and forth across the living-room carpet, watching Maisy curled up on the sofa, picking silently at the piece of toast on her plate, rolling little pieces into doughy balls and popping them mechanically into her mouth. I'd turned on the news while she'd been in the bathroom, driven by some sick, morbid need to see if Ava was mentioned, and had seen the freeze-framed image of the woman on the bus, with an appeal for anyone who knew her to come forward. I'd snapped a photo on my phone, determined to figure out why I thought I recognised her, then, hearing Maisy's footsteps in the hall, had turned off the TV, wanting to protect her from the horror of finding her own family featured front and centre. I had to believe that this woman had my daughter, that she could still come back to me, and yet, in doing so, I was well aware that I was setting myself up for heartbreak over and over again.

Tommy had called from his friend's house as I was making breakfast, asking sullenly if he could stay there longer, and though I'd been tempted to agree, to simplify life as much as possibly today, I'd told him to come home. I needed him here. Not least so he could spark some light back into Maisy.

I didn't think there had ever been two siblings closer than he and Maisy. There had never been a moment of jealousy on his part when I'd presented him with a sister when he was just three years old. He'd taken to her without the slightest prompting, and from the moment she'd been able to roll across the carpet, she'd had her sights set on him, making a beeline for wherever he was sitting, slotting herself into his games with utter confidence that she would be welcomed, cherished.

I loved standing outside the bedroom door, listening to them laugh and whisper and yell in delight over whatever game they were absorbed in. Loved how he unconsciously protected her in uncomfortable situations, and how she in turn did the same for him. In fact, lately she'd become quite feisty, especially if she heard Tommy's friends going a bit too far with the playground banter, and I'd been secretly proud to see how bravely she could stand up to a group of pre-teen boys, taking herself out of her comfort zone to pay back her brother for his years of support. She was always the first to do the right thing for others, and I saw myself in her so often, little sprinkles of my own personality emerging from her, confident, outspoken, unafraid. She and Tommy were the best of friends. If anyone could help her break through the trauma of what she'd seen yesterday and begin to talk, it was him.

Not that I expected Tommy to take the news of Ava's disappearance without his own difficulties. I'd had a quick chat with the mother of his school friend, who'd reassured me that he didn't yet know anything about what had happened, in part because she'd had no idea what to tell him. 'They're saying they have teams of divers out there,' she'd said in a horrified whisper that had made me want to drop the phone and stamp all over it. 'Oh, love, what you must be going through.'

'Yes, well,' I'd replied stiffly, stabbing a knife into the butter with more force than necessary. 'Do you need me to come and get him, or can you drop him here?'

We'd ended the call awkwardly, with her agreeing to bring him to me, but now, the reality of having to talk to him, knowing he'd have questions I wouldn't be able to answer, was making me anxious.

'Maisy, please,' I snapped, feeling tense and sick. 'Eat your toast properly. And the banana too. It's going to be a long day, and you'll be hungry later if you don't have something now.'

She continued to stare down at her lap as if I hadn't spoken, and I felt my patience waning dangerously, the stress too much. Every time I paused, even for a second, the waves crashed over me, the smell of salt water, the burn of my lungs, the phantom screams of my baby. It would drive me mad if I let it...

I glanced at the window as I heard a car pull up outside and saw Tommy, slouching and unsmiling, clamber out of the back. A second later, a dark-haired woman got out of the driver's seat and began following him up the path. Did she really have to come with him? What could we possibly have to say to each other? I'd never even met the woman, and now here she was, trying to be included, involved in the trauma that was ripping me apart with every breath. Did she really expect me to make small talk right now? It was the last thing I needed.

I went to open the door and Tommy shrugged past me, heading into the kitchen as if I was no more than a hatstand. 'Thanks for having him... and for dropping him back,' I said, already closing the door.

'Oh, it was the least I could do. He's been good as gold. Such a polite boy. A credit to you.'

I nodded, wondering why he could manage to be a reasonable human being with everyone but me. 'Good,' I managed.

'Have the police said anything? Any leads?'

'No.'

She sighed dramatically. 'I'm sure they'll get there. You know, it's funny. I could have sworn I saw *you* walking up to the car park with a little one yesterday, not long before it all happened.'

I narrowed my eyes, meeting her wide, innocent gaze. 'What exactly are you trying to say?'

She folded her arms, looking uncomfortable. 'I'm not trying to say anything. I just thought it was odd... you know, we were on the blanket just behind you.'

I frowned. 'You're mistaken.'

She pursed her lips, then, after a long pause, nodded. 'I'm sure you're right. I apologise. Look, you're busy, and I need to drop Kieron off at judo.'

She turned, walking back to her car, and I stared after her, wondering why on earth she would say something so dangerous. If the police got wind of an accusation like that, it might derail their entire search.

Furious, I closed the door and headed back inside to go and talk to my son.

'Thanks a lot for dumping me on Kieron last night. His family are vegan and I'm nearly dead from starvation,' Tommy said, not turning from the kitchen counter to face me as he used a fork to scrape chunks of cold chicken off the carcass, piling the meat into an open baguette on the plate beside him.

'And what about Dad?' he continued, biting into his sandwich and finally turning to look at me. He spoke with his mouth full to the brim and I pretended not to be bothered by the half-chewed flecks of bread spraying across the floor. 'He was supposed to have us last night. And Leah said she had a surprise for us this weekend. I was looking forward to it.' His eyes met mine, and I wondered if he intended to sound so malicious, or if it was just the wicked combination of hormones and hunger fulling his anger towards me.

I took a breath, determined not to be drawn into another toxic argument. 'Darling, something happened yesterday...' I swallowed, feeling the wedge of emotion swelling like a damp sponge in the back of my throat, making it hard to speak. 'Ava was playing on the sand with Maisy. And somehow she got lost.'

'Right?' he said, raising his eyebrows as if he was losing patience with me. 'So? She's fine now, isn't she?'

I shook my head. 'No,' I whispered. 'We... they... can't find her. There's a chance she went into the water.'

The sandwich was clamped in his palm, and I saw his fingers turn white, his grip tightening as he stared wide-eyed back at me. 'But she can't swim! She's only a baby!'

I nodded, unable to offer a response.

'So what are you saying? She's dead? My sister is dead?'

I stepped towards him, conscious of Maisy sitting in the living room just across the hall. 'Shh, please, Tommy, we don't want to frighten Maisy. This has been really traumatic for her, and we don't have any answers yet. Ava might have wandered off, or—'

'Why the hell weren't you watching her? What kind of mother are you, to let her just disappear like that?'

I gasped, his words cutting through me – words I'd thought to myself on repeat since the moment I'd realised she was missing. I'd berated myself, and yet to hear it from my firstborn, his accusation so raw and full of vitriol, hurt more deeply than I could ever have imagined. How could he hate me so much? Didn't he realise I would have done anything to keep this family together? That it was his father, not me, who'd ripped his world apart?

'She wasn't by herself,' I said softly. 'She was with Maisy, and I was right beside them. I only turned my back for a moment. I never expected her to just disappear like that.'

'Well, you were wrong!'

'Tommy, *please*,' I said, reaching for him. 'I need you to be brave, to be on my side. We have to stick together – now more than ever. I'm going to call the police again for an update, and then we're going out to look for her.' I hoped I wasn't about to take my nine- and twelve-year-old children into a horror story where they would be the ones to find a washed-up body, but I couldn't let my mind go there. I had to think of the positive outcomes.

He slapped my hand away. 'I want to go to Dad and Leah. I'm not going anywhere with you. You're fucking crazy!'

'Tommy!' I froze, stunned that he even knew a word like that. I couldn't recognise him right now, couldn't understand how the boy who'd been my sweet little sidekick just months ago could suddenly speak to me so disgustingly. I took a deep breath. 'Watch your language,' I said, my voice shaking. 'I won't have you talk to me like that. I'm having a hard-enough time right now without you treating me like the villain. I'm your mother and you'll do as you're told!'

'Some mother,' he sneered. He held my gaze defiantly, and then, still clutching his sandwich, pushed past me, heading into the living room and closing the door behind him.

I pressed my hands to my face, instantly regretting that I'd laid out an ultimatum, making him feel backed into a corner. I'd learned enough by now to know that when he got himself worked up like that, he was looking for a reaction – he *wanted* me to snap so he could storm off. Quietly, I padded across the hall, listening at the door, hoping to pick up Maisy's voice, but all I could hear was Tommy asking if she was okay, getting nothing back from her. Despite my anger, my hurt, I was relieved he was at least being sweet to her.

I walked back to the kitchen, picking up my phone to call the police station. There was a missed call, and I wondered how I hadn't heard it. When I clicked on it, seeing the voicemail notification, my heart skipped a beat as I saw the saved contact – the hospital – and for half a second, I wondered if they might have found her.

The thrill of hope was dashed the instant I clicked on the message, pressing the phone to my ear and hearing the clipped, hurried tones of my colleague, Dr Maxine Ross, asking why I hadn't turned up to work, telling me to get there as soon as humanly possible, that they were run off their feet. I was shocked to realise I'd forgotten to even contact them to let them know what had happened, to give them time to get cover. In all my working years, I'd never called in sick, never missed a shift. If you didn't go, someone else had to keep working when they'd been up for twenty-four hours straight. It put lives at risk and increased the stress in an environment that was high pressure on the best of days. I'd been due in first thing, and the fact that it had slipped my mind made me realise just how much shock I'd been in. And as much as I knew I had to stay present, I realised that what I wanted to do most in this moment was to go to work and lose myself in the pain and trauma of strangers, so that I didn't have to face my own.

I was about to call her back but instead found myself clicking on the photograph I'd taken of the woman on the news earlier. Ava wasn't visible in the picture, but I zoomed in on the woman's face, willing myself to remember. And then, like a bucket of cold water to the face, I realised who she was. Why she had done this. I swayed, gripping the kitchen counter for support. Leah had warned me what she was planning, but I'd never taken her seriously. And now, I thought, bile rising up from my empty stomach, burning the back of my throat, I understood what a terrible mistake it had been to let her anywhere near my children.

ELEVEN

LEAH

Then

My arms were folded tight across my chest, my jaw set as I stood barricading the door of my home to the witch who was shouting at me.

'Jimmy will be back in an hour,' I said firmly, meeting Carrie's irate expression. 'Come back then if you have a problem.'

She shook her head, stepping closer. 'Absolutely not! I want to take my own children home, and you don't have any right to stop me.'

'It's Saturday night!' I exclaimed. 'We *always* have them Saturdays.'

She gave a dramatic sigh. 'Yes, but what my husband has failed to tell you is that we made arrangements for me to collect them early this weekend. I'm taking them on a day out tomorrow. I want to set off first thing.'

'You can collect them in the morning in that case, if Jimmy agrees. Not that he should have to. It's *our* time with them.'

She shook her head. 'I'm taking them now! It's Maisy's birthday tomorrow, and I want her to wake up in her own bed.'

'She has her own bed here. And Jimmy has planned a lovely morning for her,' I said, though it wasn't true. *I'd* been the one to remember the date. To buy and wrap the presents. There was a pink iced cake decorated with edible silver balls and glitter hidden on the top shelf of the larder, and I had tickets booked to see the new Disney movie at the cinema tomorrow afternoon. I'd spent ages planning it all for her, sure that Carrie wouldn't make an effort. Jimmy knew what I'd been doing. How could he not have mentioned a change of plan? The only answer was that Carrie had known he would be out this evening and was lying to me now. 'I'm sorry, Carrie, but you can't just turn up at my home like this and change the rules. I think we need to establish some boundaries. You'll see the kids Monday, as usual.'

I turned to go back inside, hoping the children hadn't heard the disagreement. They'd been painting in the kitchen when I left them, and I was sure Ava would be covered head to toe if I didn't get back in there soon.

'If you don't bring them out, I'm coming in. They are my children. Mine and Jimmy's. You don't have the power to keep them from me,' she said fiercely. 'Jimmy and I have discussed this. He never bothered with birthdays. He *knows* I'm coming. The decision's been made, Leah.'

'Mummy!'

Maisy's shout of delight came from behind me, and she ran outside, a painting of a butterfly clasped in her hands. 'Look, I painted this side, then folded it over, and now it's perfectly symmetrical! Is it beautiful? Do you like it?'

'Oh, it's gorgeous! That must have been so much fun to do,' Carrie said, taking the picture from her. 'Do you want to bring it home?'

Maisy nodded.

'I'll pop it on the parcel shelf to dry. Go and tell Tommy and Ava it's time to go.'

'Carrie—' I broke off with a gasp as I saw someone getting off the bus that had just pulled up opposite. The grey-haired woman, though I hadn't seen her in years, was instantly familiar as she fixed her dark eyes on me, walking purposefully across the road. I felt my legs turn to lead, the ground gluing my feet in place, though I wanted to turn and run inside, then slam the door tightly shut.

'Leah!' she called as I turned away.

'Actually, Carrie,' I said, 'I really don't want us to fall out over this. Take them for now and I'll get Jimmy to call you later. We just need to be on the same page, right?' The words came out too fast, my nerves making my voice sound strained and unfamiliar.

Carrie looked at me, then to the woman. 'Who is she?' she asked as Ava ran to the door, purple paint smeared across her cheek. Carrie scooped her up and kissed her forehead, but her eyes were still darting from me to the woman, who'd come to a stop on the path in front of me.

'I'm her mother.'

I felt my heart drop, my spine tensing as her voice brought back a thousand memories I'd tried to delete from my mind. Ignoring her, unwilling to get into a conversation with an audience hovering nearby, I turned my back on her and tried to smile as Tommy emerged, bags in hand.

'Why are we leaving? I didn't know you were coming,' he said, smiling warmly at Carrie.

Carrie frowned in confusion at my mother, as if she wanted to ask something, then dragged her gaze to Tommy. 'We're going to pick up a takeaway, and then tomorrow we have a busy day of celebrating for your sister's birthday.'

'That sounds good. Bye, Leah. Tell Dad we'll see him next week.' Tommy gave me an awkward hug, and I nodded stiffly in return, watching the kids get into the car. Carrie put Ava in her seat.

I met my mother's eyes. 'What the hell are you doing here?' I hissed through gritted teeth.

Carrie straightened, closing the car door, and I pasted on a false smile. 'Glad we were able to sort out that confusion. I hope you have a lovely day tomorrow,' I said, clasping my hands together, willing them to leave quickly.

I realised I hadn't given Maisy her presents to take with her and glanced over my shoulder to the house, but it was no good. I didn't want to risk leaving my mother alone to talk to Carrie, to tell her all my secrets – and I knew that she would. She'd never been good at holding her tongue. I would have to give them to her another day. The cake would go stale, and the moment would have passed.

Maisy wound down her window. 'Bye, Leah!' she called.

'Bye, darling! I'll look forward to celebrating with you very soon. Have a lovely birthday.'

Carrie gave us one final, speculative glance, and I knew I'd aroused her suspicion in changing my mind so quickly, letting her win so easily. To my relief, though, she climbed into her car without another word to me and drove away.

I turned slowly to face my mother and found her staring at me. Her expression was consumed with expectation. I was struck by terror that everything I'd worked for was about to be ruined. Whatever it took, I had to make her leave. I would do anything to make her fade back into the shadows. *Anything.*

TWELVE

CARRIE

Then

I washed my face over the tiny ceramic corner sink in the toilet cubicle, rubbing hard with a rough paper towel at my skin. After tossing it into the pedal bin, the black metal lid closing with a thump, I looked up at my reflection, seeing how my cheeks had turned pink and angry from the abrasive hand soap – the only option available to me. The ward was sweltering this afternoon, and having rushed from one patient to the next since I got here, I had spent the past twenty minutes holding the penis of an exceptionally overweight man with poor hygiene who'd come to the hospital complaining that he hadn't been able to urinate for more than a day. He'd been writhing in agony, and though my duty to help him was at the forefront of my mind, it was a task I would have happily passed off to a colleague if I could have got away with it.

Everyone who went into medicine had that one thing they'd rather avoid if at all possible. For the majority of my colleagues, it was vomit. I'd lost count of how many times I'd found a student nurse or a junior doctor hiding in the staff room, retching over a disposable cardboard sick bowl they'd pilfered from the stock cupboard, chunks of someone's decomposing dinner melded into their hair, splayed across the front of their shirt. Over time, they learned to control the revulsion, suppress their nausea, but they never really let it go.

I, on the other hand, had never been fazed by sick. Even before I'd had children and grown accustomed to the tummy bugs they picked up at nursery, the smell of Dettol lingering in my carpets, I'd been able to take it in my stride. No, the thing that turned *my* stomach was urine. It was the heat of it I couldn't stand. The way the droplets seemed to condensate, become airborne, the smell inescapable. That feeling that with every breath, I was absorbing tiny particles into my lungs, the ammonia hitting the back of my throat, making me want to lose my professional cool and demand the patient drink some water before expecting me to deal with *that*.

I'd spent the best part of twenty minutes crouching down in front of the man's genitalia, my calves burning, the catheter refusing to go in, the musky smell of unwashed skin making my stomach turn, when, without warning, he'd urinated right into my face. There had been no apology from him as I'd rushed from the room, just a jovial announcement of 'That'll do the job!' And now, I longed to leave, to go back to my clean, comfortable house, climb into a scorching-hot shower and wash obsessively until all traces of him were gone. I shuddered, resisting the urge to rinse my face again. There was no time for that. I had to get back out there.

Heading away from the toilets, I walked quickly down the corridor and through the double doors into pandemonium. I stopped to take in the scene, feeling instantly guilty that I hadn't been on hand. I should have been here.

A couple of paramedics accompanied by a junior doctor and three nurses were wheeling a wailing woman towards a side room, talking back and forth in clipped, urgent voices. I caught the unmistakable scent of blood, knowing without needing to look that there would be a lot. Mikayla, the consultant on duty, hurried past me in their direction.

'Where the *hell* have you been? You're needed!' She pointed to the external doors, and I saw a second ambulance unloading another patient, a junior doctor already rushing forward to meet them.

'Domestic incident,' Mikayla continued. 'Stepfather went mad with a knife. You take the nine-year-old; I'll take the mother. I think mine is going to be heading up to theatre, but the paramedics said yours might not.'

She turned from me to go into the side room, and I glanced back to the entrance, catching sight of the tiny figure lying too still on the trolley as it came towards me, the blood splattered across her milky-white thighs, staining her bright yellow sundress.

For a second, I couldn't speak. The desire – the absolute need – to beg Mikayla to swap with me, let *me* take the mother instead, swept over my body, and it took all my strength not to shout my pleas after her. The blood didn't bother me. The fact that the mother's wounds were presumed to be far worse didn't scare me. But that bright yellow sundress, those piercing blue eyes staring up at the ceiling as if she could ignore the drama unfolding around her, the pain she was undoubtedly in... I couldn't stand it.

I swallowed, clasping my hands in a tight ball, taking in her little face surrounded by a tangle of dirty-blonde hair, and was dragged back to a moment in time I longed to erase. If I could have, I would have sliced open my head and cut the memory from my brain with a scalpel. Given myself the gift of amnesia, though some would say I didn't deserve that. That the memories of the past were there to serve as my punishment, a reminder of how far I had come – and how easy it would be for me to slip again, destroy another innocent life.

I closed my eyes, willing away the past, reminding myself that things were different now. People relied on me.

I looked up, realising the paramedic was talking to me, sharing what she knew so far, and put my hand into the pocket of my trousers, pinching hard at my thigh to drag myself back to the present and focus on her words. As if I'd flicked a switch, I swatted away the past and stepped into the role I was born to do. I was a professional. I was good at my job.

And, I reminded myself, lifting up the sundress to assess the damage, with the exception of a couple of people, both of whom had a lot to lose if they revealed the truth, not a soul knew my secret. I would do anything to ensure that didn't change.

THIRTEEN

Now

I gripped the kitchen counter, feeling myself sway. From behind me, I could hear the sound of a ping-pong ball hitting the living-room wall over and over. Tommy knew the sound drove me to distraction, not to mention it was wearing away several patches on the wallpaper, but right now, I didn't have it in me to go to war with him over it. I had bigger worries.

The doorbell rang, and I heard the ball fall to the ground as I rushed down the hall to open the front door. I flung it open and was hit with a wave of relief at seeing my husband standing there, his outfit dishevelled, his expression worried, but still as handsome as ever. I flung myself into his arms, my fingers embedding into his shoulder blades. 'I knew you'd come,' I breathed.

He held me for just a moment, then eased out of my grasp, holding my forearms as if he was trying to keep his distance. I frowned, shaking my head in confusion.

'I've come for the kids,' he replied. 'It's the weekend.'

'But... I replied to your text... I said no. I want them with me.'

'It's the weekend,' he replied, as if that answered everything.

I gripped his wrist, holding on to him. 'Did you speak to the police? Did they tell you about the lady on the bus?'

He shook his head. 'I'm planning to head to the station after I take these guys home,' he replied, and I cringed at his use of the word.

'*This* is their home,' I reminded him.

He raised an eyebrow. 'What lady on the bus?' he asked.

I pulled out my phone, showing him the photograph, waiting for him to confirm what I already knew. He took the phone from me, looking closely at the picture.

'The detective came here last night and showed me some CCTV footage of this woman getting on a bus. I'm sure he'll show you too. She had Ava. This woman has our baby, Jimmy!'

'What?' He shook his head, confused. 'Are you certain?'

I hesitated. 'It looked just like her. You couldn't see her face, but I'm sure... It *has* to be her. Don't you see who the woman is though? Can't you recognise her?'

He looked at the photo again. 'I don't think so.'

'Jimmy, it's Leah's mum! Look again!' I said, wishing the image was clearer. I doubted he'd spent a lot of time with Leah's family. He'd never been one for playing that role, but still, he had to have met her at least a few times over the past six months.

'No,' he said slowly. 'You're mistaken. It's not her.'

He handed back the phone. I stared at him. 'I know it is. Why are you protecting her? I told you what Leah threatened last month, didn't I? That she was going to take the children from me.'

He pulled his wrist from my grasp and folded his arms, stepping back and giving me a hard stare. 'You and I both know you overembellished that story. I spoke to Leah about it, and all she intended was to take the kids for a few weeks so you could go to that conference you mentioned. She said you were looking exhausted and she would rather the kids came to her than be put into wraparound childcare. She was trying to help, Carrie, and as usual you twisted it into something sinister.'

'Jimmy, listen, you've got it wrong. I think Leah might have Ava hidden somewhere... I think she planned this—'

'No, I won't listen. All I know is that my baby girl is missing. And there's a damn good chance she's floating face-down in the sea because *you* weren't watching her. It's not the first time you've put one of our children in danger, is it?' he accused, his eyes narrowed into tiny black bullets.

'You said we wouldn't talk about that again. You know what happened... that it wasn't my fault.'

'Yeah, right,' he spat. 'Nothing ever is, is it, Carrie?' He stepped closer. 'You're to stop with the accusations towards my fiancée,' he said, putting an emphasis on the word, making me feel sick. 'It only makes you look jealous. I won't have you sending the police on a wild goose chase with false information. I don't know who that woman is, but she's nothing to do with Leah. Let the police do their job, and pray to God that Ava turns up unharmed because if she doesn't, Carrie...' His voice cracked, and despite his anger, I reached for him, consumed by the need to comfort him. He sidestepped my hug, holding up a warning hand and clearing his throat. 'If she doesn't, I'll never forgive you. And neither will her siblings.'

I clasped my hands beneath my chin, trembling, unable to fathom how he could be so cruel. It wasn't at all the response I'd anticipated. He'd never been so unkind. Even during the affairs – and there had been many – he'd always been charming and sweet to me. Perfect, other than the obvious flaw. This had to be Leah's doing. Her influence.

Was he telling the truth that he didn't recognise the woman, or was he protecting her? And if so, why? Could it be that he was in on Leah's plan to take the children from me? I took a shaky breath, trying not to cry, not to show him how hurt I was, how afraid of what might be coming soon. I felt suddenly unable to be vulnerable in front of this new, harder version of the man I'd once adored. I'd imagined him coming inside. Holding me while we both sobbed. Working together to find our daughter, bonded by tragedy. But his allegiance had clearly changed, and it was frightening to realise how alone I was.

'Kids!' Jimmy shouted. 'Daddy's here.'

'I don't want them to go!' I exclaimed. 'I need them with me. I don't want Leah around them. Not until we know for sure who that woman is.'

'I won't tell you again. She's nothing to do with us.'

'I want the children here!' I made to close the door in his face, and he stepped forward, wedging it open with his foot.

'That's not up to you.'

I looked over my shoulder, hearing the living-room door open. Tommy ran straight to the porch, picking up the bag filled with his things and handing Maisy's purple holdall to his dad.

'I'm not staying here,' he said, clearly having overheard my plea. 'I want to go to Leah,' he added, giving a quick nod to Jimmy before heading to the car.

I watched, hurt, as he climbed in, pointedly looking out at the road rather than face me. Maisy slipped silently past me, and I reached out, grabbing her hand.

'Darling, you don't have to go... Won't you stay? I can take you to your dad's later. Or better yet,' I offered, 'we can all stay together.' I looked up at Jimmy, lowering my voice. 'Don't you think it best? They need stability right now – they need us to be a family,' I reasoned, even as I heard the car door slam, Maisy having walked away without bothering to listen to me.

'Jim,' I whispered, gripping his hand and squeezing it tight, 'she hasn't said one word since yesterday. Not a word! She's in shock. I can't send her away like this. She needs to be here, where I can take care of her.'

'Like you took care of Ava?'

I stepped back as if he'd slapped me, his accusation cutting through the numbness, making my eyes well up with pain. 'That's not fair,' I whispered.

He looked away, silent for a moment, seeming to try and calm himself down. 'You can't imagine how much I'm blaming myself for what's happened. I never wanted to leave the kids with you in the first place. If I find out you—' He broke off, looking away.

'Jimmy, *please!*' I said, trying to make him understand. 'It doesn't have to be like this. Let's go to the beach now, together, *all* of us, and figure this out.' I reached for him again, needing to feel his heartbeat against my chest, regulating my emotions, the way he'd always been able to do. I wrapped my arms around his neck, holding on tight as I pressed my cheek against his. 'Don't leave... I need you.'

He stepped out of the embrace and shook his head. 'I'm going to take Tommy and Maisy to Leah now, and then after I speak to the police, I'm going out to look for Ava myself. *Alone.*'

I pressed my lips together, trying not to cry, seeing that he meant it. Every time he left was no less painful than the first. Over the past six months, since that awful day, I'd done everything I could to win back his affection. I'd lost a stone and a half. I'd bought a new wardrobe, sexy tight-fitting tops and lingerie to remind him who he'd married, making sure to let my satin dressing gown slip open when he came to the door. I'd got my hair highlighted, and even remembered to put on make-up in the mornings, but it hadn't made the slightest difference. The only choice I had now was to wait out this obsession with the other woman and hope he started to see what a terrible mistake he'd made. Reverted to the kind, charming man he'd always been. This stranger wasn't my Jimmy. I had to make him see how much of himself he was losing in pandering to his mistress.

He threw Maisy's bag into the boot of his car, then, his focus on the children, asked if they'd put their seat belts on before starting the engine. I saw him glance at me as he pulled away, his eyes blazing with accusation, blame, and hugged myself tightly, feeling afraid and uncertain. If he spoke to the police while he was still angry with me, I couldn't be sure what he might say. And that, I thought as I headed back inside the empty house, terrified me.

FOURTEEN

LEAH

I poured hot water slowly over the instant coffee in the mugs, hyper-aware of the two men in smart suits standing behind me, both having refused to take a seat while they waited. I felt scrutinised, watched, and it was taking all my willpower not to talk nineteen to the dozen in an attempt to distil the awkward atmosphere. You had to be careful with the police. Guarded. I'd learned that lesson the hard way. You couldn't trust them, no matter how at ease they tried to manipulate you into feeling.

I turned, placing the mugs one by one on the counter in front of them. 'Jimmy should be back any minute. But I wish you'd waited for him to come to the station. It's frightening enough for the children to know Ava is missing. I was hoping to protect them from all this.'

'Of course,' said the one who'd identified himself as DCI Farrows, looping his finger through the thick ceramic handle and taking a sip of the scalding coffee without so much as a wince, his eyes trained on my face. From the way he'd sounded on the phone, I'd pictured him to be older. He looked around Jimmy's age, and there was something about him that felt off. His eyes were cold, even when he smiled, and the way he looked at me made me feel like I was on display. I was glad I'd had time to get changed out of my nightwear before he turned up.

He scratched his ear, wiping his finger on his shirt. I folded my arms, unsure what else to say. When the two of them had turned up on my doorstep, the terror I'd felt had been instant and, I feared, obvious. The blotchy red rash that always bloomed when I was afraid, spreading up my neck, making my cheeks prickle uncomfortably; the way my voice trembled and my hands shook. I could feel sweat beneath my arms and nausea pooling in my belly. I'd asked after Ava, if they had news, if they knew what had happened to her, and predictably been met with clipped, unhelpful responses that spared any details, other than the fact that the search was still going full throttle.

'Where were you yesterday between the hours of four and six p.m.?'

The question knocked me off balance, but I set my jaw, determined not to show it. 'I was here, and then I went to Carrie's to pick up the children. Obviously they weren't there, so I came home.' There was a tremble to my voice and I hoped the two detectives hadn't noticed.

'You came straight home?' DCI Farrows repeated as his colleague wrote something down on an electronic pad.

'That's right.'

'You didn't happen to stop by your mother's house?'

I frowned. 'What? No. I'm estranged from her. I haven't seen her for a very long time.'

'Right,' he said, the word coming out slow and lazy. His eyes remained trained on my face, and I felt myself squirm internally under his scrutiny.

The sound of Tommy's voice out the front, still high and childlike, made relief wash over me. 'That's them now. Wait here, please. I'll send the children upstairs so they aren't upset by seeing you,' I said pointedly, not bothering to hide my irritation with them for invading my home. I could have refused them entry, of course, but I didn't want to do anything that might cause them to take a negative view of Jimmy – or me.

I didn't wait for a response as I rushed to meet the children at the front door. It opened just as I reached it, and I smiled as they came through. 'Hi, sweetheart,' I said, hugging Tommy first, then Maisy, who looked pale and frightened. I kept my arm around her, squeezing her shoulders gently as I looked up at Jimmy. 'You have some visitors in the kitchen,' I said, meeting his eyes, seeing that he understood my meaning.

He frowned. 'Why did you let them in?'

'I didn't think it wise to make them leave. Sorry.'

He sighed. 'Right, fine. I want to talk to them anyway.' He walked past me, and I turned my attention back to Tommy and Maisy. 'I missed you last night. How are you both doing?'

Maisy seemed to shrink into my side, remaining utterly silent as Tommy shook his head. 'I don't understand what happened. Ava can't have just disappeared. Mum should have been watching her!' He looked down, concealing his face, and I knew he was hiding tears.

I pulled him into a hug with my free arm and pressed a kiss to the top of his head. 'It's a scary time for all of us. But we have to stick together and keep holding on to the hope that Ava will be found safe and we'll see her soon. We're a family, right?'

He nodded, clutching at me like a boy much younger than twelve, needing my support. It made me feel like I had a real place in his world, and that was something so special.

'Listen,' I said as he pulled back. 'I have to go and help Daddy for a minute, but I've put some treats in your room, Tommy – for both of you,' I added, smiling down at Maisy, who met my eye briefly. 'There are home-made muffins, and I *might* have been to the Lego shop this week. Why don't you both go and investigate what I got for you, and I'll come and see you in a bit?'

Tommy nodded, and I could see him fighting between sadness and curiosity. 'Thanks, Leah,' he said, turning for the stairs.

Maisy didn't move.

I crouched in front of her, brushing her hair back from her eyes with my fingers. She wouldn't be so easy to distract, but I wouldn't stop trying. 'You've really had a hard time, haven't you?' I said softly. 'But you're safe here, okay? And we're going to do everything we can to find our little Ava. We'll all be together again soon – I'm sure of it, darling.'

She stared at me wide-eyed and unsmiling, and I saw the dark rings under her eyes. The moment the police were gone, I was going to run her a nice bubble bath and get her into bed to watch a film. She was clearly exhausted. I kissed her cheek and took her by the hand to the bottom of the stairs. 'Go on up, darling, before Tommy gets carried away with those muffins.'

I watched her go, hoping she'd be okay, knowing that if Ava wasn't found, she might never recover from this. Then I turned towards the kitchen, curious to hear what Jimmy had to say for himself.

FIFTEEN

As I headed back into the kitchen, I heard Jimmy's voice morph from the cool irritation he'd gone in there with to a defensive, angry bark. I slipped silently in, taking a seat at the round wooden table, my back to the patio doors as I took in the expressions of each of the three men, none of whom had acknowledged my arrival.

'No need to get worked up, James,' DCI Farrows said with a half-disguised smirk, and I wondered if his use of Jimmy's first name was to show a lack of respect. Surely, given the horrific circumstances, he should be talking to him with compassion, empathy, not bringing this antagonistic energy. Unless, of course, he was trying to get Jimmy to bite back. 'I simply wanted to know your relationship to Carrie Gold. She's your wife, isn't that right?'

'Like I told you, we're separated.'

'And the divorce is under way?'

Jimmy met his eyes with malice, and I wondered what I'd missed in the few minutes I'd been in the hallway with the children that had set everyone on edge. 'My fiancée is sitting right there,' he said, gesturing to me. 'As far as I'm aware, bigamy was outlawed in this country quite some time ago.'

DCI Farrows gave a nod. 'What's your custody agreement? Would you say there have been occasions when you and Mrs Gold have come to blows over who gets the children?'

I noted that he used *Mrs* instead of *Dr* and wondered if that was intentional on his part. Jimmy glanced briefly at me, and I knew he was thinking of all the times Carrie had refused to hand over the children on a Friday night – refused to even tell Tommy and Maisy that we had arrived, instead distracting them somewhere inside the house, so that Jimmy couldn't even give them a hug.

In those first few weeks after he walked out on her, before Tommy and Maisy had got to know me, there had been multiple occasions when she'd convinced them to stay with her, leaving Jimmy to drive home alone, broken-hearted at the realisation that in walking away from his wife, he'd lost his children. The idea that he might go back to her just to keep up his relationship with them had terrified me, but as time had passed and I'd formed my own bonds with them, they'd come willingly, despite Carrie pulling out all her tricks to keep them by her side.

It hadn't been so simple with Ava, of course. She was still practically a baby, and it was only natural that she wanted to be close to her mother. Every time she got a new tooth, or a fever, Carrie insisted she couldn't come to us. Jimmy had commented privately to me that it was baffling to see his workaholic ex suddenly so interested in parenting. When they'd lived together, she hadn't shown nearly so much dedication to the role.

He glanced away from me now, and I wondered how many of his old neighbours would admit they'd heard the two of them arguing on the driveway. There had been that one horrible time when Carrie had pushed him to the limit of his patience, and he'd taken Ava, wailing and red-faced, from her mother's arms and driven back here with her. They might not understand that it was his love, his desperation to spend time with his children, that had forced his hand. Carrie had to learn that the children were not solely hers. She had to share. But why were the police asking about all of this? What did it have to do with anything anyway?

'The children come to me every weekend, on a Friday night. Sometimes we have to adjust for Carrie's work schedule, but if I'm away on business, Leah is always happy to step in and have them. And we have a couple of trusted babysitters who come over, mainly to Carrie, when needed too.'

I nodded, waiting for the next question to be directed at me, but instead, the second police officer chimed in. 'I don't imagine it's something you're used to.'

Jimmy frowned. 'What's that?'

'Having to ask permission to take your own children. Not getting your way. We looked you up,' the officer continued, his voice smooth and slick, like oil. 'You have quite the reputation in the courtroom. They call you the Dragon, don't they? Because you spit flames when you feel like you're starting to lose.'

Jimmy stared at him, his expression inviting battle. 'Make your point.' His words were slow, dangerous, and I felt myself holding my breath, wanting to warn him not to be antagonistic. That he'd only make the situation worse.

'I think I just did,' the officer replied with a dismissive shrug.

'Are you insinuating that I would kidnap my own daughter? I told you, I was due to have her here last night. Why would I go to the trouble of swiping her off the beach when I was going to pick her up that same evening?' he sneered, clearly taking an instant dislike to both of these men, just as I had. He met the detective's eye, his stance strong and arrogant, every inch the lawyer in this moment. 'I just spoke to Carrie when I picked up the kids. She said you have a lead. Footage of a woman on a bus with a child that might have been Ava.'

'What?' I breathed, holding on to the edge of the table, my fingernails digging into the soft wood.

Farrows nodded. 'That's correct. We've been unable to locate the woman so far, but perhaps you might be able to identify her.'

'Why would you say that?' I asked.

He turned to me, his gaze on my face, and I felt my cheeks flush under his scrutiny. 'Because when it comes to kidnapping cases, the abductor is often known to the child. And considering there wasn't a scene at the beach, no witnesses to say they saw a struggle, no crying heard by Mrs Gold, it would make sense for Ava to have gone willingly, if in fact she didn't go into the water.'

I swallowed. 'Right. I see.' I remained in my chair as the second police officer brought a laptop over to the table, placing it in front of me. Jimmy walked over, standing by my side as the PC pressed play. I held my breath, watching as the woman sat down, lifting a toddler who had the same curly hair as Ava into her arms. Jimmy's fingers dug into my shoulder as we stared silently at the screen. The video ended, and I heard him suck in a breath. 'Is that all there is?'

'It's all we have right now,' Farrows replied from across the kitchen, and I realised with discomfort that he'd been watching us for our reactions. 'Do you know the woman?'

Jimmy shook his head, and I mirrored his response. 'No. I have no idea who she is. And I don't think that's Ava. She's too big.'

'Mrs Gold thought it was her.' Farrows left the comment hanging in the air. I wished he'd stop calling her that. It was a constant source of irritation that she had refused to give up

Jimmy's name, and hearing the word *Mrs* made it feel far too intimate for me. *I* wanted to be the only Mrs Gold in Jimmy's life.

Jimmy shook his head. 'I don't think so.'

'And you're certain you don't recognise this woman?' he pushed as the other officer enlarged the image on the screen. I glanced at the face, then looked down at my hands, my heart thrumming against my ribs. A wave of nausea washed over me, and I suddenly felt as though I was going to throw up. I wondered if I could excuse myself without making myself look guilty and decided against it. Swallowing, I took a deep breath.

'I'm quite certain,' Jimmy answered, his voice strong, unwavering.

'And you, Miss Rigby? Do *you* know who the woman in the video is?' Farrows' eyes bored into the top of my head.

'No,' I whispered. 'I don't recognise her.'

'Are you sure?'

Jimmy stepped in front of me, blocking me from view. 'I hope you've given Carrie the same grilling,' he said, his anger evident in his tone. '*She* was the one who lost Ava. She should have been supervising her, not letting her run wild next to the sea! Have you asked her why she wasn't watching out for our toddler?' He shook his head, making it clear that he thought very little of the line of questioning. 'Makes me wonder where you were trained. Because I'd be asking for a refund if I were you, mate.'

Farrows folded his arms across his chest. 'It's interesting,' he said in a pondering tone, 'that you were expecting the children last night, and yet you weren't aware of the fact that Ava was missing until this morning. Didn't it concern you that your children hadn't arrived?'

'I had to work late. I knew they'd be safe with Leah. She's very maternal.'

I looked up at him and smiled, soaking up the compliment. I

hadn't wanted to nag, to dig for praise, but to hear him say those words was everything I could have hoped for. I wanted him to see the potential I had as a mother; to know I was worlds apart from his cold, detached ex. That I could give him the family, the home he'd always longed for.

'Sure,' Farrows said, tilting his head as if he were thinking on the spot, 'but when Leah called you to say the children weren't there when she went to collect them, didn't it worry you?'

Jimmy was silent.

'Did you speak to Carrie last night?'

He continued to stare daggers at Farrows, and I knotted my fingers in my lap, watching him closely, curious to hear his response. I'd felt sure when Carrie had called that she'd seen him, that there was something the two of them were keeping from me.

Farrows continued. 'According to the security guard at your office, you weren't on the sign-in sheet for the building at all yesterday. And yet you didn't arrive home until this morning. That's what you told my colleague on the phone earlier, isn't it? So where were you, Jimmy? And why wouldn't you call your ex if she'd disappeared with your children the night you were due to have them?'

I held my breath, suddenly frightened of what he might admit. If he hadn't been working, then where had he been? And who with? There were things that couldn't be unsaid. Things I would prefer not to hear. I couldn't risk losing everything I'd worked so hard for.

Jimmy shook his head. 'You're wasting your time here. I want you to get back out there and do your job. Find my baby girl!' He picked up his jacket and slipped it over his shoulders. 'But since you seem incapable of focusing on the task at hand, I'm going to do it myself.'

He strode across the room, kissed me on the forehead, then

left, the door slamming behind him. He hadn't answered the question, and with a sinking feeling in the pit of my stomach, I had to admit to myself that the reason for that was obvious.

SIXTEEN

CARRIE

The pebbles crunched beneath my feet, seagulls circling above, searching for the miracle of a dropped sandwich or a handful of greasy chips. I watched them, marvelling at how simple their lives were. Eat, sleep, fight, shit. Trading intelligent thought for pure, unadulterated animal instinct. Free from the dark emotions that threatened to engulf me right now. How fortunate they were.

There had been no way I could stay at home, try to rest, without the children. I could hardly believe how cold Jimmy had been when he'd come for them. Some part of me had expected a different reaction. That as the only two people who could understand the pain of what we were going through, we might offer some level of comfort to each other. He'd been there, by my side, when she was born. He'd cried, taking the tiny flailing bundle, still streaked in blood, from my arms, promising to be the father she deserved, to protect her from danger. And as his eyes had met mine, the trust he'd always had for me notably absent, I'd known he meant it.

It was hard to reconcile the hostile stranger who'd made those threats this morning with the man who'd promised to love me for ever. The man who'd once woken me before dawn with a picnic basket ready, bundling me into a warm car and driving to this very same beach as the sun crested, a soft, peachy orange, so we could eat croissants still warm from the oven and drink sweet, milky coffee out of the old plastic Thermos his grandma had gifted us when we'd bought our first house together. He'd been so thoughtful back then. Romantic. Caring. Where had *that* Jimmy gone?

Despite his habit of getting distracted by the next shiny thing, I knew deep down that he hadn't been entirely erased, though that bitch of a girlfriend had tried to change him beyond recognition. If it hadn't been for me getting carried away, telling him things I shouldn't have, he might still be living under my roof. Not hers.

As I got closer to the bright yellow tape cordoning off the section of beach where Ava had last been seen, I slowed, spotting a huddle of what looked like reporters standing on the perimeter. A sombre-faced woman in a smart burgundy blazer was holding a microphone out, listening intently to a dog-walker as if the elderly lady with her poodle might have solved the investigation. A man in jeans was packing a heavy-looking camera into a bag. By the end of the weekend, the whole country would be talking about Ava, speculating, casting blame, and I knew exactly who would bear the brunt of that.

I paused, watching as the man's companion, a second reporter in a grey suit, looked out to the shore, to where I could see a couple of people talking. There wasn't nearly as much activity as I'd anticipated. Where was everyone? Shouldn't they be doing forensic tests? Of course, the tide had already washed over the first section of beach, but surely there had to be *something* they could do. Why was it so quiet? I never should have left.

Pulling the hood of my rain mac up to shield my face from view, I avoided the little group and walked beside the yellow tape directly down to the water. There was an icy breeze coming in from the sea, and I shivered, imagining Ava out here in this weather in just a T-shirt.

The female police constable, PC Mayville, who'd spoken to me on the beach yesterday spotted me from inside the hemmed-off area and walked over. 'I'm sorry, madam, but you can't be here right now. This area is cordoned off for— Oh! Carrie, sorry,' she said as I pulled down my hood.

'What's going on? Where's the search team? Have you got any news?' I asked, clenching my fists in the deep pockets of my coat.

'No, nothing yet. I'm sorry. Alerts have been put out to all the passing boats within a fifty-mile radius. The coastguard was out again at first light. We've been door-to-door along the bus route.'

'And nothing?'

She shook her head.

'What about the old lady? Has she been identified?'

'Not yet, I'm afraid. Nobody's come forward with any helpful information.'

I frowned, feeling utterly helpless. 'Did you check the cameras from the car park? You have to cross through it to get out to the road. What was on those?'

She glanced away, and I sensed there was something she wasn't telling me.

'What? What is it?'

She sighed. 'I'm not supposed to tell you. I'm sure you'll get a call later today...' She seemed to hesitate, and I continued to stare, willing her to go on. 'A fault was discovered with the CCTV in the car park. The cameras have been off for two days. It wasn't reported, wasn't fixed.'

I looked back up the beach to where I'd parked, remembering arriving there yesterday. The way Ava had thrown her biscuit onto the tarmac when I'd said she had to have suncream on, then screamed when she realised she wouldn't be able to eat it. She'd had thick streaks of cream over her cheeks and was throwing herself around, wiping it close to her eyes, when Maisy had stepped in, seeming to sense that I was close to losing my patience. She'd sung a silly rhyme, distracting Ava as she rubbed the cream in like a little mother hen, then produced a toffee from her pocket and presented it to her. I hadn't had the heart to tell her Ava was far too young for the sweet, too grateful that the tears had stopped.

I'd always struggled with regulating my own emotions during the children's toddler years – and beyond, if I was honest – though I'd done the best I could. Ava had chewed the sweet, sticky dribble trickling from the corners of her mouth, letting Maisy take her by the hand, the battle already forgotten, though my nerves had felt frayed for some time afterwards.

Beyond the car park, there was nothing but shingle... sand... an empty expanse of uninhabited land. If someone had taken my daughter from the sea to their car, there would be no evidence of it. Nothing to point to a suspect. To give me and Jimmy a scrap of hope that she might be found. Even with the sighting on the bus, the police were providing to be worse than useless at figuring it out. Jimmy had been adamant that the woman wasn't Leah's mother, but I was sure he was lying. I knew what I'd seen, and more than anyone else, Leah had a motive. She'd want to make me look like a bad mother – the kind that didn't supervise her own child on the beach, though I'd barely taken my eyes off her. She'd want to discredit me publicly, so that when she swooped in and tried to take the children from me, the world would be on her side.

Would she have it in her to coerce her elderly mother into luring Ava away, hiding her until she miraculously turned up unharmed, after well and truly dragging my name through the mud? The idea that my daughter could be alive made me almost hope for that scenario to be true. For me to be given the opportunity to fight for her – and I *would* do just that.

I looked back to the sea, the alternative conclusion too painful to acknowledge. Jimmy had told me to drop it, but I hadn't been able to. Not when there was the slightest chance I might be right.

I'd stopped at a payphone the moment he'd left with the children and made an anonymous call to the police saying I recognised the woman. I wasn't sure of her last name, only that she was called Maggie, and I knew Leah's surname was Rigby. I hoped it was enough. I didn't want Jimmy finding out that I'd gone against him. Then again, if I was right, he'd be begging my forgiveness, filled with gratitude that I'd found our daughter and exposed Leah's true nature in the process.

PC Mayville touched my hand, and I looked down, feeling like I was in a dream. 'Don't give up,' she said softly. 'We don't know anything for sure yet.'

The sound of the waves breaking – a sound I'd always found so soothing – was making my head spin, anger fizzing through my veins, filling my mind with the urge to make it shut up, to somehow stop the motion, part the waves and see beyond their blackness to what they concealed in their depths. I pulled my hand out of the policewoman's grip, hating the pitying smile she bestowed on me, and turned away, striding wordlessly in the opposite direction.

My phone rang in my pocket, and I grabbed it, my hopes that it might be DCI Farrows telling me he'd found Ava by some miracle quickly dashed when I realised it was work again. I still hadn't called the hospital. I knew I should have done. When you were a doctor, there wasn't a choice. People died if you didn't turn up – there was no such thing as taking a cheeky day off to watch movies on the sofa, or even a mental health day. Normal rules didn't apply in the world of medicine. Breaks were forgotten, contracted hours just a starting point, and unless you'd lost a limb, you showed up for your shift, early and open to whatever would be coming your way. I wanted to answer, to justify my absence, but I couldn't seem to summon the energy, find the words to explain what had happened.

Rejecting the call, I wondered if I should ring Jimmy again. I wanted to hear his voice despite everything he'd said. To know that it had only been in the heat of the moment, fuelled by panic. We hadn't had time to talk properly before he'd driven off in anger. I wanted to ask him if Tommy was okay. If Jimmy had been on the receiving end of his fury lately, as I had. I wanted to tell him that he shouldn't leave Maisy to her own devices. That it should be him, not that awful woman he'd moved in with, who spoke to her about what she'd been through.

And I wanted to ask what we would do if Ava wasn't found. How we would survive the pain. How we would keep going. The idea that she might be alive was almost as frightening as the alternative. She wasn't a confident child. She shied away from strangers and hated it every time I left to go to work. She'd be terrified if someone had taken her. I closed my eyes, not wanting to think of the reasons why someone might abduct a two-year-old girl. I wouldn't let my mind go there.

My fingers moved without my say-so, navigating to Jimmy's contact details and pressing the call button. I held the phone to my ear, staring out at the bleak ocean, until eventually the ringing cut out to go to voicemail. I called again, and when the same happened a second time, I gave up, putting the phone back in my pocket. I was numb, I realised. I hadn't slept, hadn't eaten, and despite the knowledge that I should be feeling a thousand things, I couldn't seem to reach those emotions.

I'd experienced this once before... a long time ago. The pain of what had happened, what I'd done, so great, so overwhelming, that my mind had shut it out, cushioning me from the reality of my situation. Perhaps that was why, when I'd confided in Jimmy a few months before Ava's birth, he'd accused me of being cold. Unremorseful. Because while I'd detached myself from my past, the secrets that had long since soured deep inside me, he'd been hearing it with fresh ears, all of a sudden looking at me as if I were a stranger to him.

I would have done anything to take back what I'd told him. Would he still be with me if I had? Or would he have gone searching for a fresh start anyway, leaving at the first opportunity that came his way? The idea that he was no longer on my team made me anxious, worried over what he might say, who he might tell. I couldn't risk that. I needed him to see the good in me, remember how deeply he'd once loved me.

'Carrie!'

I looked round, seeing Shannon heading towards me, her long grey jumper wrapped tight around her petite body, protecting her from the breeze. Her shiny blonde hair was blowing wild, whipping against her cheeks, and I stood still, waiting for her to reach me, more relieved than I wanted to admit that she'd found me. That despite how little I deserved it, I had a friend to stand by my side right now.

'I knew I'd find you here,' she said as she got nearer.

'What are you doing here? I thought you'd be at home catching up on your sleep.'

She shook her head. 'I wanted to see if I could find you. To make sure you were taking care of yourself. Where are Tommy and Maisy?'

'With their dad,' I replied, feeling embarrassed at having to admit he'd taken them. 'Don't you have work today?'

'No, actually I have two weeks' leave. I booked it ages ago. I'm sure I told you.'

'Oh yeah, I think you did. Aren't you going away?'

'Carrie.' She pulled me into a hug. '*Stop*. Stop trying to be polite. Making the small talk you think you have to. Your daughter is missing. You don't have to pretend to care about me, about anything else. I know how hard it must be to even try right now.'

'I'm not, I—' I broke off, then gave a resigned nod. 'Thank you,' I whispered, taking her hand and squeezing gratefully.

'Don't be. I'm right where I want to be. Come on – you look like you're about to collapse. Let's sit for a minute.' She didn't give me a chance to argue as she led me up the beach to the very same bench we'd sat on yesterday. Hearing the distant engine of a speedboat, I looked up, unable to help the prick of hope as I watched the horizon, longing for the coastguard to deliver my baby back to me.

'She's not there,' I murmured, watching the boat continue past, the happy voices of young people laughing on the wind.

Shannon said nothing, simply sitting beside me, a supportive presence. She probably didn't realise quite how much I'd relied on her. That despite her own circle of friends she'd had since her school days, I had nobody but her. It had played a part in my holding back from telling her that I'd split up with Jimmy. I hadn't wanted her to think I was someone to be pitied. Some lonely single mother with no friends, no husband, more pleased by her friendship than I dared to admit. I hadn't found a social circle at work, though I realised there was a camaraderie amongst the other doctors there. Dinner parties, tennis matches, weekends away together even. I'd turned down so many invites in the early days that now, nobody included me on their guest lists. It was easier that way.

I hadn't wanted Shannon to know she'd become so important to me when I couldn't tell if she felt the same strength of friendship for me. I sucked in a breath, a ball of emotion breaking free in my chest, a sob ricocheting through me, tears blurring my vision. I couldn't speak, the pain of the last twenty-four hours hitting me in one fell swoop: the loss of my daughter, the blame Jimmy had hurled at me. And my own toxic guilt that at the root of this, it was all my fault. Had Leah taken my baby because she knew deep down what I'd done? How could she possibly have discovered the truth? Unless Jimmy had shared my darkest secrets with her... As much as I didn't want to believe it possible, I knew it wasn't beyond him.

I felt Shannon pull me into a hug, holding me close as she whispered calm, soothing words into my ear, and knew that if I'd been a better mother, a better person, we wouldn't be here now.

SEVENTEEN

LEAH

I took the stairs slowly down from the loft, pausing as I reached the closed door below, listening for sounds beyond and hearing nothing but the tinny music from Tommy's video game coming from his bedroom. I felt a wave of nausea overcome me and sat back on the steps, holding my face in my hands, breathing deeply for a moment, then glanced up the narrow staircase behind me at the locked door, feeling the reassuring weight of the key in my pocket. I was glad Jimmy had gone out. It wasn't the right time to talk to him about this... to show him what I'd done. Not yet.

Bracing my hand against the banister, I yanked myself back to my feet and pushed open the door leading to the landing. I tiptoed out, closing it as quietly as I could, then, feeling a prickling sensation on the back of my neck, turned and let out a gasp as I realised Maisy was standing in her bedroom doorway, her eyes flat as if she were staring right through me.

'Oh, hi, sweetheart,' I managed, stepping away from the door, distancing myself from what I'd been doing up there. 'Are you feeling better now? Did you have something to eat?'

She continued to stare without acknowledging that I'd

spoken, and I realised I was out of my depth here. When it came to the children, I was great at the fun stuff. Listening to them talk in the back of the car when we went on days out, taking note of every toy or game they mentioned they might like and surprising them with those very things – watching their little faces light up. Baking treats and letting them stay up late to watch TV, heedless of crumbs and melted chocolate dropping over the expensive upholstery. I'd managed to avoid becoming the stuffy, irritable stepmother fairy tales were made of, and I hoped they liked me, wanted me around, as a result. But this was the first time I'd been faced with something complicated, something big, and I had no idea where to begin.

I stepped forward, taking Maisy's hand and finding it cold inside my own. 'Let's go downstairs, shall we?' I glanced back at the door, paranoid that I might have left it open, an invitation to go exploring, and looked down to find Maisy watching my face carefully. 'Best not to mention to Daddy that I was up there,' I said, smiling, though it felt tight and false on my face. I bit my top lip, trying to dispel the tension fizzing through me and for a second was grateful that in her current state she was unlikely to say anything. 'Come on, sweetie.'

She followed willingly as I led her down to the kitchen, to the open back door. I pointed to the trampoline on the lawn. 'I got you guys something,' I said, looking down at her, waiting for the hint of a smile to appear on her pale little face, some sign that she was excited, pleased. 'Tommy hasn't seen it yet. I expect he'll be playing in his room a while,' I added, thinking of how tightly wound he always was when he arrived here. I did my best to give him some space to decompress – his mother had such high standards, such strict rules, he needed a moment to let all the stress go before he was ready to be with the family, and now, with Ava missing, I was sure he'd need that downtime more than ever.

I waited for Maisy to head outside to look at the gift I knew she'd dreamed of having, but she made no sign of moving. 'If you wanted to go out now, you could have it all to yourself for a little while, before your brother notices and takes over?' I offered with a conspiratorial smile.

She gave a tiny shrug and looked down at her feet. I could see that this time, it wouldn't be an easy fix. There was no distracting her out of what she was going through, and I couldn't blame her. She must have been so frightened when the police turned up at the beach, when she had to leave there without her little sister.

Lowering myself to her level, I pressed my hand to her smooth cheek, trying to meet her eyes, though she kept hers downcast. 'Maisy, what happened yesterday...' I paused, looking out at the garden, wondering if I was likely to make things worse. 'You mustn't give up hope. *I* haven't. I know it all seems really scary right now, but you might find things turn out all right in the end. You just have to be patient, okay?'

When she gave no reply, I pulled her into a hug, closing my eyes. Kids were resilient. She'd bounce back soon enough. I was sure of it. And then the two of us would go back to the way we'd been before. Practically mother and daughter.

EIGHTEEN

CARRIE

I slumped down on the low wall at the top of the beach, all the energy seeming to leave my body at once.

'Here,' Shannon said, handing me something. I looked down to see that she'd placed a chocolate bar in my palm. Despite my reluctance to eat, the guilt at carrying on as normal under the circumstances, my stomach growled and I found myself ripping open the foil. I finished it in three bites, feeling the sugar give me the boost I'd so desperately needed.

'Thank you,' I muttered, looking down at my feet.

'You need to take care of yourself,' she said softly. 'You can't just let yourself fade away, Carrie. No matter what happens. You have Tommy and Maisy to think of.'

She was right. I was a mother to three children, and I had to stay strong, to remember my responsibilities, but it felt impossible when the world seemed to be collapsing around me. I gave a resigned nod, screwing the paper wrapper into a ball, then smoothing out the green foil before folding it in a concertina. The motion was a good distraction. I'd always liked to keep my hands busy, finding it meditative. I loved doing stitches, always volunteering when a particularly nasty cut was presented at

A&E. I loved the rhythmic motion, and the way I could zone out, knowing there was nowhere else I needed to be. It was soothing, and one of the few occasions when I could let myself be fully present in the moment.

The wind had turned colder, fine droplets of seawater catching on it and landing on my face, making my lips taste salty. Shannon pulled her cardigan closer around her body, but I left my jacket open, wanting the bite of the cold, denying myself comfort.

'Have you heard anything more?' she asked. 'Do the police have any ideas who that woman was?'

I shook my head, concentrating on the foil, unfolding and refolding it again. 'They're at a loss. And the PC down there just informed me that the CCTV in the car park has been off for two days.' I nodded towards the little group still gathered beyond the yellow tape, as if they might be of some help there.

She let out a long breath, and I felt the gravity of my situation weighing on her shoulders.

'What about the children's dad? Jimmy? I take it he knows about everything. How's he taken all this?'

I shrugged, not wanting to tell her that I thought he blamed me for not supervising Ava properly. 'It was a shock, obviously. He's a good dad – well, I mean, he is when he bothers to turn up. He's taken them to his place today. He probably sees them more now than he did when we shared a home, if I'm honest.' I bit my lip, thinking of Leah, how Jimmy probably left her with my babies all the time, so he could enjoy his freedom still. He'd never be loyal to her. I hated to think of them with that woman when they should be with me.

'So... he moved out a while ago?'

Her words were gentle but probing, and I sighed, not wanting to discuss it but realising I would have to. *This* was why I'd struggled to maintain friendships. People always wanted more than you were willing to give, as if they were entitled to your secrets.

'Yes, he left... it was just before I met you, so that's why I lied. I'm sorry about that. It takes a lot for me to open up,' I admitted.

She nodded, her eyes sympathetic as she held her silence, and I swallowed. 'I caught him with another woman after we'd been going through a bit of a rough patch, and I think he felt so bad, he couldn't bring himself to ask my forgiveness. He didn't think he deserved it, I suppose. But we were together a long time before that. And who knows what might happen in the future. Maybe losing Ava...' I swallowed. 'Maybe this will bring us closer again,' I said, though I couldn't help but picture the way he'd looked at me earlier.

'Do you think he'd come back? Would you *have* him after the way he's disrespected you?'

'He's a man,' I said, shrugging, 'and we both know what *they're* like. I never met one who could keep it in his pants.'

'Really? What about your dad?'

'Nope. He left my mum when I was five for a nurse half his age. When things fizzled after a year, my mother took him back, but it became a pattern. I lost count of how many girlfriends he had over the years. Happens all the time in hospitals. Long hours. And he was a surgeon back then. He had a hell of a God complex. Thought he was above nonsense like fidelity. But don't all men?'

She stared at me, her eyes widening in shock, and I wondered if she was so naïve that she'd missed the signs with her own partners. She'd never mentioned a man, not even an ex, and being respectful of her privacy, I hadn't asked. It was possible she was gay – that might explain her lack of under-standing when it came to the opposite sex – but again, it was none of my business.

She seemed to be waiting for me to go on, but when I didn't, she said, 'That must have been hard. Growing up with a father who cheated. Having your husband repeat the pattern.'

I shrugged. 'It's a compromise you have to make. My mother taught me that. Look the other way and don't get worked up about things you can't control. But Jimmy and I are married. And when I said my vows, I meant them. Till death do us part.'

'I don't think I could live like that,' Shannon said, picking at a loose thread on her jumper. 'Never trusting the person you're living with. Always waiting for them to hurt you again. Isn't it better to be alone?'

'Not for me,' I said, feeling a little sorry for her. 'One day perhaps you'll meet someone who makes you feel the same as I do about Jimmy. You'll have a family of your own. And then you'll understand that there's a bigger picture to consider. It's about what's best for all of us.'

'But aren't you going through divorce proceedings? Haven't you agreed to it?' she asked.

I shrugged. 'Sometimes you have to play along to get to where you want to be. Jimmy is a stubborn man... I know how his mind works. I haven't given up hope just yet.'

Shannon opened her mouth, as if to ask something else, and I suddenly realised I'd said too much. She wouldn't get it, couldn't possibly understand how I felt. I was relieved when, instead of probing further, she looked away, her arms crossed tightly over her chest, not offering a reply as she stared out to sea.

I looked down, realising I'd sliced through my skin on the sharp edge of the foil wrapper, and watched as a trickle of blood ran down the side of my finger, dropping onto the ground below. I couldn't feel a thing.

NINETEEN

LEAH

I turned down the TV, listening as I heard the unmistakable sound of Tommy's bedroom door slamming, his footsteps as he walked across the floor overhead. I sighed, an ache throbbing behind my eyes. The moment of peace I'd so desperately needed was obviously not going to happen.

It was almost 11 p.m. Jimmy hadn't come back, nor had he answered his phone – *again* – and I'd given up waiting for him to put the children to bed, taking them up myself a few hours ago. I hoped they'd be brighter after a good night's sleep. That tomorrow might be easier.

Maisy's silence had frightened me, and as I'd tucked her in after reading a story, I'd found myself hurrying to leave the room, as if I'd been keeping company with a ghost, a cold, uneasy dread engulfing me, making me desperate to get away. I couldn't help but think there was more to her silence than the shock of Ava's disappearance. It made me wonder what she might have seen or heard in the days leading up to their trip to the beach.

I hadn't been able to stop myself from picturing Jimmy, wondering if he was with Carrie while I was here, putting his children to bed. He'd been angry that she hadn't been supervising Ava properly, but I wondered if he would soften. Seek comfort in their shared grief. I'd shoved the intrusive thought from my mind, horrified at myself for letting my imagination run wild, then closed Maisy's door, hoping that tomorrow she would wake up ready to talk.

Her reaction was so different to her brother's. Tommy had said goodnight with his usual easy-going manner, asking for an extra snack and flashing a cheeky grin, with a promise to brush his teeth, but now I could hear him padding around, and knew I had to go up and check on him. I'd been waiting for the moment the bravado slipped, the emotions of the situation pouring out. Was this it?

I picked up my phone for what felt like the thousandth time, checking I hadn't somehow missed a call from Jimmy, then, seething at the blank, empty screen, threw it aside and heaved myself up from the sofa.

I padded softly up the stairs, twisting the smooth round brass handle to the loft stairwell as I passed to check it was locked – a habit I needed to break if I knew what was good for me – and knocked gently on Tommy's door. He gave a grunt that I took for a welcome, and I pushed it open, stepping inside, taken aback to see him wiping roughly at damp cheeks, his eyes bloodshot and puffy, his face red. I had never seen him cry before. Never known him to be anything other than a boy who could laugh his way out of any situation.

'Oh,' I whispered, suddenly hyper-aware that he'd be embarrassed at my seeing him like this. I resisted the urge to rush forward and overwhelm him with my need to mother, as I'd witnessed Carrie doing far too many times. I'd watched how he squirmed away from her grasp, how her sympathy made him clam up all the more, turning him almost angry towards her. I wouldn't make the same mistake. Instead, I walked casually over to his window, opening it a little to let some fresh air into the room, blasting away the musty smell of his socks and sweaty armpits. He needed a shower, but I hadn't wanted to nag him.

I lingered, adjusting the curtains to give him time to compose himself, then lowered myself onto his bed, offering a little smile. 'Been a rough couple of days, hasn't it?'

He swallowed, his head bowed, and gave a tiny nod. When he replied, his words were thick with tears. 'Maisy still won't talk to me. I went in to ask if she had my book, and she looks like a robot. She's just lying there staring at the ceiling. And she won't speak! It's horrible.'

I winced, thinking of her in there, not sleeping, unable to shut off her mind. I took a deep breath in through my nostrils. 'It won't last. She's had a shock. We all have.' I pictured Ava's little face, the way she always fought my affection. Even when she was on the verge of falling asleep, she'd force her eyes open and let out a scream if I tried to hold her, comfort her. It was frustrating to have to pass her off to Jimmy and watch her relax into his arms, knowing that if she'd only let me, I could love her so much. I could take care of her the way she deserved to be cared for.

'Because my mum couldn't be bothered to look after us,' Tommy said fiercely. 'I reckon she's relieved Ava's missing. She always says she has too many children. She'll be glad, I bet.'

'Tommy,' I said, taking his hand, knowing that no matter what had happened, I shouldn't let him think that way.

He cut me off. 'It's true. I won't ever forgive her for this. If Maisy isn't okay... if they don't find Ava... it will be all her fault. She isn't a proper mum.'

'Oh, sweetheart.' I edged across the mattress towards him and pulled him into a hug, tucking his head under my chin, wishing I could find the words to defend Carrie, but somehow, none would emerge.

'I'm really glad you and my dad got together,' Tommy

muttered softly, interrupting my train of thought. 'At least we have you.'

'I'm glad too,' I said, unable to stop the smile from pulling at my lips. I pressed a kiss into his hair, giving him the comfort he'd never had from Carrie, and felt warmth spread through my veins. If Tommy felt he could confide in me over her, she only had herself to blame.

Jimmy turned into the drive, and I hurriedly checked my reflection in the hallway mirror, tugging the strap of my dress down over my bare shoulder, knowing he'd notice. No matter what he was going through, he always noticed. The dress was his favourite: red, tight-fitting, low-cut, with a pencil skirt that he'd once said made him feel like a caveman – the desire to rip it open making his blood turn to fire. It had survived the last romantic date night at a candlelit restaurant, and the drunken fumble in the taxi afterwards, and I was glad. I wanted him to look at me.

I knew I was being ridiculous, but I couldn't stop thinking about Carrie, and the possibility she would use this as an opportunity to beg him to come back. After leaving Tommy's room, I'd been hit by the memory of what I'd seen just a few weeks ago – a memory that had kept me up at night more than once over the days that followed. I couldn't get it out of my head, though I was glad in a way that my eyes had been opened, that I could make my own plans.

It had been a Friday night, and Jimmy had texted last minute to ask me to go and pick up the kids as he was running late. He'd warned me Carrie might be irritated to see me, and that she'd called on his lunch break to tell him to come alone, that she wanted to talk to him about something important. I'd pulled up in his car, seeing the light on in the living room, the wintry night already velvety dark, but when I'd knocked, nobody had come to answer. There had been no sign of the children, but a little note stuck to the front door said to come inside. So I'd gone in. The absence of the children's chatter had been the first thing I noticed, and the living room was empty, but then I'd heard the music coming from upstairs, and, feeling sick, already suspecting what I might find, I'd gone up.

Carrie had been lying in her underwear on the bed, her eyes fixed on the open bedroom door, clearly hoping for my fiancé rather than me. I'd never seen her move as fast as she did in that moment, grabbing her silky dressing gown and rolling off the mattress, out of sight. I'd made a conscious choice not to afford her a moment of dignity by looking away. I'd watched the blush spreading over her chest, the anger in her eyes. And the hurt.

She'd babbled on about falling asleep after her shower, a long shift, but it was just noise. Pointless. Her intentions couldn't have been more obvious.

The children, it had turned out, were with a bewildered neighbour – an old lady who seemed stunned to have been called upon to help – and I'd picked them up, taking them back to my house, trying not to let on just how livid I was with their mother. The only reason I hadn't told Jimmy when he made it back was the tiny voice in my head that couldn't help but wonder what he might have done had he been the one to go there. Would he have considered it a free pass, since he was still her husband on paper? I wanted to trust him, but it was still so new. And he had a track record that didn't exactly shine a positive light on him...

In time, I was sure he'd prove himself to me and I'd relax. But I needed him to remember why he'd left. Carrie was more beautiful than I'd realised, more competition than I liked. I was shocked she would even think to try to seduce him like that.

It was past midnight now, and the kids were finally both asleep. I'd almost considered giving them a little something to help. The bottle of antihistamine in the kitchen cupboard had been on my mind – a good night's rest was exactly what the two of them needed – but when I'd gone back in to check on them, I'd heard the reassuring sound of snoring and tiptoed back out, relieved.

I'd come down to a text from Jimmy to say he'd found nothing and was on his way home, and had rushed to change out of my jogging bottoms and baggy T-shirt, knowing he'd need a distraction right now. I smiled at my reflection, my hair curled in loose waves, my make-up done perfectly. It was something I did often, even when we were just staying home. I wanted him to walk in the door and find me waiting, cooking his dinner or reading to the children, the perfect mixture of sexy and wifely, the woman he'd always craved in his life. I wanted him to see that there would never be a need to go looking elsewhere, that he could have the best of everything with me.

I opened the front door and watched as he clambered out of the car, looking exhausted, his shirt crumpled. I couldn't help but glance past him into the back seat, where Ava's pink car seat was fitted, my stomach flipping uncomfortably as I saw it, my thoughts going to the little girl everyone was searching for so desperately. I swallowed the ball of emotion that seemed to wedge itself in my throat, determined to give Jimmy a moment of reprieve, to be the escape he needed right now.

He walked slowly across the drive, and I scrutinised his handsome face, feeling sure he'd been crying. He looked just like Tommy had, only he was better at hiding it.

I thought of my mum, how she'd taught me that the only way to control a situation was to let others think they were in the driver's seat – the star of the show. The brief image of her kissing my dad and waving him off for work in her red lipstick, followed by the instant change as she kicked off her kitten heels and walked barefoot out to the back garden, lighting a cigarette to go with her waiting cup of coffee, flashed into my mind. I'd come to sit beside her on the back step and, prompted by some comments made by a few girls at school, asked why *she* didn't work. Why she didn't want her own independence.

'Surely you're too clever to just be a housewife?' I'd pushed, watching as she took a long drag on her cigarette.

She'd tilted her face to the sun and smiled. 'Leah, everyone thinks feminism is being able to do what your father does,' she'd said, her expression the picture of serenity. 'But it's a lie. If I went to work at some office, I'd still have to come home afterwards, cook dinner, fit in the school run and all the other little tasks that come with being a mother and running a home. I'd be a wreck, and whatever agreements we might make, the reality is that your father would never take on more than he already does. I'd resent him. We'd forever be bickering about something.

'What your school friends don't understand is that by making my husband happy, putting on the show that men love, I get to *enjoy* my life. I can walk you to school without rushing and stressing. I get back, run the hoover round and chuck a load of washing in the machine, then the day is mine. I can do whatever I want. I'm free in a way I could never be if I had a job to go to. And your father supports me because I always smile. I make his life easier. I cook his dinner and wash his clothes, but I also get to go to the beach on a weekday afternoon and swim in the sea, and read for hours, and meet my friends for a glass of wine at lunchtime.'

She'd put her coffee down on the concrete step and taken my hand, her eyes sparkling. '*That's* the kind of feminism I want,' she'd said, grinning. 'Now let's get you off to school so I can go and spend your dad's money on a new dress.' We'd both stood up, laughing, and I'd realised she was right.

I'd really believed her. Thought she had it all figured out. But what I'd discovered in the years to come was that she'd missed the most important part. She'd trusted him too much to keep her safe, and in the end, her life hadn't turned out anything like she'd expected. I had never forgotten that... the mistakes she'd made in keeping her blinkers on. The choices that had affected me too, torn me from the home I loved and made me hard in a way she could never have been.

I blinked away the memory, seeing Jimmy's shoulders slumping as he met me at the door.

'Hey,' I said, reaching out my arms towards him. He leaned into me, wrapping me in a tight hug, and I pressed my face into his neck, subtly sniffing for traces of perfume. I felt my body tense, sure I could detect something that hadn't been there earlier, but forced myself not to react. 'Did you speak to the police again?' I asked as he pulled back.

'No, why? Did they call you? Do they know something?' he asked, straightening, his face filling with panic.

I shook my head, cupping his cheek with my hand, the dark stubble rough against my palm. 'No, they haven't been in touch. No news is good news, right?'

He nodded, his eyes glassy, unfocused for a second. Slowly, they began to clear, and I saw the moment he noticed my outfit. He ran a hand unconsciously down my bare arm, then leaned in, kissing me hard. I could feel his desire to lose himself. He stepped back, his gaze sweeping over me, lingering on the curve of my breasts, forced up by a bra that pinched but looked fantastic. He cleared his throat. 'I need to take a shower,' he said, squeezing my shoulder in a silent promise. 'Pour some wine?'

'Okay. Don't be long,' I said, smiling seductively.

He stepped inside, hanging his jacket on the hook beside the door, and I followed, watching him walk up the stairs, noting that he hadn't asked after Tommy or Maisy. I heard the shower turn on and waited, then stepped towards the hook, slipping my hand into his jacket pocket, my fingers making contact with the smooth case of his phone.

I pulled it out and keyed in the passcode he had no idea I knew, scanning his messages and then checking his call log. There were four missed calls from Carrie this afternoon. And an hour after her last call to him, there was one fifteen-minute call he'd made to a private number.

I clicked on it, hoping to see something that might tell me who he'd been talking to, but there was no other information. He hadn't managed to send *me* so much as a text. And he had just told me he hadn't spoken to the police. So who had he called? And where had he been all this time?

I slipped the phone back in his pocket and went to open the wine, humming a tune my mother had sung to me as a small girl. It brought me comfort and reminded me of who I was. And what I had to do.

I woke to the sound of knocking and rolled over, finding Jimmy's side of the bed empty, the red numbers on the little clock on his bedside table telling me Monday morning had arrived. It was 9 a.m. Sunday had passed in a blur, Tommy quiet, Maisy utterly silent, Jimmy making increasingly furious calls to the police station and barely speaking to me as he grabbed his keys and left me to care for his kids. He'd said he had to go out to search for Ava again, and despite my concern, I had let him go without argument. He'd come home late last night, long past midnight, as if he couldn't bear to be here while Ava was missing. I'd spent the day trying to hold down the fort with Maisy and Tommy, though they'd mostly kept to their bedrooms, unwilling to talk about what was happening. I hated that a part of me was relieved by their lack of engagement. I was so afraid of making it worse, saying the wrong thing.

Rubbing my hands over my face, I slowly sat up, feeling dizzy and disorientated. I'd forced myself to stay up until Jimmy came home, then spent nearly an hour tending to him, comforting him, waiting for him to fall asleep so I could sneak back up to the loft, unable to let my obsession lie. I'd been exhausted, emotionally drained and it had taken all my effort to keep from falling asleep first, but I'd needed to... I reminded myself that soon there would be no more secrets. I could tell Jimmy everything. We would be a happy little family, and Carrie would no longer have a hold over him.

It wasn't as simple as that though. I pictured Ava's little face and felt tears well up, unable to stop them from cascading silently down my cheeks. She was so very young. So vulnerable. I gave a shaky sigh, wiping away the tears, not wanting my eyes to be puffy and red when I made the children their breakfast. I had to be strong for them. It was what a good mother would do. Sacrifice her own needs for her family.

I couldn't help but think bitterly of my own mother. How, when push came to shove, she'd let me down, unable to summon the strength to be what I needed. I didn't want to think of her now. Instead, determined to focus on the positive, I thought again of sweet, feisty little Ava and made a silent wish that she would be reunited with her family very soon.

I leaned back against the pillow, listening for the sound of Jimmy's footsteps downstairs, heading to answer the front door, but there was nothing. The knocking came again, and I swung my legs over the side of the mattress, wondering where he could be. Massaging my throbbing temples, I saw a note on my bedside table and picked it up.

Morning, sexy,

Didn't want to wake you. Have taken the kids to school. Think it's best we keep things as normal as possible for them. Be back late, don't wait up.

J

I stared at it incredulously. I hadn't even considered the possibility that he might take them there today. Tommy was in a state, Maisy still hadn't said a word, and the kids at school would be buzzing with gossip that might frighten them and do far more damage to an already fragile situation. I could only assume he hadn't bothered to consult Carrie about his decision. She'd have put her foot down immediately. I hadn't had a chance to make them breakfast, or to hug them goodbye. I wondered if they'd be coming back here tonight, or heading home to *her*. The thought made a sick feeling swirl up inside my belly. I wanted them here, with me, where I could take care of them properly. Keep them safe.

I reread the second part of the note. *Be back late.* Why? For what possible reason? He couldn't be heading into work with Ava still missing, the search still forging ahead. I'd assumed that for the time being, he'd be here, with me and the children. That we'd figure out how to get through this together, supporting each other. That it would make us stronger. Closer. But someone else had landed on that very idea too, hadn't she? Was *that* who he was spending the day with? The woman who'd caused this mess in the first place? Were her tricks beginning to work?

I shook my head, wanting to call him and demand he come home, but knowing he wouldn't answer. And that even if he did, he wouldn't bend to my will. He'd never taken kindly to being told what to do.

Standing slowly, I pulled on a pair of leggings and a jumper over the camisole I'd worn to bed, then made my way down the stairs, opening the door to find a pretty, petite blonde woman waiting on the step.

'Can I help you?' I asked coldly, keeping a hand on the door, ready to close it if she tried selling me something.

She flashed a pearly smile and I instantly felt that awful sense of jealous competition hit me, relieved that Jimmy hadn't been the one to answer the door to her after all.

'Hi,' she said, her hand moving to the thin leather strap of her shoulder bag, her fingers fiddling with the gold buckle, giving away her nervousness. I had a sudden horrible premonition that she was about to tell me she'd been sleeping with my fiancé and gripped the door harder, wanting to slam it in her face and stop the words from ruining everything.

'I'm so sorry to disturb you,' she continued. 'My name's Shannon. I'm a friend of Carrie's. I... I was hoping to talk to Jimmy.'

'What do you want to talk to him about?' I asked, folding my arms across my body.

'Well... it's delicate... I'd rather not discuss it on the doorstep. Is he here?'

'No, he isn't. I'm Leah, his fiancée. Anything you need to say to Jimmy, you can say to me. We don't keep secrets.'

She bit her lip. 'Can we go inside?'

'I don't think that's a good idea.' I held her gaze, unmoving, and she sighed.

'Okay,' she said with a resigned nod. 'I'm not sure how to put this... I'm worried about Carrie.'

'Well, her daughter is... missing,' I said, stumbling over the word. 'It makes sense that you would be.'

She shook her head. 'No, that's not what I mean.' She twisted her mouth, then looked over her shoulder as if she was checking nobody could hear us. Turning back to me, she spoke in a low voice. 'Up until this weekend, I thought she and Jimmy were still together... She let me believe their marriage was strong.'

I blinked, a mixture of impotent rage and shock flaring in my belly. '*What?*'

Shannon shrugged. 'That's not all.' She pressed her lips together, and I realised I needed to know everything this woman had to say. '*Please*,' she said. 'Can we talk about this inside? I have questions I need answering before I go to the police with my concerns. I don't want to make a mistake I won't be able to take back.'

I felt my eyebrows shoot up, suddenly realising what a gift had arrived on my doorstep, and tried to school my features into something more serene. Slowly, I stepped back. 'You'd better come in,' I said, curiosity burning through me. She stepped into the hall, and I turned back to the door, closing it on the outside world.

'So,' Shannon said, 'you see, when Carrie told the police your address, I was listening, and I thought I really had no choice but to come here and find out your side of the story. And Jimmy's. Will he be back soon?'

'No,' I replied, my tone cold. 'He'll be out all day.'

'That's a pity.' She took a seat, watching as I put the kettle on. 'I'd love a coffee,' she piped up hopefully.

Grudgingly, I took a second mug out of the dishwasher. 'I'd like to hear what Carrie's been telling you about her and my fiancé,' I said, watching her face closely.

She nodded, her blue eyes meeting mine without hesitation. 'Like I told you, up until Ava went missing, I truly believed that the reason I hadn't met Carrie's husband was that he was working away. She said he was on the oil rigs.'

'*What*? Jimmy's a lawyer. And he gets seasick.' I frowned, confused. 'She said those exact words to you?'

'Yes. But when the police arrived at the beach on Friday, it came out that they're getting a divorce. It was a shock... I thought we were close, so to discover she's been lying... it makes me wonder what else she's capable of.'

'Maybe she was embarrassed?' I offered. 'It can't be easy to have your husband leave you for someone else.'

'Yes, she said that... Well, sort of...' She hesitated.

'What do you mean?'

'Even after we spoke, she never mentioned he was engaged. She made it sound like he might...' She looked down at her lap, tucking a strand of blonde hair behind her ear nervously.

'Might *what*?' I pushed, trying to keep my tone measured – not an easy task when all I wanted to do was yell at her to spit it out.

Shannon sighed, meeting my penetrating stare again. 'She made it sound like there's a chance he might come back to her. That this horrible thing that's happened to Ava might be something only *they* could understand.'

I gripped the jar of instant coffee in my hand, my mouth turning dry. 'He wouldn't go back to her,' I replied, though the truth was, it was my greatest fear. A nightmare that plagued me more often than I cared to admit. They shared so much history. It was sometimes hard to feel I could compete with that.

I cleared my throat, then put the coffee back on the counter and handed her a steaming mugful. 'I won't divulge Carrie's secrets,' I said, trying to keep my dignity, 'but there's no way Jimmy would go back to that woman. She wasn't a good wife to him. She's not a good person, no matter what she might try and convince you of. I'm sure anything she's made out to you was said in a state of grief for poor little Ava. And because of that, I'll let it pass.'

'I'm not here to meddle in your relationship.'

'So why *are* you here?'

'I'm worried,' she admitted, her voice quiet, soft. 'Carrie isn't acting normally. I don't mean she's grieving. More like... oh, I don't know.' She shook her head, looking me in the eye. 'I get the feeling she's hiding something. There's something off about the whole situation. I overheard a witness at the beach saying that Maisy and Ava were nowhere near the sea.'

'That's got to be a good thing, right?' I asked, confused.

'But then why would Carrie put on such a—' She broke off, fiddling with the handle of her mug.

'Go on,' I pushed, desperate to hear her thoughts on what had happened that day.

'It's a terrible word to use, but I was going to say *performance*. Because that's honestly what it felt like. Her swimming out to sea, screaming like that, drawing all the attention her way when the chances of Ava even getting to the water in the supposed few seconds Carrie had her back turned were pretty slim. There were families camped out on the beach between Carrie and the shore. Ava would have had to walk right past them, and it's not like she's big for her age... It just doesn't ring true. Someone would have spotted her, stopped her. Then there's the footage on the bus. You've seen it?' she checked, and I gave a nod. 'Carrie was convinced it was Ava... that she recognised the woman from somewhere. But it was barely a glimpse, and to me, the child looked so much bigger than Ava. It was like she was trying to send the police in the wrong direction, on a wild goose chase.'

The hairs on my arms rose and I turned away, opening the larder, making a show of looking for a packet of biscuits. 'What are you suggesting?' I said, keeping my back to her.

There was a moment of silence. 'I... I think someone took Ava. And I think... I think Carrie meant for it to happen.'

I turned slowly, gripping the custard creams tight against my chest. 'Have you told the police this?'

'I told them the truth. That I wasn't sure the child was Ava.'

'And the rest?' I stared at her, seeing the way her cheeks had flushed, her fingers knotting and unknotting in her lap.

She stood up abruptly, grabbing her bag and slinging it over her shoulder. 'I'm probably being silly. I shouldn't have come. Forget I was here, okay?'

I stepped towards her, shaking my head, not wanting her to leave. 'No, please, stay,' I said, placing the biscuits and my own mug of coffee down on the table and taking a seat, gesturing for her to do the same. Slowly, the awkwardness of the situation seemed to become too much for her, and she lowered herself back down, another sigh escaping her lips.

'The police obviously haven't ruled out that possibility. They're still searching for her,' I said.

She nodded. 'But if Carrie believes that losing Ava might somehow bring her husband back...'

'He's not her husband any more,' I snapped, irritated that Jimmy was being linked to another woman.

'Right, yes, but you know what I mean.'

I swallowed, my throat suddenly dry, the echo of my own fears, the eerie similarity, making a chill sweep down my spine. How strange that we should both think the same thing. Hadn't I shared that exact sentiment with Jimmy? That Carrie had somehow planned this whole situation to get him to come back to her.

'So,' I replied, my words slow and careful now, 'are you suggesting that Carrie took Ava somewhere herself? Or got someone to take her while nobody was watching so that she could stay on the beach and play the role of the grieving mother? You think she's orchestrated this whole drama to get Jimmy back?' I raised an eyebrow. 'What kind of mother would that make her?'

Shannon looked down at her mug and then raised her eyes to meet mine. 'I'm not suggesting anything,' she whispered. 'But I'm afraid that whatever's happened, she's not thinking straight. And I don't know how to help.'

I nodded, picking up my cup.

'She would never do anything to hurt them... any of them,' Shannon said. 'Being a good mother means everything to her.'

I snorted.

'What?'

'Is that what she told you?' I asked, unable to hide my surprise.

'Yes, why?'

I placed my cup purposefully on the table and pushed the pack of biscuits towards Shannon, who shook her head, looking pale. 'I don't know how much I should say. You're her friend, after all, and if it got back to her that I've been telling you things about—'

'It won't. I swear. I just want to know the truth, so I can help her. I'm afraid she's going to make a mistake that could destroy her life if she's not careful.'

I nodded slowly, taking a biscuit and nibbling the corner of it. 'Obviously, I only know what Jimmy's told me. Carrie and I aren't exactly best friends.'

Shannon nodded, though she didn't reply.

'You know she's a doctor?'

'Yes,' she said, 'I know that. I work at the same hospital. That's where we met.'

'Did you know she took Tommy to a different hospital in November with a broken arm?'

'No.' She shook her head, her expression confused as she tried to understand the relevance of that to this situation.

I pursed my lips, wondering if I was making a mistake in talking to this woman. She was a stranger, and I was sure Jimmy wouldn't appreciate me sharing our private family matters with her. But to have someone here who could see through Carrie, see her flaws like I could, was something I'd craved. Shannon was someone who not only seemed able to voice the concerns I'd been trying to communicate to Jimmy about Carrie, but was ready to speak up and do something to stop her. I took a deep breath, making up my mind. 'Social services were called, and there was a lot of drama about it. Tommy had one version of events and Carrie had another. It was a mess, Jimmy said. It happened just after I met him but before he'd left her.'

Shannon shook her head. 'I don't understand. Children break bones all the time. Why would social services care?'

I pushed the rest of the biscuit into my mouth, chewing

purposefully, then took a gulp of coffee, instantly regretting it. Wiping my mouth with the back of my hand, I shrugged. 'Carrie said he fell. That he was so excited when Jimmy arrived home from work that he went to run down the stairs to meet him and tripped.'

'And Tommy?' she asked, though I could see the fear in her eyes as she began to put two and two together. 'What did he say?'

I crossed my arms. 'That she pushed him.'

'Down the stairs?' Shannon asked, her eyes wide.

I nodded.

'But why would she do that?'

'I don't know. What mother would do that to their child? Tommy had been overheard by one of the nurses at the hospital saying she was jealous because he didn't want to spend time with her and only wanted Jimmy. Later, when it all blew up, he took it back and said he only said that because of some argument they'd had. But Jimmy... he didn't ever trust her after that. He said it rang too true. He thinks she did it to get him to stay... that she had an idea he was seeing someone behind her back. I know she thinks *I'm* the reason he left her, but I'm just the last puzzle piece. He was always going to leave. It was just a matter of when.'

I took another biscuit from the packet and looked up, meeting Shannon's shocked eyes. 'Carrie's a workaholic. An absent mother. A selfish woman. And all she ever cared about was not losing Jimmy. She's used the kids as pawns plenty of times before. And I'm not surprised she lied to you about the divorce.'

I pictured the woman who had shared my fiancé's bed for so long before me, envy rearing up inside me. Even now, even after all the horrible things he'd told me, I knew he still felt something for her. When I brought her up, there was a look in his eyes that made me afraid he really might leave me, go back to his life, in order to keep the peace. He'd once told me there were secrets he could never share, and though I had pushed hard, determined to know everything, he'd remained frustratingly loyal to her. I was sure that whatever he was hiding, whatever his reason for protecting her, was the last tie, the final rope I had to break. Once I found out the truth, he'd finally be free of her hold over him. And if it was worse than the stories he had shared, it was imperative we go for full custody. The children – all of them – should be with me... us.

'And Ava?' Shannon asked. 'Given Carrie's past, do you think it's possible that she could have taken her? That she might have hidden her somewhere? She couldn't have done it alone – there wasn't time.'

'Only you can make up your mind about that,' I replied. 'I wasn't there.'

She put her hands over her face, her shoulders stiff as she sighed. Finally, she dropped them, looking at me helplessly. 'I don't want to make the wrong choice here. I could ruin her life. But I don't want to waste precious time either.' She looked at me as if I held all the answers. 'Should I tell the police my concerns? What would you do in my situation?'

I bit my lip, then reached across the table, taking her hand. 'That,' I said, 'is entirely up to you. But if something happens to Ava and you didn't speak up, could you live with that?'

I sat back, popping the rest of the biscuit in my mouth and crushing it between my teeth, feeling a calmness spreading through me that I hadn't felt for quite some time.

TWENTY

CARRIE

I pulled into the school car park, shaking with anger as I spun the car into a space. There was a grating screech of metal on metal, and I froze, my hands tight on the wheel as I realised I'd misjudged the distance, taking a chunk out of the car in the next bay. I breathed in deeply, trying to calm myself but finding the task impossible. With slow, deliberate movements, I put the car in reverse, backing out of the space, studiously ignoring the wide streak of red paint on the white chassis of the neighbouring vehicle.

I drove around the car park to an area that was empty, backing into a space under a tree, then turned off the engine, yanking the keys from the ignition and dropping my head to the wheel. Jimmy had taken them to school. I still couldn't get over how he had come to such a decision. He always took them to school on a Monday morning, but surely even he could grasp the fact that this was no ordinary week.

I'd phoned just after ten, having already had a wholly unsatisfying update from the police station, resulting in an argument with DCI Farrows during which, in a fit of grief and rage, I'd called him an incompetent waste of space when he'd informed me they'd still been unable to locate the woman on the bus. He'd made a comment about it being an unlikely line of inquiry anyway and mentioned that Jimmy had been sure the child wasn't Ava – a fact that made me wonder what on earth Jimmy was playing at.

I hadn't wanted to admit that it had been me who'd made the call to the station identifying the woman as Leah's mother, but he'd given me no update about receiving any sort of tip-off, and desperate to know what he'd found out – if he'd even bothered checking for himself – I'd asked outright, heedless of the consequences.

'So,' he had said, 'that was you, was it? That's interesting. Well, we've been to visit Ms Rigby, and I can confirm she's not the woman in the video. Look, I don't know what kind of games you and your ex are playing, Carrie, trying to make each other look guilty, but you're wasting our time, and Ava's too, with this nonsense.'

I'd tried to get a word in, to explain that I wasn't playing games, that I really did think the woman was Leah's mum, but he'd hung up and I'd been left feeling like the scrap of hope I'd been clinging to had been ripped out from beneath my feet, leaving me free-falling. I had been so sure I was right. And even though Farrows said it wasn't the same woman, I couldn't help but feel he'd made a mistake. My instincts were screaming at me that somehow Leah was involved in this, and if I could just figure it out, I'd find my baby. I *had* to find her. The emptiness that had hit me in the wake of the conversation had made me want to crawl into bed and never come out. I was so tired, so very, very tired. The adrenaline that had carried me through the weekend had long since dissipated, and now I just felt broken.

I'd needed to hold Maisy and Tommy, to have them in my arms, the only comfort available to me right now, so when I'd assumed they'd be out of bed and done with breakfast, I'd phoned to arrange going over to pick them up, only to be told by

Leah that Jimmy had taken them to school. It was hard to understand why he would make a decision like that without so much as consulting me.

I squeezed the steering wheel, taking a few calming breaths, not wanting to walk into the building looking like I was on the verge of a breakdown. I had to make another call before heading inside anyway – I'd put off contacting work for too long. The voicemails had grown increasingly concerned, and if I was going to tell them what was happening, I needed to do it without Tommy and Maisy as an audience. They didn't need to hear me rehash the whole awful story.

I swallowed, watching through the windscreen as a woman pushing a buggy headed across the car park towards the nursery unit, then lifted the phone to my ear and turned my face away, the sight of the chubby-cheeked toddler too painful to bear.

The phone rang five times, and for a second, I thought it might connect to the answerphone and I'd be saved from having to talk to a real person. Then a male voice answered and I felt my heart sink. Of all the people it could have been, it had to be bloody Nick Jameson.

'Carrie? Where have you been?' he demanded, his tone impatient. 'Do you have any idea of the stress we've been under here? You've missed two shifts without so much as a call. We even tried your emergency contacts, but nobody's got back to us.'

I pressed my lips together wryly, unwilling to admit that the phone numbers I'd listed on my contacts sheet were fakes, that they could call my parents as many times as they liked, but they'd never get an answer. I hadn't spoken to them in decades. They hadn't been at my wedding. Had never even *met* their grandchildren.

A good therapist would tell me that my relationship with them had shaped the way I viewed people, influenced my inability to trust, my assumption that if someone came into my life, it was inevitably going to bring pain sooner or later. I wasn't ignorant of the psychology behind it. My dad had cheated in plain sight on my mother, digging at her to do better, step up to the competition and make him look her way.

I was sure that she, in turn, had blamed me for ruining her body, making her a monster, or so she believed. I'd been born via emergency C-section, and the surgeon had inadvertently made a cut in her bladder during the rush to get me out safely. It had resulted in her needing a permanent catheter, a bag of urine strapped to her leg, and I was sure this was the source of her resentment towards me.

I'd only tried once to bring a classmate home to tea, as far as I could remember. We were five years old, and I was so excited to finally have someone who liked me, who talked to me as if I was worth her time, who made me laugh – something I couldn't recall ever doing before. My mum had walked into the dining room and lifted up her dress, showing my new friend the bag and pointing to me, telling her to look at what a mess I'd made. She'd begun ranting, shouting about how I didn't deserve to be sitting around her table eating and drinking and chatting away without a care in the world when I'd wiped out her social life in one fell swoop.

My friend had left in tears, and by the following week, the story had spread about her awful experience and the whole class suddenly seemed to look right through me. No more invites. No more company in the playground. I was alone, just as my mother wanted.

I'd thrown myself into my studies, determined to escape their toxic world as soon as I could, and I'd done well for myself. But the worst part about taking up medicine was meeting other women who'd had similar injuries through childbirth. Bladder and bowel perforations, back problems; even a woman who'd been thrown into early menopause from the confusion in her hormones. I'd been wary of them. Frightened of how bitter they would be – a mirror of my mother. But it had been so much worse than that. Because as it turned out, not one of them blamed their child. They brought them along to hospital appointments. Cuddled them close. Told them loudly and without shame that they would do it all again if it meant having them, that they were lucky and grateful and all the words I'd never imagined possible.

When, at eighteen, I'd left home to support myself through university, my father had been having yet another affair, my mother losing weight and selling my things to buy new dresses to win him back, and I'd known that the pattern would never change for them. But I would no longer be around to be her emotional punchbag. I'd hoped for a fresh start. To erase their influence from my life. But it seemed it was impossible to break free of those patterns. Why else would I have put up with Jimmy all these years? I'd become the woman I most despised without ever realising it, though I was a far better mother to my children. At least, I hoped I was.

I cleared my throat, annoyed that Nick had made me think of them. It was the last thing I needed right now. 'Yeah, sorry about that,' I said, hearing the hostility in my tone. I closed my eyes, wishing I could ask to speak to anyone else. I didn't want to have to tell him what I'd been going through. We didn't exactly see eye to eye, and given that he was my superior, it was impossible for me to tell him just how much I disliked him. 'I've had a family emergency.'

'I'm sorry, Carrie, but that won't fly. You're a *doctor*. You're needed here!'

'Nick.' My tone was sharp. 'Ava's missing.'

'Ava?'

'My daughter. My *two-year-old* daughter. She... she went missing on the beach on Friday evening.' I glanced at the display on the car clock, which read 10.48 a.m. Almost sixty-eight hours out there alone. I let out a shaky breath. 'The police are searching still, but...' My words drifted off, and I sank my teeth into my bottom lip, desperate not to break down, to let him hear me cry.

'*Shit*... Holy shit, Carrie. That's... well, that changes things. I had no idea... Take a leave of absence, starting immediately. I'll sort everything here and let the team know you won't be on shift for the time being.'

I gripped the phone, blinking back tears at the unexpected kindness. If a man as clinical and cold as Nick Jameson could find a scrap of empathy for me, it just went to show how dire the situation was. 'Thanks, Nick,' I managed, my throat tight with emotion.

'I hope you find her soon, Carrie.'

'Me too.'

I hung up, tossing the phone onto the passenger seat and bowing my head over the steering wheel as I tried to gather myself. After a few moments, and several deep breaths, I climbed out, trying to keep my focus on Tommy and Maisy for now. It was the only thing I could do, the only area where I could summon any sense of control and offer something of value. If I could have done anything to aid the search, I would have – whatever it cost me – but every time I tried to think of something that might help, I just ended up feeling utterly useless.

I walked across the car park to Tommy's school first. The campus was split between the infant, junior and senior schools, and I liked the idea that they would always have the familiarity of the same location, always know their siblings were just across the playground. It felt more nurturing to me.

I pressed the buzzer and waited before being let in by the receptionist, who I'd only met once before, at parents' evening.

'Can I help you?' she asked, peering owlishly at me from behind a stack of registers. The photocopier was working loudly behind her, and I stepped closer so she could hear me.

'I'm here to collect my son, Tommy Gold. His father brought him in, but I—' I broke off, suddenly unable to find the words to keep going. 'I just need you to get him for me, please.'

She pursed her lips as if she was going to demand a reason, then, seeming to take in the boiling emotion I was fighting to contain, gave a short nod and stood up. 'Just a moment, please.'

I nodded, turning to look at the walls behind me, trying to distract myself with the brightly coloured Monet imitations the children had painted for the school fair. A few minutes passed, and then I heard footsteps. I turned, seeing Tommy slink through the door behind the receptionist. 'Hi, darling. Do you have your bag?'

He shook his head. 'No, why?'

'We're going home. I don't know what Daddy was thinking bringing you here today. It's too soon, what with everything that's happening. You must be feeling so confused. Let's go home. We need to be together at a time like this.'

He scowled at me. 'I don't *want* to go home. Why do you think I'd want to leave my mates so I can come and mope around the house with you?'

'Tommy!'

The receptionist turned to the photocopier, pretending to be occupied but clearly still listening. I wondered if he simply didn't understand. Didn't realise that there was a real possibility his sister was dead. Or that she'd been taken by someone who was right now doing awful things to her. The very thought of it made my skin crawl. Did he not get how terrible the situation was? Did he not care?

He folded his arms. 'I'm staying. This is just another example of you trying to undermine Dad's parenting choices. You can't stand that you're not getting your own way, can you?'

The way his eyes bored into mine, cold and hard, like all the love he'd once had for me had just evaporated, broke my heart. I didn't think I had any remaining capacity for pain, but somehow he managed to summon a fresh wave of it. How could this unfeeling, emotionless boy be the same baby I'd cradled in the dead of night, whispering lullabies to, when he couldn't sleep? How could he be the child I loved with all my heart? I couldn't hold his gaze. Because a part of me knew he was right to hate me. That it was exactly what I deserved. Knowing that didn't make it any easier to bear though.

'I have to go back,' he said. 'Don't bother coming to pick me up later either. I'll walk.'

'Tommy,' I pleaded, my voice pitiful even to my own ears. I watched his hunched shoulders as he disappeared through the door, then I turned and headed back outside before the receptionist could say anything.

Feeling like a robot, a shell of a human being, I walked across to Maisy's school. I couldn't take much more. My nerves were frayed, and I'd been holding everything in. Now I felt like the smallest prod would make me fall to pieces.

'Hi, I'm here to pick up Maisy Gold. I'm her mum,' I said as soon as the receptionist, young and frazzled this time, let me in.

'You're Maisy's mum? Oh, thank goodness. I was just dialling your number.'

'Has something happened?' I asked, my stomach tensing.

She sighed. 'She's in with the nurse. Her teacher had to walk her there. She's not said one word, and she's just been sitting in the book corner all morning, ignoring everyone. Mrs Fritz said it was like the rest of the children were invisible to her. Like she wasn't even aware of them being there with her.'

I shook my head. 'I knew she wasn't ready. Did her dad at least tell you what's happened?'

She nodded. 'Yes, he did. I'm so sorry. But he didn't say Maisy was in this state. I think she needs to see someone. Maybe you should take her to the GP this afternoon.'

'Thanks,' I said, 'but I actually know someone who might be able to help. Will you go and get her for me, please? I'm so sorry her father brought her in today. He must not be thinking straight.'

'Don't be silly – you're all going through a tremendously tough time. You don't have to apologise. I'll get her now.'

She disappeared through a door, and I scrolled through my phone looking for Fiona Lees' number. We'd trained together in medical school for a while, until she'd gone down the psychotherapy route and we'd lost touch. I'd never particularly liked her; she was obsessed with her work, but we had that in common. And from what I heard, she was very good at what she did.

I hesitated, suddenly frightened of what opening the doors to therapy might mean for my family, but it was too late to pretend Maisy would be fine on her own. It wasn't normal for a child to go this long without speaking. Whatever my private fears might be, I *had* to get her help. The school were involved now. It was no longer just down to me. As I pressed call, I hoped I wouldn't regret it.

TWENTY-ONE

LEAH

I paced back and forth in the living room, wishing I knew what to do. I couldn't leave the house, I might be needed here, but with Jimmy refusing to answer my calls and no word since Shannon had left to indicate she'd reported her concerns to the police, I felt trapped in limbo. I hated the waiting, the feeling of being shut out of what Jimmy and Carrie seemed to be treating as *their* business – a family matter. It burned to realise that Jimmy wasn't acting in the way I'd anticipated in the wake of Ava's disappearance. Shouldn't he be confiding in me? Crying in my arms? Asking how I was coping with the sadness of it all? It was like I'd suddenly become invisible to him, like he didn't even see that I could be a support to him, that we could help each other.

I picked up my lipstick from the mantelpiece above the wood-burning stove, looking into the mirror and applying it just for something to do. I wasn't expecting Jimmy to walk in and include me in whatever the hell he'd been doing. I'd called his office and confirmed that he hadn't been in. Wherever he was, it wasn't there.

The house had been scrubbed from top to bottom. I'd made

a casserole and left it warming in the slow cooker. I'd ordered a book Tommy had mentioned wanting to read, and been back up to the loft – more than once. And now I was fizzing with the need to get out. It wasn't fair. The way he was treating me... it wasn't right.

The sound of my phone ringing jolted me out of my thoughts, and I grabbed it from the coffee table, answering hurriedly. 'Jimmy?'

There was a moment of static, as if someone had dropped the phone, then a voice that sent chills through me spoke. 'It's me.'

I held the phone away from my ear, as if I could separate myself from her, from the memories that churned within me at the sound of her voice. 'Why are you calling me?' I asked, glancing over my shoulder as if someone might hear me, though I knew it was impossible. 'I have nothing to say to you.'

She gave a throaty laugh that sounded spiteful and cold, and I could picture the cigarette clamped between her thin lips as she sat by the little window in her third-floor flat. She tutted. 'After all I've done for you, Leah? I'm your mother, and if I want to call you, that's my right. Besides, I thought you might like to tell me why the police have been knocking at my door. Asking questions.'

I felt myself sway. 'What?' I whispered. 'When?'

'Earlier this morning.'

I thought of that CCTV footage from the bus, the way the detective had asked about my mother when he'd come to the house, and felt suddenly sick.

'What did you say to them? What did you tell them about our family?'

She gave a laugh. 'You have a lot of questions for someone who seems incapable of answering any of mine.'

I closed my eyes, hating how unrecognisable this mean, bitter old woman was from the mother who'd raised me. I wished there was even a trace of that version left, but there was no point dwelling on what I'd lost now.

I was yanked from my thoughts by the sound of a car pulling up on the drive, and without bothering to make an excuse or say goodbye, I ended the call and rushed to the window. Relief flooded through me as I watched Jimmy climbing out of his Jaguar. The elation was short-lived, though, as seconds later, Carrie's battered red Volvo bumped up the kerb behind him, blocking him in. She climbed out, and I could see Maisy sitting in the back seat, staring straight ahead as if in a trance.

What was going on? Why were they arriving together? Had they been out searching for Ava without me? Lately, even before Ava had gone missing, I'd had an uneasy feeling that something was going on between them. I'd caught Jimmy looking at her when he didn't know I was watching and seen something in his expression that made me sick. Scared. The thought of them talking behind my back made me want to drag him inside and lock him up, to stop him making the mistake that would cost me my happiness. I turned from the window and stormed through the house, flinging open the front door.

Carrie was squaring up to Jimmy, and I saw him glance over her shoulder, his gaze landing on me, suddenly aware that he was being observed. 'What on earth were you thinking?' she was saying. 'She should never have been in school today. She's in no fit state – you can't just expect her to carry on as normal.'

'I was seeing if it might help. Tommy was happy to stay, wasn't he? He texted me to let me know you'd tried to take him home.'

'That's not the point. Tommy's obviously dealing with what's going on in his own way. But Maisy is struggling.'

I walked across the driveway to where the two of them stood, taking my place by Jimmy's side. Carrie flashed me a quick glare, then pointedly turned her attention back to him.

'I've booked her a session with a therapist tomorrow. Fiona Lees. She specialises in childhood trauma. If anyone can help, it's her.'

'She doesn't need a bloody therapist, Carrie. It's only been three days. She needs a bit of time. And you assuming the worst isn't helping anyone.'

'What do you mean by that?'

'I mean you're projecting your fears onto everyone else. I don't believe my daughter is dead. Someone would have seen her if she'd gone into the water. Someone would have heard something!'

'So where is she then, Jimmy? Why haven't they found her?'

He stared into her eyes as if he were seeing into her soul. The intimacy of the moment made me uncomfortable. It was like they were communicating without words. 'You tell me, Carrie,' he said softly.

'If I bloody knew something, I would!' she snapped.

I stepped forward, placing a hand on Jimmy's arm, reminding both of them of my presence. 'We'll take her,' I said.

Carrie frowned. 'What?'

'Jimmy and I will take Maisy to the therapist. You have enough on your plate. You might be too busy with the police.'

'They aren't exactly calling every five minutes with updates,' she replied snidely. 'Unless you know something I don't?' she added, turning the focus onto me, her eyes aflame as they met mine. I was certain that Carrie was the one who'd thrown my mother's name in to the ring, making accusations she had no way of proving. Who else would be so calculated, if not her? If she'd told Jimmy she suspected my mother was involved, he certainly hadn't mentioned it to me, but she had to know by now that the police had been to see her and ruled her out. I wondered what that must be doing to her, how she must be feeling right now. It was apparent that she had no intention of raising the issue with Jimmy standing by listening to every word, and I wondered if that was because she knew she'd been wrong, or because she was worried he'd take my side and couldn't bear to see that.

I took a breath, determined to be the voice of reason when the two of them clearly couldn't. It was good for Jimmy to have an opportunity to see just how calm and reasonable I could be under pressure. 'Be that as it may,' I continued, ignoring the second half of her response, 'I think it best we take her. It might help her to loosen up if she's not worried about upsetting you.'

'Excuse me?' Carrie stepped closer, and Jimmy looked between the two of us. 'I think you're forgetting your place. Why don't you go back inside and let me talk to my husband about *our* children, okay?'

Her words were like a slap across the face, and I folded my arms defensively. 'Jimmy,' I said softly, 'what do *you* think is best for Maisy, given the upset she's been through in the wake of Carrie's trip to the beach?' I slid my hand around his forearm proprietorially.

'Are you trying to make out this is my fault? That *I'm* to blame for Maisy being in this state? For Ava going missing?'

'Well, they *were* in your care, weren't they?' I asked, meeting her eyes.

She stared at me, hatred radiating from her very being, and it took all my courage not to let go of Jimmy's arm and back away.

He cleared his throat, nodding at me. 'Leah's right. We should be the ones to take her. You're busy.'

As if he hadn't spoken, Carrie turned, heading for the car and opening the door, pausing to look at Jimmy over the patchy red roof, her face flushed, her mouth pursed tight in anger. Maisy didn't even raise her head in acknowledgement as the door creaked on its hinges. 'I'm not too busy for my child!' she said fiercely. She got in and revved the engine, heading down the road without a backward glance at us.

'Well, I guess there's a first time for everything,' I said under my breath.

Jimmy flashed me a warning glare, and I swallowed, wondering why he wasn't agreeing. Why he wasn't saying it himself. He was hiding something from me, and I wouldn't rest until I'd discovered what it was.

TWENTY-TWO

Jimmy yanked his arm from my possessive hold and stalked across the driveway, heading for the house. I stood staring after him for a moment, wondering if he was planning to stay for a while at least, then followed him inside, closing the front door quietly behind me. He walked into the living room and slumped down on the sofa, throwing his head back with an exhausted sigh. His pale blue shirt was unbuttoned, his throat exposed, and I could smell strong aftershave. I briefly wondered if he might be trying to cover the scent of another woman with it. He looked nothing like a father who had just lost his child. His charcoal trousers were pressed, his shoes shiny, his complexion tanned and devoid of any signs of the stress of the previous few days.

I walked over to him, taking a seat at the other end of the sofa, not wanting to make him feel like I was crowding him. I was glad now that I'd bothered to reapply my lipstick. 'That was... strange,' I said, watching him stare up at the ceiling, giving off a strong vibe of wanting me to leave. I wasn't about to do that though. 'Did you two arrange to meet here to talk?' I asked.

He shook his head. 'No, that was a coincidence. I would have stayed away longer if I'd known she was coming. You know, sometimes that woman talks to me like I'm a piece of dirt on her shoe. I don't think she even realises how she comes across.'

'Maybe not.' I picked at a loose thread on the cushion cover. 'Where were you? After you took the kids to school, I mean?'

He closed his eyes, his mouth pinched in an expression that I was fast recognising as irritation. 'Did the police call?' he asked, ignoring my question.

'No.' I swallowed, thinking of Shannon. I should tell him about Carrie's friend turning up here. The things she had said. But perhaps not just yet. 'You didn't answer my question,' I pushed, my voice gentle. I reached out, taking his hand in mine and squeezing encouragingly.

He snatched it back, his eyes snapping open. 'For God's sake, Leah, I don't expect to have to give you a step-by-step itinerary of my day. I was at the office, trying to get some work done – not that it was much use. It's not exactly easy to focus right now.'

I met his angry glare, hoping he'd take back the lie. The admin assistant had told me that Jimmy wasn't in. That he hadn't been in the office since last Thursday, in fact. I didn't know where he had been or with who, but it damn sure wasn't at work.

'Do me a favour, Leah,' he said, rubbing his hands over his face. 'Stop trying to police my every movement and just focus on taking care of stuff around here. Take some of the stress off my hands – it's what you're good at.'

I pressed my lips together, trying to bite back a retort. Was that all he saw me as? A skivvy? Someone to scrub his floors and cook his meals? I pinched the edge of the cushion hard and reminded myself that we were *all* experiencing some strong emotions at the moment. It was to be expected that he'd be snappy and say things he might later regret.

I smiled sweetly at him. 'Of course. If I can make things easier, I will. Which is why I really think it should be me who takes Maisy to therapy. You know how close the two of us have become. Even before all this happened, she talked to me far more than she does to Carrie. She tells me her secrets.'

He nodded. 'I know you care for her.'

'*Care* for her? I *love* her, Jimmy. I love them all. And I want to help. You and Carrie need to focus on Ava. Be ready if the police have leads, able to drop everything and go if she's found.' I looked down at my lap. 'You can't help Maisy if you're only half present. Let *me* take her. Besides,' I added, 'don't you want to do your own research to check that Carrie has chosen a decent therapist? Shouldn't you have a say in who gets to delve into Maisy's issues? The wrong person could inadvertently do more harm than good. They could make her silence last longer, and none of us wants that. You're the one who should be making these decisions. You're such a good father, I know you'll make the right choice.'

He gave a heavy sigh, but I saw the tension leave his expression and knew I was making headway. 'You're probably right,' he conceded. 'These are all questions I'd be asking myself if I weren't so distracted.' He leaned over, kissing my cheek.

Men were so simple. So easy to distract with a bit of flattery. It was like flicking a switch. It was laughable that he might think he was in control, when I could play him like a puppet, make him dance to my tune.

'So you'll sort it?' I asked, squeezing his hand.

'I'll see what I can do,' he replied. 'But Carrie can be bloody stubborn when she wants to be,' he warned.

So can I, I thought, smiling into his collar. So can I.

TWENTY-THREE

CARRIE

'Fiona, thanks so much for seeing us at such short notice,' I said, taking Maisy's hand and following the doctor as she guided us from the waiting room into a smaller room with a window running the full length of one wall. Fiona had changed considerably since I'd last seen her, eight or nine years ago. She'd gained a lot of weight on her once petite frame, her short legs struggling as she walked, and her black wavy hair had wide streaks of grey running through it. There was no wedding ring on her finger, but I decided not to go down the route of discussing what we'd been doing since we last met. It wasn't the time for small talk.

'You called at the right moment,' she said, fixing me with a flat smile that didn't meet her eyes. 'I had a cancellation and my receptionist hadn't got round to offering the appointment to anyone else on the list. You understand this will have to be filed under private cases. I can't put it through the NHS unless you're willing to wait a year, or more, to be seen.'

I shook my head. 'I don't want to wait. Send me the bill.'

Maisy dropped my hand, clasping her fingers together as she stared down at the ground.

'Well, Maisy,' Fiona said, 'we're just going to head through to that room there.' She pointed to the other side of the window, where I could see colourful toys placed temptingly on low tables: dolls, teddies, pirate swords and muskets, wooden bricks, a jumble of Lego. It looked like a child's dream come true, but there was no spark of excitement in Maisy's eyes, no indication that she'd even noticed.

I forced myself to smile encouragingly, trying to convince myself that by the time we walked out of here in thirty minutes, there would be some change for the positive, no matter how small. I just wanted her to be okay.

I felt a sudden wave of irritation as I remembered the phone call that had woken me at the crack of dawn. I'd lurched out of bed, grabbing for my mobile in the dim half-light, unable to remember falling asleep. All I could think was that this was it. This was the call I'd been dreading. The cold finality of some stranger telling me they'd found a body... that my little Ava was never coming home. I'd been shaking so much I could barely keep my grip on the phone as I sat on the bedroom carpet, my knees pulled tight to my chest. And though I didn't dare admit it to myself, I'd been hit with a sudden jolt of hope that instead of the worst, it might be the best. Ava's little voice would be calling for me in the background as a police officer told me in amused tones to come to the station and pick her up.

But neither of those was the case. Instead, Jimmy's voice had filled my head, and after a few seconds of confusion, I'd realised that he was calling to lecture me on my parenting choices; to tell me that he'd given it some thought and actually he agreed that it *was* best for Maisy if Leah – that young, barely-out-of-school slut, who had no experience of being a mother – took our daughter to her therapy session. 'If she even *needs* to go,' he'd tacked on to the end.

The disappointment of not having the news I'd let myself so briefly hope for and the audacity of Leah making demands on how I cared for my own daughter had been too much. I'd cut the call and, shaking, gone to have a long, hot shower before getting Tommy up for school.

I would not let this woman insert herself into my life, my *children's* lives, no matter how easily she seemed to be able to manipulate my husband to her will. I shook away the surge of rage, looking over to see Maisy walk slowly through the door to the second room. Taking a steeling breath to prepare myself for what was about to come, I made to follow her.

Fiona put an arm in front of me, shaking her head. 'Not you for now, Carrie,' she said in her clipped tones.

'Excuse me?'

She gave another bland smile. 'I find that when the parents hang around, it stops the child from opening up. You'll be able to watch through the window.' Her tone was no-nonsense, leaving no room for argument, but the idea of her probing into Maisy's mind without me there to step in if needed made me want to pick my daughter up and walk away. She didn't give me a chance to argue though. She turned, striding into the room and shutting the door behind her. I stood, staring through the window, sure that it must be mirrored on the other side so as not to distract the patient.

Patient... my daughter was a patient. I swallowed, my heart beating fast. I watched Fiona lower her bulk into an armchair and begin to talk. With a horrible trickle of realisation, I stepped closer, pressing my hand to the window. I couldn't hear a thing. I could see her lips moving, but I couldn't make out a word. The window was soundproof! It was hugely unsettling.

Maisy remained standing on the rug, her head bowed, her fingers laced tightly in front of her. She looked so tiny standing there, so broken as she ignored the play opportunities all around her. It was like she'd gone. Like I'd lost her too. And if the call finally came to confirm what I already feared in my heart – that her baby sister was dead – any chance of Maisy breaking out of this state would be crushed for ever. Both of my daughters would be lost to me.

The weight of the realisation hit me with such force, it stole the breath from my lungs. I'd been so determined to keep going, keep searching, keep believing this was all just some awful nightmare that I might wake up from soon. To cry would give power to the notion that I believed hope was lost – it would be self-indulgent when Ava needed me to be strong for her. But seeing Maisy standing there, silent and lost in her grief, knowing I might never again hold Ava in my arms... it was agony.

I turned from the window and broke into a sprint, rushing back through the main waiting room, shoving past a handyman with a toolbox clasped in his hand to push through the front doors of the clinic. Outside, I darted across the wide pavement to where a tree-shaded green offered a scrap of privacy from passing onlookers.

The moment I reached the sparse line of trees, I felt my legs give out beneath me, my body overcome with tremors. The sobs seemed to come from somewhere so deep inside me it felt as if a part of me was breaking away as they ripped through my chest, choking me in their urgency to escape. The intensity, the sheer inability to control or stem the pain as I muffled the screams with the balled-up sleeve of my jumper, took me back to the birth of my children, the knowledge that I could do nothing but submit, that my body had taken over now. Sharp needles of twigs and tiny rocks bit into the backs of my legs, but I couldn't move, couldn't breathe, my forehead pressing against the rough trunk of the closest tree.

Eventually, though I couldn't guess how much time had passed, the tears subsided and I raised my head, wiping my soaked cheeks and puffy eyes with my sleeve. My throat was tight, raw, my body aching as if I'd been beaten black and blue. I had to get back inside. Maisy needed me to be there for her. I was letting her down – again.

Legs shaking violently, I heaved myself up, brushing the mud and pine needles from my trousers. I held on to the tree until I was sure I was steady enough to walk, then froze, staring across to the entrance to the clinic as a familiar figure emerged from the door, looked over her shoulder as if she was checking nobody was watching, then walked straight to the waiting taxi and climbed in.

I stepped out from behind the tree, feeling suddenly focused... alert... hyper-aware that this wasn't normal behaviour. I'd made it crystal clear to Jimmy that I would be doing this alone. So why the fuck was Leah here now? And what had she been doing inside the clinic while I'd been giving in to my emotions out here?

TWENTY-FOUR

LEAH

I unwound the towel from my hair, the smell of roast chicken wafting up from the kitchen below. I'd spent the afternoon cooking. Jimmy hadn't had much of an appetite of late, but his words during our disagreement yesterday had struck a nerve, reminding me of what I needed to do – the small sacrifices I needed to make in pursuit of the bigger picture. Frustratingly, he had left the house before I'd woken up this morning, and this time, I hadn't bothered to call his office. He was right that I shouldn't be demanding to know where he was every minute of the day. A sensible woman would deduce that he was out there looking for his daughter.

In his field as a defence lawyer, he'd met a lot of people who might now be able to offer some help in the search. Some of the people he'd helped to walk free might even consider themselves in his debt. Perhaps he was contacting them now, asking for assistance in this time of need. Of course he wouldn't want me involved in that. He'd want to protect me.

My stomach tensed as I thought of what lengths he might go to to find his daughter. I hoped he wouldn't take it too far, put his freedom in jeopardy. The thought of him spending his days contacting retired detectives, ex-cons and insalubrious people was still far preferable to the alternative of him being with another woman though.

I turned on the hairdryer, absently blasting it through my damp hair, hoping he'd come home soon. I planned to talk to him over dinner about Shannon's visit. I didn't want him to find out later and think I was keeping secrets; besides, if he felt that I'd concealed information, suspicion about Carrie being involved in Ava's disappearance, if there was truth in what Shannon said about her still wanting him back, I wanted to make sure he knew it. That he understood the depths she was willing to sink to, the ways in which she was trying to manipulate him. I wouldn't let her take him from me – I wasn't naïve enough to allow that to happen.

My phone lit up on the dresser in front of me, and I switched off the hairdryer, seeing an unknown number. I was half tempted to ignore it, but curiosity got the better of me and I picked it up.

'Hello?'

'Leah, it's me.' Jimmy's voice sounded urgent, and I wondered why.

'Whose phone is this? I thought you were coming home for dinner. It's going to be ready soon,' I said.

'My phone died. I'm at the police station. They called earlier and asked me to come in to answer some questions... I think they're looking at me, Leah.'

I frowned, sitting up straighter. 'What do you mean? Have they arrested you?'

'No, nothing like that, but I just wanted to warn you. They're acting really strange. They've said I'm free to go, but' – he let out a panicked sigh – 'I don't know what's happening.'

I held my breath, wondering why they'd suddenly turn the spotlight on him. 'Come home,' I said. 'Come now, and we'll talk.'

'Okay,' he answered softly.

The line went dead, and I stared at my reflection in the mirror, my eyes wide as I realised this could be bad.

I hadn't been able to bring myself to serve the roast chicken just for myself, and now it was drying out in the oven, the potatoes no doubt turning wrinkly and hard. The sound of Jimmy's key in the lock had me rushing for the door. 'You're back!' I gasped, pulling him into my arms. He let his head rest on my shoulder, hugging me tightly for a moment.

Straightening, he looked at me. His expression was one of exhaustion rather than fear, far calmer than I'd anticipated in the wake of his call. 'Well, that was a strange afternoon,' he said.

'Tell me everything.'

He nodded. 'I will, but can we eat? I'm starving, and whatever you've cooked smells delicious.'

'Oh, of course.' I nodded, taken aback. 'I wasn't sure if you'd want to. Come and sit down,' I said, taking his hand and heading for the kitchen.

He slumped heavily into a chair and I opened the oven, taking out the covered trays of food, hoping it wasn't completely ruined. The gravy should mask the worst of it at least.

'So?' I probed, looking over at him. 'What happened?'

He gave a heavy sigh. 'That detective, DCI Farrows, called me this morning and asked me to come back in. He wouldn't say anything else on the phone, so I was worried, you know...' He swallowed, looking up at the ceiling as if he was trying not to cry. 'I thought maybe they'd found something... someone.'

'Oh, Jimmy,' I breathed, pausing my carving of the chicken, gripping the handle of the knife tight in my palm. 'You should have called me. I would have come to support you. That must have been awful.'

'It wasn't great,' he said. He cleared his throat. 'When I got there, I was made to wait for nearly an hour in a little side room. It was like they were trying to make me uneasy or something. And then finally DCI Farrows and another guy turn up, and instead of reassuring me that they're still searching for Ava, he starts throwing all these questions at me, demanding proof of where I've been, who I've been with.'

'What did you tell them?' I asked, trying not to let my own desire for the answers seep through my tone.

He shook his head like he couldn't understand the question. 'The truth, obviously. Work, here, at the beach and surrounding areas, knocking on doors and searching for my daughter. I told them I'd been doing *their* job, by the look of things. They didn't take too kindly to that.'

'But they let you go,' I said. 'You were able to convince them.'

'They had to. They have nothing on me. They can't find evidence for a crime I didn't commit, can they?' He folded his arms. 'I can't believe how bloody useless they've been over this whole situation.'

I walked across the room, placing his dinner on the table in front of him. He'd lied to the police if he'd told them he'd been working. And if *I* knew that, it was only a matter of time before they did too. 'Do you want a glass of wine?' I offered.

'Go on then.' He picked up his fork, not waiting for me to join him. 'It's not fully over,' he said through a mouthful of food. 'There was mention of a search warrant. I don't think I was supposed to hear it, but like I said – *useless.*'

'A warrant. To search where?'

'Here, of course. But they can be my bloody guest. I have nothing to hide.'

The bottle of wine slipped from my hand, the dark green glass exploding on the tiles, fragrant red liquid splashing over the cream-painted wall.

'*Leah!*' Jimmy yelled, jumping up from his seat.

'No!' I exclaimed. 'You can't let them come here with a warrant! You *can't*, Jimmy!'

'It's not something we get a choice over, darling. I don't like it either, but sometimes you have to just play along. Fuck, you're bleeding!'

I glanced down, seeing a piece of glass protruding from my shin, blood running down my flesh-coloured tights. 'They *aren't* searching the house!' My words were a scream, fear sweeping through me like wildfire, igniting every sense along the way.

The warmth evaporated from his expression, his eyes darkening. 'What's the matter with you? You'll make things ten times worse if you act like a petulant child! Grow up, Leah. I know you're young, but you're embarrassing yourself. And it's a massive fucking turn-off. You hear me?'

I lurched forward, my hand ricocheting across his face so hard his head was thrown to the side. Slowly, he turned back to look at me, and I gasped, seeing that his bottom lip had split open. I must have caught it with my ring.

I regretted my outburst instantly. 'Oh God, I'm sorry!' I cried, grabbing a towel and moving towards him. 'I didn't mean—'

'Don't!' He held out a hand to keep me at bay. 'Don't come near me.' He touched his lip, staring down at the blood on his fingertip, then looked back up at me. 'You're a fucking lunatic.'

'Jimmy, I'm so sorry!'

He stalked out of the kitchen, and I heard the front door slam behind him. I squeezed the towel, trying to calm my breathing, feeling dizzy and disorientated, panic coursing through my veins. Then I bent down slowly and pulled the shard of glass from my flesh, pressing the towel to the cut.

Ignoring the mess, the dinner congealing on the table, I locked the back door, then walked slowly through the house, bolting the front door from the inside. I felt as if I'd been thrust into a bad dream as I walked upstairs, all my fears swarming to the surface, choking me in their intensity. I unlocked the door to the loft and stepped into the stairwell, turning the key behind me. I didn't want the police here, in my house. Didn't want them anywhere near me or the children. But, I thought, heading up into the darkness, if they came, I would be ready for them. This time, I had to be.

TWENTY-FIVE

CARRIE

'How are you doing?'

I raised an eyebrow as Shannon placed a mug of coffee in front of me, and she held up a hand in apology. 'Stupid question. I'm sorry. It's just hard to know what to say.'

'I know. Don't worry about it.' I sighed, taking the mug in my palms. She'd given me the one Jimmy always used to hate – the huge one with the tiny handle that he said was a dangerous liability – but I loved it because it was the biggest cup we had. As a busy working mum, I had to keep hydrated.

She walked over to peer inside my larder. 'Shall I make something to eat? Do you want a sandwich?'

'No thanks,' I said, shaking my head. 'I'm not hungry.'

She regarded me over the counter. 'You've lost weight. I can see it in your face already.'

'Is it any surprise? My stomach feels like it's tied in knots. Food is the last thing on my mind.'

She folded her arms, her mouth twisting in disapproval. 'I get that. But you're not taking care of yourself. Let me heat you up some soup at least.'

I shrugged non-committally, not having the energy to argue. Jimmy had turned up a few hours before Shannon arrived, insisting that he was going to take Maisy out for a walk and some lunch, and Tommy had gone to school first thing, despite my offer for him to take the day off so we could spend some time together. I wanted them both here with me, and with Leah making an unwelcome appearance at the clinic yesterday, I felt more than a little uneasy having Maisy out of my sight.

I'd told Jimmy everything I'd seen, needing him to believe me, to see for himself just how far Leah was overstepping. I didn't care what that stupid detective said. There was no way I was going to believe that Leah wasn't somehow involved in Ava's disappearance. I had been relieved to get Jimmy alone for a moment, but he'd batted away every bit of evidence I put to him, refusing to even consider that he could be wrong about the woman he'd moved in with after a matter of weeks. He barely knew her! It broke my heart that after all the years we'd spent together, he'd take her word over mine. He'd said I was being ridiculous, that Leah couldn't possibly know any details of what time or where Maisy's appointment had been, and even if she had, she was hardly going to turn up and make things uncomfortable for her, but I knew what I'd seen. Fiona had looked at me like I was mad yesterday when she finally emerged from the room with my daughter, to find me blotchy-faced and asking if anyone had tried to get into the room with Maisy while I'd stepped outside. She'd told me no, of course not, but still I felt on edge.

Jimmy had gruffly insisted that I needed to drop it but had mentioned in passing that he wasn't planning on taking Maisy to his house today anyway. He'd seemed more subdued than usual and didn't look nearly so put-together. His shirt was crumpled as though he'd slept in it, he'd somehow cut his lip open, and he hadn't bothered to shave. I could see the grief written on his face; recognised it because I was sure my own features were a mirror image of his. The pain of losing Ava was killing him, as it was me.

I couldn't grasp why he wouldn't confide in me. Why he wouldn't let us break down together. It took every scrap of my self-control to hold my emotions in check, refusing to show my vulnerability to a man who had so clearly shut his own off from me. But even so, even with the rejection jabbing me in humiliating blows, I couldn't ignore my need to comfort him. He looked like he wasn't being taken care of, and despite our bickering, I'd wanted to hug him, tell him we'd get through this together. That I was here if he needed to talk because *I* certainly did. I'd held my tongue, though, knowing full well the response I'd get.

'How was the therapy session?' Shannon asked, opening a tin and pouring the unappetising-smelling contents into a pan.

I sighed, my hands fidgeting in my lap. I hadn't been able to sit still in days. My skin was raw and broken from the scratching I couldn't help – a thousand tiny wounds as punishment for letting Ava down. 'I don't think it's going to be the quick fix I'd hoped for. Maisy didn't say a word, and she seems more closed off than ever.' I didn't want to admit that I was having second thoughts over hiring Fiona. Perhaps she didn't have the nurturing side needed to make Maisy feel comfortable. It was an alien situation and she'd gone straight up to her room the moment we arrived home, refusing to come down to eat dinner. I hoped Jimmy wasn't putting pressure on her right now on their walk. It would only do more damage.

'Oh, Carrie, you must be out of your mind with worry. And now Tommy is pulling away right when you need him too.'

I gave a tiny nod, trying not to cry again. I couldn't be sure I could regain control and didn't want a repeat of yesterday's breakdown outside the clinic. 'He won't talk to me. It's like he's blaming me. I know it's partly down to his hormones, and teenage boys are *supposed* to hate their parents, but he's *just* turned twelve. I wasn't expecting it yet. He was my shadow for years.' I pressed my knuckles to my eyes, trying to force back the tears that felt dangerously close to the surface. 'I feel like I've lost all three of them. It's breaking me apart, Shannon. I don't know how I'm going to survive this. It's too much.'

Her blue eyes widened. 'Don't you talk like that. You're stronger than you think. And you *will* get through it because they need you to. But that doesn't mean it's going to be easy. With Tommy, you just have to be patient. I remember my cousin at that age – he was awful to my poor auntie, and he didn't have any reason to be angry.'

'*Reason?* You think I've done something to bring on this attitude?'

She turned her back to me, stirring the pan of soup. 'Oh no... that's not what I meant. Just, he's been through a lot this year. The separation, the shared custody, and... he mentioned he was in hospital with a broken arm.'

'He told you that?'

She gave a nod, and I felt myself flush. 'Well, it was hardly a major trauma. Kids break bones. It's just a fact of life. But he was... unsettled by it.'

'What happened?' She turned from the pan, her eyes suddenly fixing on mine, making me feel as if I was under inter-rogation, and not for the first time. She couldn't know how hard it was for me to discuss. I had to remind myself that this was how friendship worked. The trading of secrets and stories. It was an aspect I could have quite happily lived without.

I glanced out the back window to the garden, shaking my head. 'Just a silly fall. An accident,' I said quietly.

She didn't speak for a moment, and I hoped she wouldn't ask more.

The silence continued, and I held my shoulders stiff, refusing to break the awkward moment, knowing she expected me to go on. Finally, I heard the pouring of liquid into bowls, and felt my stomach lurch. I knew I wouldn't be able to eat a thing.

TWENTY-SIX

LEAH

My whole body was shuddering violently as I made my way slowly down the stairs. The cricket bat clasped tightly in my sweaty hands offered a mild sense of reassurance, but I knew I wouldn't be able to protect myself for long with it. I didn't have the strength.

I'd ignored the banging for more than half an hour, but it had grown increasingly demanding, and somehow it had become the less frightening option to leave the safety of the loft and face whoever was out there. It had taken me a long time to realise it might be Jimmy. He hadn't come back last night after our argument in the kitchen, and I'd refrained from calling him, wanting him to have the chance to calm down before we spoke again.

I approached the front door now, nervous and sick to my stomach. If it *was* him, he certainly hadn't calmed in his absence. I wrapped my arms around myself, the bat still clutched in my trembling fingers. 'Who is it?' I called.

The banging stopped abruptly. 'It's bloody me!' Jimmy's voice yelled back. 'Why have you deadbolted the door? I've been out here ages!'

He sounded furious, and I stepped closer. 'Who's with you?' I called, making no move to unlock the bolt.

'*With* me? Nobody! Let me in – now, Leah!'

I didn't believe him. I felt sure that the moment I opened the door, a SWAT team would come swarming into my home, wreaking havoc on my life. 'What about the police?' I called. 'Are *they* out there?'

'What? No! Of course not. Do you think a deadbolt would stop them if they wanted to search the place? Don't be ridiculous!'

I knew he was right. But that didn't stop the terrifying scenarios from playing out in my mind, making it hard for me to take a step forward and open the door. Closing my eyes, I realised I had no choice. If I kept Jimmy waiting out there much longer, he'd think I'd gone mad. He might actually call the police himself, and I couldn't let that happen.

I opened the cupboard under the stairs and pushed the bat inside, hiding it away, then finally went to the door and slid back the bolt. I left the chain on, opening the door a crack to peer outside.

Jimmy glared at me. 'All the fucking way, for Christ's sake! I'm losing my patience with this, Leah.'

Sucking in a breath, I released the chain, opening the door fully. He pushed his way inside, and I slammed the door closed behind him, sliding the bolt back over. He watched me, his expression bewildered and cold, his lip not as bruised and swollen as I'd anticipated. Maybe I didn't hit him that hard after all. It had only been the edge of my ring that had made it bleed.

He turned to face me, his cheeks red, a purple vein protruding from his temple. He was breathing hard, and for a moment, I wondered if I was in danger of *him* lashing out. If I'd pushed him too far.

'I don't know *what* you're playing at, but don't you dare do anything like that again. Locking me out of my own house – have you gone mad?'

'I'm sorry,' I said, my words quiet as I tried to moderate the shaking in my voice. 'I was frightened. When you said about the police coming here, I got scared,' I admitted, minimising my true feelings.

'And you didn't think to come and answer the door to me when you knew you'd made it impossible for me to let myself back in?'

'I... I was asleep. I only just heard you knocking.'

He regarded me coolly, then turned for the kitchen, striding through the door. I heard the sound of the kettle being filled, and walked in to find him cracking eggs into a pan. Anxiety was racing through my veins, and the sight of the food made my stomach lurch. I turned my face away, going to sit down at the table. 'Where have you been?' I asked, afraid to hear his response, to see a clue that he might have been with another woman.

'I went to a hotel, and then earlier today I was out with Maisy.'

'Oh. How is she?'

He sighed. 'No different. Still not saying a word. And before you ask, there's still no news on Ava. I spoke to the police first thing. They have no leads, *none*, unless you count the witch hunt they've started against me. It's ridiculous. If—'

He broke off, and I saw his jaw flex, the protective shell hardening around him, making it impossible for him to break down. I longed for him to show me the true extent of his emotions, but instead I felt like I was being kept on the periphery, not good enough, not trusted with his heart. It wasn't healthy to keep everything bottled up like this. I was going to be his wife soon – he needed to remember he was safe with me. That I would never let him down.

He took a deep breath, flaring his nostrils. 'I have to get Maisy talking again. It's possible she saw something. She was right there with Ava. If only she'd tell me what happened... it could give us the answers nobody seems capable of finding.'

'Do you think Carrie has told her to keep quiet?'

'Why would she do that?' There was a warning tone beneath his words, and I shook my head.

'Never mind,' I said, pasting on a smile and brushing the comment away. The last thing I needed was to get into another row with Jimmy. I didn't want to hear him taking his ex's side over mine again. 'Maybe you should ask Carrie if Maisy can come and stay here early this week. *Tonight*. Tommy too. I hate knowing they're going through such a tough time and not being able to see them, or do anything to help.'

He grunted, flipping his eggs and buttering the toast that had popped up. It was clear he was in no mood to talk to me.

'Here,' I said, standing and walking over to him. 'Let me make you a proper coffee.' He was holding a mug, and I went to take it, covering his hand with my own for a moment.

'I can make it myself,' he said, stepping back, out of my reach.

'Jimmy, I'm trying to apologise,' I said softly. 'I know I acted... out of character. I'm sorry, okay?' I moved to kiss him, and he lurched back as if I was a viper trying to strike.

I frowned, hurt. 'Have you been drinking?' The smell of rum was overwhelming now that I was close to him, the alcohol seeping from his pores, his breath sour.

'Have I been *drinking*? What reason would I have to drink? Can you think of anything?' he spat sarcastically. He turned his back on me, heaping the eggs on top of his toast, sloshed some boiling water over a spoonful of instant coffee and, picking up the plate and cup, walked past me as if I were invisible.

I stared after him, knowing I had to fix this. I couldn't lose him. Couldn't lose this family. The children I adored. I would not let him take away everything I'd dreamed of. I would fix this mess, no matter what price I had to pay.

TWENTY-SEVEN

CARRIE

The walls were closing in on me. I stood in the middle of Ava's small pale green playroom, her soft blue rabbit clutched to my chest, the sun rising, soft light filtering through the gaps in the green-and-yellow floral curtains, and knew I was dying. The pain of her not being here, of not hearing her voice, was corroding my heart, acid pumping through my arteries, burning everything it made contact with. I couldn't do this. Wasn't strong enough.

I'd been awake for hours... it felt like days. How could I sleep when she was out there somewhere, sobbing for her mama? How could I live when she wasn't with me? I *couldn't*. Every breath felt like it was being sucked through an increasingly narrowing straw, my lungs burning with the effort of simply staying here, living through the worst torture any parent could imagine.

I'd seen mothers have to walk away from hospital without their children. Heard their cries, their desperate screams and prayers to bring them back, to save a life that had been lost too soon. It had been hard to hear them. Uncomfortable. I'd learned to distance myself emotionally, shutting down. The early days on the ward had taught me that I couldn't continue to be a good doctor if I let my patients and their distress seep into my consciousness. I'd been professional. Cold, even. And as the years had passed, I'd learned to brace myself when I had to tell someone that their child had died. To shut out the tortured wailing, the shrieks of despair. I'd become hard. Unbreakable. It had been a conscious choice on my part.

But I couldn't defend myself against this pain. This agony. There was no shell I could muster to withstand the onslaught of emotion, fear, horror that smashed into me over and over, breaking my soul to pieces. I would die from this. I *wanted* to. Craved the blackness of oblivion, the peace of nothingness. The image of the woman I'd treated just weeks ago, the rope marks on her neck, the snap judgement I'd made on her character, blaming her for daring to leave her children without a mother, seared into my mind in hyper-colour. I hadn't ever thought I could empathise with her. Long for her courage to end it all. I was trapped, needing escape, and yet knew I had to stay. For Maisy and, though he wouldn't appreciate it, for Tommy too.

I clutched the rabbit tighter, inhaling its scent, squeezing my eyes shut as I tried to imagine it was my sweet Ava in my arms. But I couldn't believe the lie. Somewhere out there, my daughter was suffering. And, I thought, my eyes opening, my gaze flitting around the empty room, anger and desperation poisoning me from the inside out, if she wasn't found soon, my mind would snap. And I wasn't sure I'd be able to come back from it.

TWENTY-EIGHT

I felt like I'd been on hold for hours as I waited for someone to speak to me and tell me what the hell was going on. I couldn't believe how infrequent and unhelpful the contact from the police had been. I'd seen Ava's picture plastered across the news, but as yet there'd been no mention of a press conference, none of the fanfare I'd have anticipated in the wake of her disappearance, and I didn't understand why. Was this how it always was with a child disappearance case?

I'd seen them on the news over the years, the appeals for sightings, the photos of the children, and always assumed that behind the scenes, so much must be going on. But it didn't feel like that now. It felt as though Ava had been written off, and whatever the police were doing, it wasn't going to bring her back to me. It was like they were going through the motions when they'd already given up. Did they think she'd drowned? Hadn't *I* thought the same? It was the obvious conclusion, or it would have been if there wasn't clear footage of her on the bus just moments later. Why weren't they able to find that woman? How difficult could it be? I closed my eyes, picturing Leah's mother again, as I had a thousand times over these past few days. I wished I knew her address so I could go and see for myself if I was right.

Every night, I lay in bed looking up at the ceiling, trying to pretend to myself that Ava was in my arms, that I could feel her little body curled close to mine, her breath falling soft and sweet on my cheek. I lost myself in the fantasy over and over again, fighting against the moment I had to turn my head and discover the cold, harsh truth, see the empty space where she should have been.

The phone line sprang to life at last, and a voice – female and soft – spoke. 'Carrie, I'm so sorry to have kept you waiting. This is PC Mayville. We spoke on the beach a few times.'

'Oh, I was expecting DCI Farrows,' I said.

'He's unavailable at the moment, but I wanted to update you. I know how hard it must be to hear nothing, but the reason nobody's been in touch is because we've yet to find any evidence of what's happened to Ava. I know that isn't what you want to hear.'

'But have you given up? Are you still looking for her?'

'Nothing has changed. We still have a huge team working on this, Carrie. We've reached out to everyone at Tommy and Maisy's schools, local businesses, everyone we know was on the beach that day. Ava's father gave us a list of all the babysitters you've used and we've been in touch with all of them. We're exploring every avenue.'

'Oh, really? You haven't invited me and Jimmy to give a press conference.'

There was a pause. 'There's been some talk of it, but some of the team feel that with the obvious avenue being that Ava went into the water, it isn't fair to give you that hope. That's not to say it won't happen. I imagine in a day or two, if the situation remains unchanged, we'll have you and Jimmy make a public appeal.'

'Oh...' Her words hit me like a bucket of iced water to the face. 'I see.' I swallowed hard and felt myself sway.

'I shouldn't tell you this – I'm not supposed to – but DCI Farrows also wanted to look into a few leads first. There was someone he wanted to question.'

'Who?' I frowned.

'I can't say. But it's looking like a dead end. That's why we haven't had more to tell you.'

'I don't understand who you'd be looking at. Is this something to do with Leah?'

'Oh, Carrie, I wish I could tell you everything, but you know I can't. I'm desperate to give you some good news. This is the first child disappearance case I've worked on, and it's all I can think about. I can't imagine how you're coping.'

'I'm not,' I replied bluntly. 'I have to go. If you find out anything, anything at all, please call me.'

She hesitated, then said, 'Okay, I will. Don't give up, Carrie.'

I put the phone down, feeling numb, flat, and called to Maisy to come down from her room. It was time for another session with Fiona Lees.

'I have to tell you, Carrie,' Fiona was saying, 'I don't think I've ever seen a child as unresponsive and blank as Maisy is. She's not just mute – she's catatonic.'

'Yes, I know that,' I snapped, crossing my arms and glancing over to where Maisy sat on the far side of the waiting room after another ineffectual session in Fiona's therapy room. 'That's why I brought her here. You're supposed to know how to deal with this.'

She fixed me with a withering stare. 'I'm not saying I can't. I'm just trying to communicate to you that this is serious. The trauma of losing her sister has impacted her deeply. And I think she might be blaming herself for it.'

'Blaming herself? Why?'

'Children take responsibility for a lot of things they shouldn't. Is there any way Maisy might have contributed to Ava's disappearance? Was she unkind in the moments leading up to it? Sending her away from her game, perhaps? Telling her to play somewhere else or leave her alone? These little comments, things you and I would see as nothing important, can haunt a child – make them turn the blame onto themselves. And I do think there's an element of that going on here.'

I shook my head, stunned at the idea that Maisy could be taking responsibility for such a hugely traumatic event. 'I... I don't know,' I admitted.

'Well, have a think and try and remember if you heard anything between them in the moments before Ava went missing. Any little scrap of information could be a massive help in turning this around.'

'I will.'

'And we can consider prescribing something to help her relax if things don't improve soon.'

'Medication?' I frowned, looking over at my daughter, sitting on the edge of her seat, unmoving. She looked like a china doll. 'I don't know. I don't think her father would like that.'

'It's just an option. Something to discuss later on. You should consider bringing your son in too.'

'Tommy? Why? He's doing okay, given the circumstances.'

She twisted her mouth, tapping her biro on her lip. 'He might seem okay outwardly, but children present differently after a trauma. Whichever way you look at it, his sister is missing, and that's a lot for a young boy to deal with on his own. Bring him in and I'll have a chat with him.'

She turned away, saying goodbye to Maisy before heading

back to her office, and I realised my hands had balled into fists. I was terrified at the idea of bringing my son here. Of what he might say to Fiona. Him spilling the family secrets was the last thing we needed right now; it would complicate everything. No, we needed to be a team. To focus on Ava. Finding her was all that mattered.

TWENTY-NINE

LEAH

I groaned, tossing aside the green bodycon dress and rifling through my wardrobe, trying to find something to wear. I wanted it to be casual; not to make me look like I was trying too hard – something Jimmy couldn't stand – but something that would make him take a second glance at me, *notice* me. He'd spent the day upstairs in the spare room he sometimes used as an office, though I was sure he wasn't working – not after drinking so much last night.

Twice I'd gone up to see him, taking food and drinks to help him through his hangover. And, though I didn't dare admit it, to see if he volunteered any further information about the possibility of a police search at the house. I'd forced myself to stay outwardly calm, knowing he wouldn't dig deep enough to uncover the continual churning terror in my gut. He'd taken the offerings – sandwiches, juice, home-made cakes – but given nothing back, clearly not ready to talk.

I'd given him as much space as I could bear to, but now it was heading for evening and he was still acting like I was some alien creature he wished he could toss back into the ocean. I hated walking in and hearing him sigh, none of the warmth and sexual tension we usually shared evident in his eyes. I wanted to make it better, get him back on my side, but I hated every outfit I tried. None looked right.

With a sense of surrender, I pulled on a pale blue cotton shift dress, letting my long light brown hair hang loose down my back, hoping that if I couldn't make him see me as sexy, he might see me as sweet, in need of his protection, sparking those deep masculine instincts I knew he had inside him.

I cast a final look in the mirror, not bothering with perfume, then walked to the spare room, knocking gently on the door and stepping inside. 'Hi,' I said, reminding myself to smile at him, though it took all my effort to pretend I was okay. 'Dinner's ready. It's beef pie and broccoli. I thought you might like to come downstairs and eat with me?' I added hopefully.

He nodded, his expression very different from earlier. 'I just got off a call with DCI Farrows,' he said, his tone businesslike, confident and detached. 'The idiots don't seem any closer to finding her,' he went on, avoiding saying Ava's name, 'but I don't think they're focusing on me any more.'

The blast of relief hit me forcefully, making me blink in disbelief, but I tried not to show it too obviously for fear of letting on how tightly I'd been wound today. I let out a slow breath, holding on to the door frame. 'Oh...' I said softly. 'What makes you think that?'

He rubbed the stubble on his chin. 'He didn't ask any questions about me this time.'

'So what did he want?'

He gave a twist of his mouth, meeting my eye. 'To ask about Carrie. Her relationship with the children. Her long working hours. That incident with Tommy's broken arm...'

'How did they find out about that?' I asked, though my mind was whirring frantically. It *had* to have been Shannon. She must have gone to the police after all. And in doing so, she'd not only taken the spotlight off Jimmy, saving us from the torment of having our home ransacked by strangers, but if they found out something bad about Carrie, the result could be that the children would finally come to me. I could be their full-time mother. Take care of them like they deserved. And I knew I could make them happier than *she* ever had.

'I don't have a clue,' Jimmy said, standing up, oblivious to the thoughts spinning wildly through my head. 'But she's not going to like it if they turn their focus on her. I'm not sure she can cope with more stress on top of everything else.'

He frowned, and I saw an unexpected expression of concern cross his features for the woman who'd caused us nothing but distress for the past six months. He'd complained about her parenting, her selfishness, who she was as a person from the moment I met him. So, I thought, following him from the room, why now did he look like he didn't want the police investigating Carrie any more than he had wanted them looking into him?

THIRTY

CARRIE

The doorbell was ringing, and I hurriedly wiped my eyes and shoved my phone in my back pocket as I rushed to open it. I'd waved Tommy off to school a few hours before, though he hadn't offered more than a grunt in return, and Jimmy had unexpectedly turned up on the doorstep not long after, asking to take Maisy out again.

I'd suggested we go somewhere together, just the three of us, needing the nostalgia of those glorious family days out we'd once shared. I'd wanted to pretend we were the couple we'd been this time last year, for him to hold my hand as we walked through the fields, looking for pheasants in the long grass as Maisy picked flowers and skipped ahead. To lose myself in the past for a little while as a way to escape the torture of the present. But he'd rejected my suggestion, and in response, I'd insisted he bring Maisy back by lunchtime so I could spend some one-on-one time with her too. There was no therapy booked for today.

I'd watched him drive away with her, him talking nineteen to the dozen, her still resolutely silent, and then I'd found myself curled up on the sofa, Ava's soft blue rabbit clutched under my chin as I scrolled through every photo, every video I'd ever taken of her on my phone. The sound of her voice coming through the speaker had been unbearable, ripping a hole right through my heart, the need to reach into the screen and pull her out, hold on to her, overwhelming, impossible. And yet I hadn't had the strength to turn it off. I'd lost all track of time while I'd been sitting there, smelling the fluffy rabbit, the scent of her skin already fading from the fabric. Jimmy must be back already. I'd expected him to push the boundaries I'd laid down and come back late. He never had been great at being told what to do.

I blotted my cheeks with my sleeve, not wanting Maisy to see me in this state, then opened the door, surprised to find PC Mayville standing on the threshold, DCI Farrows by her side. His expression was serious, and I felt myself sway, wondering if this was it. If they'd finally found my baby.

'Is she...?' I breathed, the sentence fading away as the words refused to come.

'Carrie Gold, we have a warrant to search this property. We believe you may be hiding Ava Gold, and we'll be looking for her or any evidence as to where you might have taken her. You may remain here, but PC Mayville will be by your side so you can't tamper with any evidence.'

I blinked, trying to take in his words. 'Tamper with... *What?*' I asked, feeling slow and stupid. 'You think...?' I swallowed, trying not to give in to the panic that was threatening to overwhelm me, the realisation of what he was telling me making me want to throw up. They weren't searching for my daughter in the right places. They were looking at *me* instead. They were never going to find her.

I saw PC Mayville throw a look of disgust at DCI Farrows as he pushed a folded piece of paper into my palm and strode past me into the house. Several more men appeared on the driveway and, without asking my permission or even acknowledging my presence, walked inside my home. I felt Mayville's hand close around my wrist and wondered what was happening, if I was being arrested. And if so, what was the charge?

Gently, her mouth unsmiling, she led me along the hallway. 'I can't believe he did it that way. I'm so sorry,' she said, her voice barely more than a whisper as she guided me back to the living room and out through the patio doors to the garden.

The air was cold, and I shivered, wrapping my arms around my body.

'Please, sit down,' she said, pointing to the wooden picnic bench on the lawn. 'This will take a while.'

I lowered myself down, feeling numb with shock. Through the windows, I could see the police swarming through the rooms, tipping out drawers, opening cupboards. I wanted to demand that they stop, insist that they leave, but my legs wouldn't work. I felt helpless, watching the people who were supposed to be on my side, the people I'd trusted to find my baby, looking for a reason to pin her disappearance on me. Why on earth would I hide my own daughter? It didn't make sense!

PC Mayville sat down opposite me, sighing deeply. 'I'm really sorry, Carrie. I can't imagine how hard this must be for you.'

I nodded, unable to turn my gaze away as I saw two men come into the living room, upturning the toy chest where I kept puzzles and the train set. 'I don't understand,' I whispered. 'Why would they think...?'

'They're grasping,' she said. 'They haven't found Ava, nor any evidence as to where she might be, and, well...' I looked at her, seeing the expression on her face, which at least told me she was on my side. 'It's often the case that when a child goes missing, it's someone who knows them... someone with motive.'

'I am her *mother*!' I cried, the words fierce, protective as I gripped the edge of the table. 'What possible motive—'

Her hand reached across the bench, covering mine. 'I believe you.'

'*Do* you? Or are you just saying that to keep me calm while those bastards ransack my home?'

She shook her head. 'No. I had an argument with Farrows before we left the station – I told him this was ridiculous, and that he needed to approach the situation differently. It was cruel for him to turn up unannounced like that. At the very least, he should have started by telling you that we still haven't found your daughter; we don't have any answers yet.'

'I thought... I thought he'd come to tell me...'

'I know.' She pursed her lips angrily.

'Why are they doing this?' I asked, my heart thumping a hundred miles a minute in my chest, making me breathless. What if Maisy turned up now and found the house crawling with police? It would terrify her!

Mayville looked down at her lap, shaking her head. 'A tip-off,' she admitted. 'Personally, I think it's nonsense,' she added, keeping her voice low. 'But if they're seen to be following it up, it makes it look like they have a plan – like they know what they're doing. They're floundering. And the top guys won't take any suggestions that they haven't thought of themselves.'

'What do you mean?'

She glanced towards the house, then leaned closer to me, lowering her voice even further. 'Between the two of us, I've noticed a real power play at the local station. There's a culture of toxic masculinity – and Farrows is the worst. He loves to exert his dominance, especially over women. Why do you think I'm out here babysitting you? They don't see me as one of the team. I've never been an equal since I took the job. If a female puts forward a suggestion, it's instantly dismissed.'

'But... he's supposed to be helping me! Finding Ava.'

She nodded. 'I know. But I promise you, Carrie, there are plenty of people who think he's searching in the wrong places. People who are doing all they can, myself included. I know it's not easy, and you don't deserve this, but you don't have a choice now he's got a warrant in place. Let him rule you out as a suspect, and then he might get over his idiocy and get on with what needs doing.'

The door opened and two officers headed over to the shed. PC Mayville sat back, her hand sliding away from mine, and I realised that if this was the team charged with finding Ava, I would never find out what had happened to her. By the time they stopped chasing dead ends, anything could have happened to my daughter.

THIRTY-ONE

LEAH

The door slammed, and I wrapped the blanket tighter around my body, curling my legs under me on the sofa. I held my breath, trying to keep calm, to stop myself from reaching for a weapon and running back up to the loft. This whole situation had gone on for too long now. I needed to make Jimmy – not to mention that awful detective – understand that whatever had happened to Ava, Carrie was at the root of it. That she'd taken a risk, believing in her warped mind that it would somehow pay off – hiding her daughter to get Jimmy's attention – and it hadn't worked out the way she'd hoped. She was creating chaos in my world, and it needed to stop. I wanted everyone to see what I saw. That sweet little Ava deserved so much better. She should be with us, where she wouldn't be a pawn in a broken marriage.

Jimmy had texted twenty minutes earlier to say he was on his way home, and despite not wanting to go downstairs, where I couldn't help but feel vulnerable, I knew I couldn't stay hidden away in the loft any longer. He would think I'd lost my mind, and besides, I didn't want him up there, where he might see something he shouldn't yet.

He came into the living room, flicking on the light. 'It's getting dark,' he said, frowning as he shrugged out of his jacket, tossing it on the armchair.

'Oh, yes.' I nodded, pulling the throw closer around me, noticing for the first time that the sun had slipped below the horizon. 'Where have you been all day?' My voice sounded hoarse, unfamiliar, and I swallowed, trying to clear my throat.

He sat down without bothering to cross the room to kiss me, clearly still harbouring some anger. 'I took Maisy to the art café in town. I was hoping she might make something... that it might spark some life in her.'

'I take it that didn't happen?' I said, the disappointment in his expression impossible to miss.

He shook his head. 'No. She wouldn't even drink the hot chocolate I bought for her.' He sighed. 'I was supposed to take her home at lunchtime, but Carrie called to tell me the police were there.'

'At her house? Doing what?' I said, sitting up straighter, the blanket dropping to my waist.

'Christ, Leah, are you still in your pyjamas? Didn't you even bother to get dressed today?'

'I... I've not been feeling great.'

He peered closer. 'You're not wearing make-up either, are you?'

'I didn't realise I had to,' I said, though it wasn't strictly true. I knew he had high expectations of me. It was my part of the bargain, and I wasn't upholding it.

'I'm the one whose daughter is missing, but you don't see me lounging around in my PJs, barricading myself in the house, do you?' he said, leaning back in his chair with a look of disgust.

I took a deep breath, determined that no matter what he said, I wouldn't rise to the bait tonight. He was right – his daughter was missing. I had to remember that he wasn't himself right now. He didn't mean to be so blunt. 'Why were the police at Carrie's?' I asked again.

He sighed. 'She said they had a warrant. They said some nonsense about her hiding Ava.'

I raised an eyebrow. 'Nonsense? So you don't think it's possible?'

He sneered as if I'd gone mad. 'It's the stupidest thing I ever heard. First they accuse me, and now Carrie. Ava's our daughter; why would we need to kidnap her?'

I shook my head. How much had they been texting back and forth? 'Are you really so naïve about the way she tries to manipulate you, Jimmy? She wants you back! And if you're both in this together, looking for Ava, she's got a way to bond with you.'

'Are you insane? Are you actually mad?' He stood up, his hands balled by his sides. 'I really don't know who you are any more, Leah. I can't believe you'd accuse her of something so...' He shook his head, grasping for words that wouldn't come.

I was too exhausted to argue, to go over all the things Carrie had done to lure him back to her web. And I was suddenly afraid that if they didn't find what they were looking for at her house, they'd refocus their attention on us. That they'd come here after all.

'Are you even listening to me?'

I snapped my head up, realising Jimmy had been speaking as I went over the possibilities of what might happen next.

'Sorry, what?'

He folded his arms. 'I *said*, can you at least serve dinner? It's been a long day.'

'I haven't made anything. I told you – I haven't been feeling well.'

He shook his head. 'Leah, my baby girl is missing. My daughter is mute. My ex is being accused of God knows what. I've had to let down my clients and risk my reputation in the process. I'm going through hell, and now you're acting nothing like the woman I met, throwing fits and not even bothering to cook a meal after I've been out taking care of my family all day. Do you think this is what I signed up for when I asked you to move in with me? Do you think you can take and take and give nothing back?'

'Jimmy, wait!' I said, pushing the blanket aside and standing up. 'I... I'll cook. Go and shower and I'll make something now.'

He stared at me, his expression cold and angry, then turned away. I listened as he stomped up the stairs, the bathroom door slamming shut behind him, and I reminded myself that if I wasn't careful, I would lose everything.

I had to do better.

THIRTY-TWO

CARRIE

I heard Shannon's bubbly, high-pitched voice as her voicemail kicked in, and gave a sigh, ending the call without leaving a message. I'd left one already the day before yesterday, in the wake of that bleak therapy session with Fiona where she'd declared my daughter was catatonic. I'd wanted to ask Shannon if she'd noticed anything about Maisy while we were at the beach, and then overnight while she'd been at the house. Any tiny detail had the potential to make a difference at this stage.

When she hadn't got back to me, I'd sent a couple of texts, but now, two days had passed with no contact from her. It wasn't like her to ghost me. And though I knew she had every right to a life of her own, certainly no obligation to be here by my side, I couldn't help feeling hurt that she would leave my messages unanswered when she knew what I was going through. Had I asked too much of her over this past week? Made her uncomfortable in how much I'd leaned on her for support?

I was being selfish, I supposed, but I wanted her to be here with me. I needed someone who could make me feel less alone, less frightened.

Yesterday, after hours of the police combing through my things, I'd asked PC Mayville how long they were going to stay, telling her Maisy was due back soon and Tommy would be arriving home after school. She'd asked Farrows for an update, and he'd come out to the garden, grim-faced, telling me that he would take as long as was needed to ascertain the truth, and that perhaps the children should stay with my husband for a few days.

He'd smirked, then made a comment under his breath about my being in a cell overnight, which had left me simultaneously furious and frightened – a feeling that hadn't been improved when Leah had sent a message asking why the children couldn't come and stay with her, along with a long lecture on how Maisy needed to be in a stable environment right now, and how I was too wrapped up in the search to be there for her and Tommy.

It was nonsense, plucked from thin air. Taking care of them was the only thing keeping me from jumping off a bridge right now. I needed something to focus on outside of Ava, or I'd go mad. Leah was acting like I'd changed the parameters, but the children never stayed with Jimmy during the week! She was overstepping, trying to blur the lines of our agreement, and for some reason, it made a cold feeling of dread creep through my stomach. I couldn't help but worry about what would happen if Jimmy decided she was right. Would they try and take my children from me? Had Leah already been chipping away at Tommy, trying to get him to make the decision for me? The idea of losing him, of never fixing the gaping chasm that had formed in our relationship, broke my heart.

I was sure that Farrows had dragged out the search far longer than was necessary, just to torment me more. When at last they'd left, I'd found the house ransacked, nothing tidied, as if they'd done as much damage as they could get away with during their time in my home. I'd hurriedly sorted the children's bedrooms as best I could, pausing to call Shannon again, wanting to ask her to come and help me, but she hadn't answered.

When Jimmy had brought Tommy and Maisy home, having kept Maisy away all day, they'd both gone straight upstairs, and I'd spent the rest of the night trying to put the house back together. It was actually easier to have something to focus on, rather than lying alone in my bedroom, the chance of sleep next to zero, holding in the screams that begged to be released every few seconds as I thought of Ava, wondering where she was and who she was with, the smell of the sea and the memory of the endless expanse of the horizon filling me with a terror that made my guts twist into knots, bile searing my throat. I couldn't stay still. I needed the distraction. Farrows had done me a favour.

I hadn't brought up Leah's message with Jimmy, unwilling to cause another argument when he was looking so dishevelled, wearing his distress on his sleeve – though he refused to share it with me – but he'd mentioned that he hadn't taken the children home, and that he might need to change the plans for the weekend as he thought he might be too busy to have them. When I'd questioned him, he'd made some offhand comment about Leah not being well, and I'd wondered if he was hiding something from me.

I glanced at the clock and sighed. I needed to wake Tommy for school if he was going to make it on time, but the energy seemed to drain from me. The thought of beginning another day with Ava still missing, Maisy still mute and Tommy still hating me was exhausting, especially after a night of frantic tidying and no sleep.

I made a coffee and sat down at the kitchen table, breathing in the strong, comforting aroma and looking again at my phone. Why wasn't Shannon replying to my messages? I was hurt that after everything, she'd let me down when I most needed a friend. Was it simply that she had plans elsewhere? Or, I thought uneasily, was she doubting me? She'd been asking some uncomfortable questions when she was last here. Had there been more to her questioning than I'd realised?

This was what came of letting someone into your life. You began to hope you could trust them, depend on them. And that was always a mistake. My marriage should have taught me that, if nothing else.

I thought about the moment everything changed for me. The few friendships I'd tentatively begun to form suddenly fading away, never to be replaced. I hadn't tried to fool myself that it was for any reason other than my own actions. I'd hardened myself. Closed myself off. Lost trust in the world and pushed away everyone who cared about me. I'd changed overnight from a person who was finally coming out of her shell after a lonely childhood and adolescence, into someone unrecognisable: a workaholic, someone who couldn't open up, couldn't share their secrets because mine were too dark to admit – so much worse than theirs.

It was why Jimmy had begun cheating. Not that I blamed myself entirely; he made his choices, broke his vows. But I had to own up to the fact that there were long years in our relationship where I no longer let him see the real me. I became a shell, surface-deep, and when he went looking elsewhere for connection, I hadn't been nearly as surprised as I might have expected. I'd kept secrets from him to protect our marriage, to ensure I never lost his love, but my mistake had been in not realising how by shutting him out, I'd pushed him away.

Shannon was the first person I'd dared to let into my life in a very long time. I hadn't allowed her *too* close, but slowly I'd begun to share more with her. And now, sitting here with my messages unanswered, my calls for help ignored, I realised I should never have let my guard down. It was too easy for people to hurt you. And they *always* hurt you in the end.

THIRTY-THREE

LEAH

It felt good to be out of the house. I'd spent far too much time cooped up inside lately, and now, with the constant fear of the police arriving at the door, it had become a place where it was impossible to avoid my anxiety. It was no longer the sanctuary I needed from my home. I wondered if, when all this was over, we should move somewhere else. Maybe somewhere further away, offering the children a new start in a new town. Carrie would soon return to work, falling back into her old habits of taking on long shifts and missing the important things. They would be better off somewhere that wasn't filled with sadness – memories of things that needed to be left in the past. I just wanted them to be happy.

I walked from the car up the path to Carrie's house, hoping that Maisy would answer the door. I knew Tommy was at Scouts, but he should be finishing soon. I had to come now, though, while Jimmy was out and wouldn't notice my absence. I didn't want him to know I'd been here. He wouldn't like it.

I swept my hair back over my shoulder and, breathing in deeply, knocked at the door. I heard the footsteps almost instantly, and the door swung open, Carrie standing there with an expectant, almost defensive expression on her face. I tried to contain my surprise at how different she looked from when I'd last seen her, only a few days before. Her eyes were bloodshot, dark circles marring the skin beneath them. Her long cardigan hung off her frame, her collarbone jutting out sharply. Her cheeks looked as if they'd been hollowed out with a spoon, her skin pale and drawn. She looked frightening, as if she were ready to take on the world, strong and yet simultaneously fragile, broken.

It shocked me to see her like this. In a single moment, all the suspicion and doubt I'd been leaning on to make sense of Ava's disappearance was smashed into dust. This wasn't a woman who was in control, pulling the strings on the situation. This was someone who had lost something irreplaceable. Icy dread trickled down my spine. How wrong I'd been to suspect Carrie.

'What do you want?' she asked, her shoulders relaxing slightly as she realised it was only me.

'Did you think the police were back?' I meant the question to be empathetic, to show her that I understood because I'd been going through the very same thing, but from her expression, I could see that she'd taken it as a goading remark.

'No, I didn't. They made it quite clear yesterday that they'd found nothing here. And I have nothing to hide.'

'So you think that's them done? You don't think they'll keep trying to find something on you?'

She frowned. 'What I hope, Leah, is that they do something useful now. The incompetence they've displayed is unfathomable. What they've put me through... I don't deserve—' She broke off, shaking her head, then looked at me. 'Why are you here?'

I tried a smile, determined to get her onside. I didn't want to tell her that I'd needed to hear from her what she thought the police might do next. 'I don't know if you got my message yesterday, what with everything going on here,' I said, though I was sure she'd read it.

'Oh yes, asking me to send my children to you. No thank you,' she replied, her tone harsh, angry.

'Jimmy told me last night that you've refused to let them come to us this weekend. He said you can't be without them. Look, I get it, you're having a horrible time and you want them close. But Jimmy is too. And we all want what's best for the children, don't we?'

She frowned. 'What's *best* for them?'

'Yes. They *love* coming to us. And it's important to keep up with their routines. I think it might do Maisy good not to be here. I mean, she must feel a certain level of guilt over not watching her sister at the beach. She was there when it happened. I expect there's a part of her that feels like you're blaming her on some level,' I said.

'Oh, must she? Because I'm such a terrible mother I'd blame a child for something so serious, is that it?'

'No, that not what I—'

She stepped forward, forcing me to move back from the step, onto the path. 'I'll tell you why the children aren't coming to you this weekend, Leah. It's because Jimmy told me he's too busy to have them, and that *you're* not well enough to take care of them. It was nothing to do with me.'

I shook my head. 'What, no, he said—'

'And another thing. You might have been able to convince him you weren't at the clinic this week, but I saw you there. I know you were trying to get into Maisy's therapy session, to take over, insert yourself where you have no right. Did you really think the receptionist was going to let in some random woman? Because that's exactly what you are! You're *not* her mother. It's too much, Leah – it's verging on obsessive. These are *my* children! *My* family! And if you try to take them from me, I swear

I'll destroy everything you care about. I'll die before I let you do that.'

I stared at her red, blotchy face, shocked. Her fingers were trembling, and she balled them into fists.

'My only concern, Carrie,' I said, 'is making sure the children are okay. You think this is about winning? I couldn't care less. I just want them safe.'

'And they aren't safe with me – is that what you're trying to insinuate?'

I shrugged. 'Just let me see Maisy. Let me have a moment with her to ask what she wants, if she wants to come to me this weekend.'

Carrie stepped forward, an inch from my face. 'She's not your fucking daughter!' she spat. 'And you'd do well to remember it.'

My phone rang, and I yanked it from my back pocket, staring incredulously at the name on the screen. I cancelled the call, looking up at Carrie, hoping she hadn't been able to read it from where she stood, but her expression told me otherwise.

'Jimmy told me you and your mother are estranged,' she said softly.

'We are. Other than that time she turned up uninvited at our house, I haven't seen her since I was a teenager.'

Carrie folded her arms, her eyes cold and probing as she stared at me as if she were trying to read my mind. 'Is that so?' she said, her voice still quiet, dangerous, like a coiled viper about to strike.

I stepped back, feeling suddenly afraid. She looked as though she might lurch forward in attack; there was something feral and terrifying in the energy pulsing from her. 'Carrie, I don't know what this has to do with anything. I—'

Her hand darted out, grabbing the collar of my top, jerking me towards her. 'If you've taken her...' she said, the words hissing through her clenched teeth, 'if you have her hidden away—' She broke off, her breathing jagged and harsh, and shoved me backward.

I stumbled and cried out, but managed not to fall on the ground.

'Bring Ava back to me,' she demanded. 'Today. Right this moment. Or I *will* destroy you, Leah. I fucking promise you that. I will ruin your life the way you have mine.'

I folded my arms protectively around myself, shaking my head. 'Carrie, you've got it wrong. I don't—'

But before I could finish my sentence, she spun around, storming inside and slamming the door hard, leaving me on the path, my phone clutched tight in my palm. I let out a long breath and wondered what to do next.

THIRTY-FOUR

CARRIE

I stormed back into the kitchen, shaking with anger at the audacity of my husband's girlfriend to turn up at my house and criticise the way I raised my children. It was frightening to hear her speak, to see how deeply she believed in what she was saying. How could she claim to be estranged from her mother – from the woman I'd so clearly seen with my daughter on the bus – when she was still getting calls from her? What was she hiding, from me and from Jimmy? I couldn't cope with the deception, the stress of not knowing. Couldn't stand the way she refused to unravel herself from my business. She was too involved now, and it had to stop.

I picked up my phone, seeing the screen still blank; no messages from Jimmy or Shannon, and – I supposed something to be grateful for – nothing from the police either. Was no news still considered good news in this situation? I closed my eyes, Ava's face filling my vision, her voice so loud in my head it was as if she was in the room.

My eyes snapped open. I couldn't do this now. Couldn't fall apart, not while Maisy was upstairs. I had to keep moving forward, keep my mind from going to those dark places. I might never allow myself to grieve if I was left trapped in this purgatory. I needed answers – answers I might never get.

Sighing, I keyed in my passcode, calling the clinic to book another session for Maisy.

The receptionist was warm, asking me to wait one moment, and I heard the tap of her fingers on the computer keyboard. She made a clicking noise as she waited for the page to load, apologising for how long it was taking. 'Oh,' she said at last, 'I can fit you in next Wednesday, and there's a note on the system to give you an appointment for your son, Thomas Gold, too. Would you like me to make it after school so they don't have to miss classes? I know schools are cracking down on absences now, aren't they?'

'Actually, I won't be bringing Tommy in just yet. It will just be Maisy,' I said, squeezing the phone tighter, hoping she wouldn't ask me to explain myself.

'Not a problem.'

I booked her in for two sessions with Fiona, then hung up the phone, feeling more lost than ever. All the hope I'd had prior to her first session was conspicuously absent now. It had been a week since Ava had vanished from the beach, and Maisy had yet to say a single word. I knew how she felt. It was impossible to move forward while waiting for answers that might never come. Was Ava lost? Taken... dead? If I could barely cope with the weight of it, how on earth could I expect my nine-year-old daughter to?

I walked into the living room to turn off the TV. Tommy had gone to Scouts, seemingly in need of a slice of normality, and as usual, he'd left a pile of crisp packets on the living-room carpet, the cartoon he'd been watching long since over, the local news on in its place. I'd heard what he'd been watching as I'd passed the door, surprised at the sound of the high-pitched voices of the animated, cutesy toddler programmes Ava always asked for. The familiar theme tunes had made my stomach wrench, reminding me of how excited she would get, how deadly quiet the living room was without her babbling away to herself. I'd found her knitted rainbow cardigan – the one she always wore – in Tommy's bedroom, tucked under his pillow, a few days before. He might not be saying much – anything – but I knew he was hurting as much as the rest of us. I wished he'd open up to me.

I dropped the handful of empty packets onto the coffee table, suddenly too tired to keep going. It felt as if there wasn't a scrap of energy left in my entire body. I wanted more than anything to collapse, to give up and lose myself in the darkness that was surrounding me from all angles.

Lowering myself to the armchair, my gaze glassy, I stared at the television, watching with detached numbness as a reporter appeared on screen, standing in the middle of a town centre. I recognised it as one I'd been to a handful of times before, about an hour's drive from my home. She stared into the camera, sharing the details of a gas explosion from a bakery that had caused immeasurable damage to the surrounding businesses.

'So far, there have been seven casualties, but as far as we know, there are no fatalities,' she said in her clipped, professional tone.

I was about to turn off the TV, not wanting to listen to any more misery, afraid that my own family might be the next feature, when my hand froze on the remote, hovering above the button. I heard it clatter to the ground, hitting the table leg, then suddenly I fell to my knees, crawling fast towards the screen. Behind the reporter, an old woman was walking across the square, holding the hand of a little girl. My whole body was on fire, the urgency pounding through my veins as I touched the image, sure that this was the woman from the bus. And that child... that curly-haired toddler holding her hand, was my sweet little Ava. I knew it with all my heart!

In a second, they were gone from the frame. I gave a yell,

smacking my palm against the TV, wanting the camera to pan right, to follow them, show me more!

I jumped up, rushed into the kitchen to where my laptop was sitting on the table and, trying to control the tremor in my fingers, keyed in my password, getting it wrong twice before successfully logging on. I navigated to the news website and clicked on the live video at the top of the page, rewinding it to the moment the old lady had walked behind the reporter, this time drinking in the details of the little girl at her side: the strawberry-blonde curly pigtails, the blue eyes. It *was* her. I'd never been more sure of anything in my life. That child was my daughter! Either that or I was going mad.

Breathing heavily, I paused the video, zooming in on the girl's face, certainty setting in. But it made no sense! Why would her kidnapper just brazenly walk across the town with her while the search was still going strong? The only reasonable explanation was that this wasn't Ava. I was mistaken. I was letting my need to find her convince me of what I wanted to see. The clothes weren't hers. I didn't recognise the long-sleeved pink dress and purple tights. The white Mary Jane shoes. But still... I wished the image was clearer, less pixelated. If only they'd been closer to the reporter.

I rubbed my hands over my face and then leaned forward again, my heart in my throat. I zoomed in on the face of the old lady until it filled the screen, trying to jolt my memory. *Was it* Leah's mother? Looking at her now, I couldn't be sure. Her silver hair was short and unkempt, the waves falling over her eyes as if she'd had a perm a long time ago but hadn't bothered to keep it up. Her expression was blank, her dark eyes unread-able, her dress a thin-looking blue smock dotted with a yellow pattern that might have been flowers. It was old-fashioned and didn't look warm enough for the weather we'd been having this week. I wished I'd spent more time taking in the details of

Leah's mother that one time I'd met her. That I could be certain.

I panned back to her face, scrutinising it again.

'I know that lady.'

I started, turning in shock to see Maisy standing behind my chair. Her face was pale and I reached for her, needing to hold on to her, to hear her voice again, though it took a moment for her words to register.

'What did you say, darling?' I whispered, afraid of shocking her, breaking the spell.

She dropped my hand, stepping closer to the computer. 'That lady... I saw her... She was at the beach the day... the day...' She shook her head and I saw the mask go up again, her lips pressing resolutely closed.

I felt dizzy, my head throbbing with tension, my heart pounding hard enough to smash through my ribcage. Maisy had spoken to me. And if what she was saying was true, it meant that I'd been right. The woman *had* taken Ava. Somehow she had kidnapped my daughter. Ava was alive!

I could see from Maisy's expression now that she was afraid. That something had happened to make her feel she couldn't tell me everything.

Rage and hope intermingled in my veins, and I pulled my daughter into a hug, relieved that at last I had a way to fix the mess that had built over the week. My baby girl was alive. I would not stop until she was back with me. Exactly where she belonged.

THIRTY-FIVE

I knew I should be feeling a self-protective sense of revulsion at having DCI Farrows back in my house again after the way he'd treated me last time, but all I could feel was a pulsing excitement that we were on the cusp of finding Ava. Despite everything he thought of me, he was about to be proved wrong. He stood a few feet away from the kitchen table, frowning at the laptop screen as I pressed play on the news story.

'Look – look there,' I said, pointing to the little girl as she toddled across the square. 'That's my daughter! And Maisy swears she saw this woman at the beach the day Ava went missing.'

He squinted, pulling a pair of glasses from his jacket pocket and putting them on. I paused the footage, enlarging the image of the woman, frustratingly so much clearer than the face of the child.

'It's her,' I repeated, folding and unfolding my arms, buzzing with anxious energy as I waited for him to speak. 'It's the same woman from the bus, the same child, the one you've been searching for!'

He stepped back. 'It's unlikely,' he said, his voice flat, not matching any of the enthusiasm I felt.

'It *is* her! Do you think I would mistake my own daughter?'

He put a hand on his hip, regarding me coolly. I could feel his dislike penetrating through me, his cold grey eyes holding my hopeful stare.

'Maisy *saw* her,' I insisted. 'She told me this woman was at the beach!'

'This would be the daughter who hasn't spoken a word since that day? The child who is currently in therapy for mutism?'

'She had a shock! But seeing this woman obviously sparked enough of a response to get her talking again.'

'In that case,' he replied, flashing an incredulous smirk, 'I'd like to hear from her. Is she here?'

I shook my head, not wanting to admit that since those precious few words, she'd clammed up again and retreated to her bedroom. 'There's no need to frighten her. She's been through enough. Please, just do your job and investigate who this woman is. I'm certain that when you find her, you'll find Ava.'

He shook his head, and in that moment, I hated him so much I could taste it. 'Please,' I begged. 'Just find her.'

He breathed in deep, his nostrils flaring wide, then gave a curt nod. 'I'll look into it.'

'Thank you,' I replied, following him to the door, watching as he climbed into his car and drove off. I didn't care if he hated me. I didn't care what he thought of me. All I cared about was him finding this woman and bringing my baby home. I just had to trust that he wouldn't let his personal feelings and misplaced suspicion interfere with his professional duties.

. . .

The evening had been endless, pacing the house, checking the volume was up on my phone with obsessive regularity, unable to eat, to sit, to do anything but wonder what was happening at the police station, what they'd discovered about the woman with my child. I'd texted Jimmy, asking him to come over so I could explain to him what I'd found, wanting him to see for himself the woman who'd taken our baby, to discover if he would recognise her in this new footage and put the puzzle pieces together himself, but he'd neglected to reply, and I didn't want to call him and risk missing a call from Farrows.

I knew I should be upstairs, trying to cajole Maisy into speaking again, to find out what else she might have seen, and, though he wouldn't appreciate it, making the effort to speak to Tommy and support him through the hormonal blaze he was currently enduring, but I wasn't in any state to be a good, present mother to either of them right now, so I'd left them in their rooms with the company of their screens and a plate of sandwiches each, silently promising myself that once Ava was back, I'd do whatever it took to be the mother they both needed.

I longed to be at work. To lose myself in the frenzy of the hospital, taking comfort in the sharp tang of disinfectant and alcohol wipes, the nurses' chatter, the sound of pumps alarming – the never-ending beep that provided the soundtrack to my long shifts. To know exactly how to respond, exactly what I needed to do. I hadn't wanted to admit to myself that the reason I sought distraction in my work was because I often found myself floundering as a parent. I was so afraid of getting it wrong. Of messing up and creating long-lasting consequences in my children's lives. I thought I'd been managing, faking it, at least, but the way Tommy looked at me these days made me sure that without even realising how, I'd fucked it all up.

I'd shut down, telling myself they were better off with me working such long hours, that I couldn't make a mistake if I wasn't there to get it wrong, but more than that, there was a part of me that couldn't get over the idea that I didn't deserve to be a mother. To step into that nurturing role. That with every baby I'd birthed, I'd given myself a gift I had no right to enjoy. It was only now that I was seeing that the choices I'd made, the unconscious need to distance myself from my children, lose myself in the dramas of strangers, stemmed from my own need for self-flagellation.

I hadn't realised it until I'd lost my daughter. But if I managed to get Ava back, things would be different. I'd suffered more than any mother deserved in the past week. I had paid my dues. And my children shouldn't have to suffer because of my past, my own self-hatred. They deserved better.

I walked over to the patio doors, staring out to the garden, watching the sun sink low over the hedge, the sky streaked with pink and orange. I couldn't bear the waiting. I felt ready to explode, to scream, to tear off my own skin. It was torture. It was gone 7 p.m. now. Would I have to endure a whole night of this endless waiting without an update?

I spun, striding over to the kitchen cupboard, flinging it open and grabbing a crystal tumbler from a set we'd been gifted for our wedding. I turned, reaching into the drinks cabinet for the bottle of spiced rum Jimmy had left behind, still half full, twisting open the cap and pouring a generous measure. I lifted the glass, enjoying the weight of it in my hand, holding it up to the light to see the amber liquid swirling, the reflection hitting the white wall beside me.

Bringing the fragrant-smelling drink to my lips, I was about to knock it back when my phone began to ring. I slammed the glass down on the counter untouched and, recognising the number for the local police station, answered, holding the phone to my ear with trembling fingers.

'Carrie, it's Paige... sorry, PC Mayville.'

'Do you have her? Have you got my baby?' I demanded, my words coming out in one breathless cry, my eyes turning wet, the tears I'd held on to all day unable to be contained any longer.

I heard her sigh and felt the weight of her reply before she'd even spoken. 'I'm so sorry, Carrie. We tracked the woman down and an officer went out to her house this afternoon. He said it's a dead end.'

'What? *No!* Did they search the house?'

There was a silence. 'They didn't apply for a warrant. The guy who went out thinks it *was* the woman from the bus but that the child isn't Ava. The lady said she had been taking care of her granddaughter. She showed him a photo and he claims it definitely wasn't your daughter, though there are similarities between them. I didn't see it, but he said she had a whole album at her house. Farrows has decided they're not taking it any further.' She lowered her voice. 'He's stuck on the idea that you did this. That you're hiding Ava somewhere in some sick attempt to get your ex to come back to you. He thinks you're trying to play a game, be seen as the victim so you'll get Jimmy's sympathy.'

'I don't give a flying fuck about Jimmy Gold!' I yelled. 'I don't care who he marries, what he does!' I was shocked to realise that it was true. He'd shown me time and again who he was, how little he cared for me, and I'd steadfastly ignored every sign, too blinded by the love I held on to for him, the dream life I'd longed for, the perfect family I'd always wanted. I'd been prepared to overlook so much.

But this awful situation with Ava, the way he'd selfishly disappeared time and again, turning off his phone and leaving me to cope alone, how even now, he hadn't been able to work with me, fighting me on every little thing to retain his sense of control, had shown me what kind of a man he *really* was. And, I saw now, any love I might have been holding on to, any hope of reuniting my family and giving my children a traditional upbringing, had gone up in smoke.

I swallowed, feeling more clear-headed than I had in years, amazed at what I'd been prepared to put up with, how weak he'd made me feel. 'I have *no* interest in getting back with Jimmy,' I said, my voice sure and strong. 'All I care about is finding my daughter. How could they have given up without even searching her house?'

There was a pause, and I leaned back against the counter, my legs shaking as I realised that I might never see her again. I couldn't let that happen!

'Carrie,' PC Mayville said softly, 'I wanted to tell you... I've handed in my notice today. I can't stand the misogyny, the way some of the staff treat the women they're supposed to help. There are some real gents, don't get me wrong, and I know I should stick it out and try and force a change in their attitudes. But I can't do it any more. I'm going into childcare. I want to foster. To make a difference in a field I know I can be better in.'

I shook my head, wondering why she was telling me this, how I was supposed to respond. She was the only one on my side, and now she was leaving. It was hard to be happy for her, given the circumstances. 'Right,' I said, my mouth dry. I looked down at the glass of rum, longing to feel the burning alcohol numbing my veins.

'So,' she continued, 'since I'm leaving anyway, I don't feel bad about breaking the rules, just a little bit.'

'What do you mean?' I replied, suddenly alert.

'Get a pen and pad.'

I sucked in a breath, hardly daring to hope as I rifled through the kitchen drawer.

'The woman we tracked down is called Janice Sotherton. She's eighty-two years old. I'm going to give you the address now. Are you ready?'

'Yes,' I said. I wrote it down, making her repeat it twice. 'Why are you telling me this?' I asked, unable to comprehend what had just happened.

'Because I believe you. I know you think that woman has your daughter, and I want you to have the opportunity to find out, one way or another, if you're right. Even if she isn't there, it will rule out that avenue and you'll know for sure. I want to do something good before I leave this fucking job. And honestly, Carrie, those incompetent bastards aren't going to find Ava unless she's delivered to the station with a brass band to announce her arrival.'

'I can't believe you've done this for me... Thank you,' I whispered.

'I'd offer to come with you, but... well, I *do* need a reference and I'd rather not be in the thick of it. I'd appreciate if you didn't let them know where you got the information.'

'Of course. I'm sorry the job hasn't worked out for you,' I said softly.

She gave a wry bark of laughter. 'I was never cut out for it. Be careful, okay? Don't put yourself in danger. Is there someone you can take with you?'

'I'll be fine.'

'Okay. And Carrie, be prepared that Ava might not be there, okay? I know it's not what you want to hear, but it's easy to convince yourself that you've seen someone in cases like this. Steel yourself for the possibility that you were wrong.'

'Thanks, Paige. For everything,' I said, ending the call and picking up the pad.

Whatever she said, whatever her doubts, I didn't care. I was going to find my little girl. And I would not leave without her, whatever I had to do to make that happen.

THIRTY-SIX

LEAH

The room was dark, comforting, and I curled my legs tighter beneath my body, making myself small, as if I could hide from those who made it their mission to seek me out. The armchair tucked into the dusty alcove had once been my mother's. It didn't belong downstairs, in the main part of the house. Didn't fit with the expensive, artfully designed pieces Jimmy liked to buy – the kind that wordlessly displayed his wealth, his success, to everyone who passed through our door. No, this was less vintage, more plain old-fashioned. The velvety rose-coloured upholstery was worn in patches, the once polished oak frame now dull and scratched, and no amount of upcycling would make it special. But to me, it was simply the chair where I'd once sat and listened to my mother tell stories. The place I'd felt safe when everything around us was turning to chaos.

It had been the first place she'd sat after they came for my father. After our lives changed for ever. The only piece of furniture we'd taken with us to the tiny flat we'd had to move to when we discovered there was no money left, that despite all his promises, he wouldn't keep taking care of us. I'd stood in the middle of our new living room, the walls grey and ugly, the window tiny and blown, and with tears streaming down my face, I'd longed to have him back, to hear the sound of my mother singing as she baked in the kitchen, my dad laughing at some story he was relaying – he always laughed at his own stories – to be in the big bright bedroom with all the toys I'd taken such good care of.

My mother had come out of the bathroom, having unpacked the toiletries, taken one look at me standing there with wet cheeks and beckoned me to the chair, which she'd placed beside a flimsy-looking electric fireplace with a cracked wooden mantel above it. She'd lowered herself into it, then dragged me onto her lap, wrapping us both in a blanket, and, in her soft, comforting voice, had told me that this was just another adventure. That we were going to be fine. That Daddy would come home soon and make everything all right.

It had been a lie, of course. She had to have known that. But at the time, it had helped. The chair had felt like a piece of the life I craved, a tie to the past. And no matter what anyone might think of it, I couldn't let it go.

I hated thinking of her. Of the way I'd watched her slowly disappear until there was nothing left of the woman I'd aspired to emulate.

Casting a look at my dim surroundings, I suddenly saw the similarities in our situations. The way that, despite all my promises to myself, I had taken the very same path, hiding away from the world because things hadn't gone to plan. I wouldn't let myself become a shell. Not like she had.

Making up my mind, I stood, tossing aside the blanket and shaking the cramp from my feet, then picked my way across the thick carpet to the heavy door and headed down the stairwell, leaving the loft behind. I paused at the bottom, carefully locking the door and pocketing the key, then went into the bathroom, splashing cold water on my face and pulling a brush through my tangled hair.

I went into the bedroom next, trying not to mind that the strong smell of Jimmy's aftershave still lingered in the air, despite him having been out of the house since the crack of dawn. My fingers wrapped around the bottle, running over the ridges, picturing the way he'd looked, unable to meet my eye as he doused himself liberally then checked his hair in the dresser mirror. Placing the cap back on the top, I replayed the words I hadn't meant to say out loud. 'What kind of man bothers with aftershave and hair gel when his baby is missing? Why are you even going to work?'

He'd turned, a little too quickly, his smile too practised, too charming as he came over to the edge of the bed where I was sitting. I'd stared up at him, thinking I knew the answer, and he'd leaned down, pressing me into the mattress and kissing me hard.

'A man who has well-paying clients to keep hold of and a family to feed,' he'd replied as he pulled back. 'I don't want to see you all on the streets, do I? But,' he added, his voice gravelly as he tucked a strand of hair behind my ear then slowly eased me up from the bed, standing with his legs between mine, his brown eyes locked on my face, 'don't think that means for a second that I don't care. That Ava hasn't been the only thing I can think of every waking moment. Don't think that of me, Leah.'

He'd picked up his wallet, shoving it in his pocket, leaving me feeling confused and guilty. I'd always believed him, but this time, I was struggling to. I couldn't stop myself picturing the way he'd smiled at his reflection in the mirror. It had reminded me of a man getting ready for a date with a new girl. A man who was playing away, I thought, unable to prevent the intrusive mantra from starting up again.

I slammed the aftershave bottle down, then turned for the stairs. The doorbell rang when I was halfway down, startling me, and I froze, my feet welded to the step.

'Jimmy!' came a shrill voice, and I saw Carrie pressing her face to the glass, the bell sounding loudly again.

Frowning, I went to open the door.

'Carrie, what are you doing here?' Tommy and Maisy were by her side, and I smiled warmly at them, then noticed they both carried overnight bags.

She grabbed my wrist, and I yanked it back as if she'd burned me. 'Where's Jim?' she asked, her words coming out in a breathless rush. 'I need to speak to him now!'

She looked unhinged, her eyes wider than usual, penetrating as she stared expectantly at my face, and I felt my belly drop, a wave of nausea slamming into me.

'He isn't here,' I replied, blocking her view as she craned her neck to look past me. I wanted to shove her away, to tell her to get some manners. This wasn't and had never been her house. She had no right to disrespect my personal space. 'I don't know when he'll be back,' I said, folding my arms across my chest. 'What's going on?'

'*Fuck!*' she yelled, bending double, her hands on her knees. She gave a cry of frustration, and Maisy cringed back, stepping behind her brother as if she couldn't bear to witness her mother's distress.

'Carrie! For Christ's sake, rein it in, will you?' I demanded, disgusted at her inability to compose herself. It was a skill – one that she clearly needed to work on. 'Kids,' I said, softening my tone, 'go on inside. I'll just chat to your mum, and then I'll come and find you.'

'Thanks, Leah.' Tommy nodded, taking Maisy's hand and guiding her past me, along the hall towards the kitchen. I noted that neither one of them bothered to say goodbye to their mother, and she barely seemed to notice they'd gone.

I waited until they'd disappeared, then turned back to her. 'I take it you want me to have them tonight?' I asked, my tone clipped.

'No, I want their bloody father to be here when I need him. To answer his phone once in a while! But it seems like *that's* too much to ask, so yes, I need you to have them. *If* it's not too much trouble,' she finished, her words dripping with venom.

'You know they're always welcome here. In fact, I think we should have that discussion about us going for full custody. They're so much happier with me and Jimmy. It can't have escaped your notice.'

Her mouth dropped open, her eyes wide, and I smiled.

'We'll talk later – you're clearly in a rush,' I said sweetly.

She went to speak, then stopped. I felt something at my hip and looked down to find Maisy standing silently by my side. She stepped slowly past me, holding her arms up to Carrie, who bent to pick her up, hugging her tightly.

Maisy leaned in, her lips close to Carrie's ear. 'You're going to get Ava back, aren't you?' she whispered, her voice small and filled with hope.

My eyes widened, shocked to hear her speak after so long, wondering how Carrie would respond to her finally breaking her mutism. She gave nothing away, and I wondered if it might not be the first time. How could she keep something like that from me, when she knew how worried I'd been? And what could have happened to make Maisy believe Carrie might find Ava now, after all this time? It made me uneasy to know there were secrets being kept from me, things I deserved to know.

Carrie let out a shaky sigh, pressed a kiss to Maisy's cheek, then whispered a reply I couldn't hear. She placed her gently down and turned, heading to her car.

I felt Maisy's hand slide into mine and looked down to find her watching me, a smile on her lips that made me sure she'd seen something on the day Ava had gone missing. Something that could have the power to change everything.

THIRTY-SEVEN

CARRIE

My hands were shaking as I drove down the narrow country lane to the address Paige had given me. A small thatched cottage came into view up ahead, and I slowed down, sucking in a breath, trying to dispel the nerves that were swirling inside my belly. On the left side of the lane, opposite the cottage, was a concealed driveway half hidden by the surrounding foliage, leading to a barred metal gate that in turn led into thick woodland beyond. I turned the car into it, then backed up behind the bushes, switching off the headlights and engine, keen to avoid being seen. I stepped out of the car, looking over my shoulder, feeling exposed and skittish. Overhead, the sky was turning from dark navy to an oppressive, inky black, a crescent moon failing to provide any comfort.

My phone was heavy in the back pocket of my jeans, and I yanked it out, calling Jimmy once more, wishing he was here with me right now. He *should* be here. If he cared even a little bit, he would be.

The call went straight to voicemail again, and I kept my voice low, not wanting it to carry in the quiet lane as I spoke.

'*Jimmy!* For God's sake, where are you? I think I've found

Ava. I'm at a house, I need you to come here. I don't know what I'm heading into – if you get this, *please* just come. If not for me, then do it for her.' I read out the address on the slip of paper, then ended the call, putting the phone back in my pocket and walking towards the cottage, keeping close to the treeline.

It was a ramshackle-looking building, surrounded by an overgrown garden. Trees lined either side of the narrow lane, blocking out the glow of the street lights from the main road. The only light to be seen was coming from one of the small windows downstairs, its frame brown and rotting, and I didn't know whether to feel relieved or scared that the place was obviously inhabited. Now that I was here, I didn't know what to do. There had been no time to plan, no time to think it through. All I knew was that if my daughter was in there, I had to go and get her. No matter what.

Casting a nervous glance up and down the lane, making sure I wasn't being watched – though the wind whistling through the boughs of the nearby trees, rustling too close, made it impossible to know for sure – I took a deep breath and pushed open the little wooden gate, heading up the path, stepping over the weeds that had burst through the cracks in the paving stones.

I reached the front door. The candy-pink paint was peeling from the wood, the brass handle tarnished. I felt like once upon a time this had been a special place. In the dim glow of the downstairs window, I could see a tangled mess of rose bushes, cracked ceramic pots, earth spilling from them, a little metal bench that had all but been lost to nettles. It had been loved once. Tended to. But not for a long time.

I knocked on the door, then clasped my hands tightly together, listening hard, wanting to hear signs of life beyond. I hoped that if I saw the woman from the news, this Janice Sotherton, I would recognise her instantly. That all the questions and suspicions that had been bouncing through my aching skull would be answered at last. I wouldn't leave until I had turned this whole house upside down, until I had Ava back in my arms.

I was breathing too fast, my heart pounding, adrenaline thudding through my veins, and I squeezed my hands into fists, my nails digging into my skin, tearing, stinging. But no one came. There was no sound of footsteps in the hall. No movement.

Pressing my ear to the door, I was sure I could hear the sound of a television coming from inside. I knocked again, harder this time, and felt the door give a little.

Straightening, I cast a quick glance over my shoulder, then, pulling the sleeve of my jumper over my hand so as not to leave fingerprints, tried the bulbous brass handle. It turned easily, opening into a cramped, dim hallway. A hatstand stood to the side of the door, a thick woollen coat hung over it, the heady smell of lavender radiating from the material. A dark mahogany sideboard held an expensive-looking vase, a bunch of dead flowers drooping over it, brown petals carpeting the floor below. There was a staircase to the right, but the light was coming from the room to the left. Was I actually going to do this? Enter a stranger's home uninvited? Could I really find the courage to go in there?

The tinny canned laughter of some comedy programme reached me, and I realised that whoever was in there wasn't expecting me. I had an opportunity now – this might be my only chance to catch them off guard and get the answers I needed.

It wasn't a choice. I *had* to do it.

I closed the front door softly behind me, then, biting my lip hard, stiffened my spine and walked softly, quietly towards the light.

The door to the living room was half open, and I stepped

closer, holding my breath as I pushed it, my eyes wide and alert as I took in the scene in front of me.

The room was a mess. Piles of books and magazines covered the floor, every surface filled with cardboard boxes of various sizes, trinkets and ornaments squeezed into the gaps. There was a powerful smell of dust and damp – and woodsmoke too, I realised, seeing the black iron stove, the glass pane glowing orange with the final embers of a log. The clutter was overwhelming. Perhaps that was why I didn't see her right away. That or the fact that she didn't move, didn't even acknowledge my presence in her home. But when my gaze landed on the frail old woman sitting in the blue upholstered armchair opposite the small, boxy television, I let out a gasp.

'Hello,' I said, discomfited by her lack of response. It was clear she was alive, her beady eyes trained on the television, though I couldn't be certain she was taking in the images.

Stepping further into the room and looking at her in person, I realised I'd been wrong. This woman wasn't Leah's mother. Her colouring was paler, her features more angular. She was tiny in the flesh; even sitting, I guessed she was no more than five feet tall. Leah's mum had been at least five foot six. I remembered her being taller than me.

I couldn't believe I'd misjudged what I'd seen so badly. Accused Leah and her mother of conspiring against my family when it had been this stranger on the CCTV coverage all along. 'Who *are* you?' I asked, stepping in front of the screen to draw her attention to me.

She raised her head, a slow, unwilling movement, staring blankly up at me.

'Do you know who *I* am?' I tried, unable to place her. 'Do you...?' I paused, not ready to ask about Ava, not sure if I should.

The woman closed her eyes, leaning back against the cushions as if she had tired of my questions. I stared at her for a moment, wondering if she'd taken a sleeping pill or if this was just normal behaviour for her. Whatever the case, it was clear she wasn't going to be any help.

I turned, unwilling to be deterred, heading back to the staircase in the hall. There was a light switch on the wall, and I tried it. I was rewarded with a harsh white light, too bright for the surroundings, but I didn't care. I was just relieved not to have to climb up in total darkness, afraid of what I might find up there. No sound came from above. There was no sign of a child, and I felt my stomach tighten, nausea churning in my belly as horrific images, premonitions, played vividly in my mind. What had that woman done with my daughter?

My mouth was dry as I moved across the narrow landing. There were four doors, and I stopped outside one that stood out. The others were all a dirty yellow colour, grime and dirt embedded into the grain. This one, however, was clean, painted a glossy pale pink and had a little name sign attached to it. The sign was white porcelain with pink flowers hand-painted around the border, and the name *Katie* was scribed in swirling letters across the centre. I realised there was soft music playing from inside. Twinkly nursery rhymes, the kind I'd used now and then to help a restless baby drift off to sleep.

I pushed open the door and let out a cry. There in the centre of the dark room was a cot, and in it, illuminated by the eerie white light from the landing, lay my baby girl. Her hair was tied in curling bunches on top of her head, her little lips pouted and pink, her eyelids closed tightly. There was no hesitation as I rushed across the carpet, hardly daring to hope as I scooped her into my arms.

The relief as I felt the warmth, the softness of her body was indescribable. My hand scrabbled to get beneath the unfamiliar pink pyjama top she wore, pressing my palm against her chest and feeling the reassuring movement as she breathed slowly in and out, deeply and peacefully.

I dropped to the ground, holding her in my lap, tilting back her head. 'Ava, my love, it's Mama. It's me, baby – wake up.'

Slowly, dragging herself from the depths of sleep, her eyelids fluttered and then opened, her gaze settling for a moment on my face. Then she broke into a smile, and I felt my heart explode in relief.

'Mama?' she asked, reaching her chubby little hand out to touch my cheek. 'I miss you much!'

I laughed, tears blurring my vision. 'I missed you so much too, my darling. So very much!' I pulled her against my chest, sobbing as she held tightly to me.

There was a creak, and I looked up, tensing as I saw the figure in the doorway. For a second, I couldn't see the face, the bright hallway light casting a dark silhouette. Then the person moved, and I gasped. '*You!*' I cried, scrambling to my feet, holding my daughter close.

The figure fixed me with an expression of pure hatred, and I held Ava tighter.

'Hello, Carrie. I'm surprised you made the effort to come. But now I think you need to put my daughter down and get the hell out of this house – before I do something to make you.'

THIRTY-EIGHT

I backed towards the wall, my arms tight around my daughter. There was no way in hell I would be letting her go again. I could feel her clinging to me, her tiny fingers digging into the soft flesh at the backs of my arms, and knew she must have been terrified. I swallowed as the woman stepped into the room, reaching to turn on the lamp. My hackles rose as she turned to face me, her expression flat and dangerous, her pretty, girlish features twisted into something unrecognisable and horrifying.

'Shannon,' I whispered, trying not to show how shocked I was to find her of all people here. How naïve I'd been to trust that she was my friend. That *anyone* could be. Of course I should have suspected her. 'Why did you do it?' I asked, determined not to raise my voice and frighten Ava any more than she already was. 'I knew you were there at the beach, but I never considered you could possibly be involved! Why did you take her from me? Make me believe that she could be lost out at sea? What kind of a woman *are* you?' I hissed, hating her more with every word I spoke.

The last week had been a living nightmare. I'd lost weight, unable to swallow, the emotion wedging itself hard in my throat as I pictured all the awful things that could have happened to my daughter, the terror she'd have felt in her final moments. I'd barely slept. I'd been grieving and angry and terrified, cast adrift, with no one to help me, and to top it all off, I'd had my home ransacked by the police, who should have been on my side. If they had focused on finding her, this could have been over long before now.

Shannon ignored my question, opening the top drawer of a pale pink dresser and pulling out a little red dress decorated with white polka dots and a matching red cardigan with heart-shaped buttons. It was only now that I was able to take in my surroundings. I'd been too focused on Ava to notice. The room was like something out of an Argos catalogue from the nineties. There was pink everywhere. A fluffy baby-pink rug beside the cot. Candy-pink curtains, pink stacking rings and teddy bears lining the low shelves. It was a nursery. One that had clearly taken a lot of time and effort to create.

Shannon turned to me, holding the red dress in her hand, fixing me with a cold smile that didn't reach her eyes. 'Give her to me.'

I shook my head. 'No. Are you crazy?'

She twisted her lips, then, without warning, made a sudden grab for her. Ava let out a squeal, clinging tighter still to me. My body reacted instinctively, my foot swinging out hard, making contact with Shannon's stomach before her hand could close around Ava's leg, terror fuelling me, unable to think of anything but keeping this madwoman away from me and my child.

She flew backward, colliding with the dresser with a loud crash, and let out a pained gasp, gripping her spine, breathing hard for a moment. I glanced at the door, wondering if the old lady would finally be roused by the noise. If I could make a run for it, reach my car before Shannon had a chance to try again. But before I'd made a move, she was up.

Ava pressed her face to my neck, and I looked down, seeing

her little lips wobbling, her eyes wide as tears pooled in them. 'It's okay, Ava – it's going to be okay,' I soothed, hoping she wouldn't have one of her famous meltdowns now. She seemed to understand somehow that she couldn't give in to that. The tension in the room was impossible to ignore, even for her.

Shannon reached for a box on the dresser, flipping the lid, and to my horror, when she turned back to me, I saw the barrel of a gun pointing straight at my face. There was a click as she cocked it. She took a step towards me.

'That is not Ava. That is my daughter, Catherine. My little Katie. And you're going to hand her over now, or I will shoot you in the fucking face. Do you understand, Dr Gold? Am I making myself clear?'

THIRTY-NINE
SHANNON

Then

The wires covered every last inch of my daughter's tiny body. I held her hand, my thumb pressed to the pulse at her wrist, needing to remind myself that she was alive. That she'd survived. Blood was crusted on her forehead, a dark, flaking brown, contrasting harshly with her porcelain skin. I was surprised the nurses hadn't thought to clean it off before letting me in to see her. *I* should do it. I was her mother. But I couldn't bring myself to move. Didn't want to have to let go of her little bruised hand, to risk missing the moment she woke up. For her to have to look to strangers to ask what had happened to her... to her father.

For what felt like the thousandth time since I'd got that awful phone call this morning, I felt hot tears spring to my eyes. They blurred the image of my daughter in the hospital bed, making the red flashing light on the pump attached to the drip stand dance in front of my eyes. How was I going to get through this? How could I survive the pain? It burned inside me. I felt as though some sharp-toothed parasite had scuttled into my belly and was consuming me from the inside out. It was unbearable. I closed my eyes, reminding myself that it could have been so much worse, though right now, that was hard to imagine.

'Mummy?'

My eyes snapped open and I was on my feet in half a second, cupping her sweet little cheek. Her forehead creased in a frown as she tried to turn her head to the side. 'Where am I?' she asked, trying to sit up.

'Wait, let me help you,' I told her, pressing the button on the rectangular handset to raise the head of the bed. It creaked as it tilted, bringing her up to a sitting position. 'Is that okay?'

She nodded. 'I'm in hospital?' she said, looking even more confused. 'But we're going to London. Daddy said he'd take me to the Tower of London so I could see the Crown Jewels—'

'Does anything hurt?' I interrupted, running a hand down her arm, pausing before I reached the cannula into which fluids and morphine were being pumped into her system via two long, snaking lines.

'I don't know,' she replied, still frowning. Her pupils were larger than I'd ever seen, round black circles eliminating the hazel irises almost entirely, and some part of me registered it must be a side effect of the drug.

She grabbed my sleeve, forcing me to stop fussing, to look at her properly. 'Mummy, what happened? Did I miss my birthday outing?'

I bit my lip. The day had been planned for months. Martin had told me how he wanted to take Katie out for a pre-birthday celebration, just the two of them. They were both massive history buffs, obsessed with the Plantagenets and the Tudors, Henry VIII, the mystery of the princes in the tower – stories that made me feel shaky and sick. It wasn't my thing at all, and we were planning to go to the local petting farm on her *actual* ninth birthday, so I'd been happy to sit this one out and get on with some stuff around the house.

I'd been intending to visit my mum too, worried that she didn't seem herself lately. There had been mention of Alzheimer's at her last doctor's appointment, and I wanted to pop in, make sure she was eating and drinking properly. Martin had always been so understanding of my bond with her, my need to take care of her now that she was no longer in a position to do the same for me.

She'd had me late in life, after her first husband had scandalously left her for his male tennis instructor. My father had been a short-lived fling in her late forties, when she'd given up hope of ever having a child of her own. He hadn't stuck around, so it had been just the two of us – until I met Martin, at least.

'I'm sorry, darling,' I said, fighting to keep my voice steady as I lowered myself to sit on the edge of the bed. 'You didn't make it to London. You were in an accident on the motorway.' Very gently, I pulled down the sheet that covered her, keeping my expression neutral as I showed her the thick yellow-toned dressing that was adhered to her abdomen. 'You had to have a little operation on your tummy,' I added, watching her eyes widen.

She kept her hands firmly by her sides, as if she couldn't bear to touch the wound. She shook her head. 'I *can't* have had an operation. I would remember.'

I pressed my lips together. I could see she was on the verge of tears, and it made it all the more difficult to hold my own emotions in check. She looked up at me, and in that moment, I could read the unspoken question on her lips without her needing to voice it. She wouldn't be able to say the words out loud. And, I worried, she wouldn't cope with hearing the answer. But I couldn't hide it from her. It would be impossible to protect her from this, as much as I might wish I could.

'Katie... sweetheart—' I began.

'No... don't say anything.' She cut me off, suddenly looking far more grown up than her nearly nine years. 'I don't want to hear any more!'

I swallowed, gathering myself as I gazed down at my lap, unable to look her in the eye as I prepared to destroy her world, rip away the reality she'd trusted would never change. 'Katie... Daddy didn't make it,' I whispered, my hand tightening around hers as if I could somehow squeeze hard enough to offer some small scrap of comfort. 'He' – I brushed away a rogue tear with my fingertips – 'he died in the crash.'

'Stop saying it! Stop it!' she screamed. 'You're a liar! My daddy isn't... he isn't...' The heart-rate monitor began to alarm, the red light flashing faster as she thrashed, and a nurse rushed into the room, pushing past me with an apology.

Katie seemed to crumple, her last reserves of energy flittering away. She slumped against the pillow, her head turned away from me, and I heard her whisper, 'My daddy is fine... he's going to come and get me soon. We're going to the Tower of...' Her eyes closed, and she drifted into a fitful sleep.

A good-looking middle-aged doctor appeared in the doorway, his blue eyes taking in the scene, and the nurse excused herself. The doctor cleared his throat, unsmiling as he introduced himself. 'I'm Nick Jameson, the surgical consultant who operated on Catherine today. I'm sorry it's taken me a while to get to you. I know you weren't here when Catherine arrived by ambulance, and as you're aware, she was whisked straight into theatre. I believe you spoke to the anaesthetist over the phone. Did someone explain to you what's happened?'

'The nurse said she had a perforated bowel.'

He nodded. 'Just a small tear, one that was relatively easy to repair. The surgery went smoothly,' he said, and I caught a smug air of cockiness, as if I should bend down and kiss his feet. A part of me wanted to, I was so filled with relief at hearing she was okay.

'I'll be heading home in a short while,' he continued, 'but

my colleague, Dr Gold, will be taking over, and I'll be back first thing to check on Catherine.'

'So she has to stay here?'

'I'm afraid so. It will be a couple of days, I should think. I don't foresee there being any complications. I can't make any promises, but once she starts eating and going to the toilet normally, we'll get you out of here.'

'Right.' I nodded, trying to remind myself that this was a good thing. That I could have lost both her *and* Martin today. I had to be grateful that I still had my little girl.

I shook my head, trying not to think of the man I loved lying on a cold table somewhere in this building. I wanted to see his smiling face again. Smell his skin. Breathe him in. I considered asking to see him now but quickly batted away the idea. It wasn't him any more. All that was left was a shell, and seeing that would haunt me for ever. It was better that I kept the good memories I had of him, without tainting them.

The surgeon stepped towards me, touching the top of my arm. 'I'm so very sorry about your husband, Shannon. You're more than welcome to stay with Catherine tonight. Parents often do. The nurse can make you a fold-out bed if you'd like?'

I nodded. 'Thank you,' I whispered.

'I'll pop in first thing to check on you both, okay?'

I nodded again, already turning back to Katie. I stared at my daughter, vowing that whatever else I did with my life, I would do whatever it took to make sure she was okay. She was all I had now, and I was going to be everything to her.

From the depths of sleep, I could hear movement somewhere nearby, whispers between two women, their presence reassuring me that it wasn't my daughter calling for me, that I could continue to sleep. Every bone in my body felt limp with exhaustion. I couldn't force my eyes open, couldn't even move.

As I stopped trying to fight it, the voices bounced around my skull. They were talking about Katie's morphine. 'She's been very fidgety,' the younger voice said. There was the sound of soft footsteps, rustling, and I imagined them standing over the bed, assessing her.

'Increase the rate,' the other voice replied. There was the sound of a pencil scratching on paper, the tear of a page, and I pictured it being handed over. 'Turn it to this and keep me updated on how she's doing.'

'Are you sure?'

There was a pause. 'Are you questioning me?'

'Oh no, not at all. I just meant—'

'Adjust the rate,' the older voice repeated, less patient this time.

'No problem, Dr Gold,' the younger woman replied.

I tried to speak, to ask a question, but exhaustion overcame me. Everything went black.

The bright light overhead burned through my closed eyelids, and I pressed my hands to my face. An alarm was beeping frantically, yells and footsteps filling the room. I sat up in one swift motion, suddenly wide awake as I saw my daughter's bed surrounded by a horde of medical staff. A man in a bottle-green button-down shirt was performing chest compressions, too hard, too aggressive, his tall, bulky frame looming over my daughter. He would terrify her when she opened her eyes.

'What's happening?' I mouthed, no sound emerging from my lips. She'd been sleeping. The doctor had said she was going to be okay. That we'd be going home soon.

'Paddles!' someone shouted, and I gripped the edge of the mattress, hardly daring to breathe as Katie's tiny chest was obscured by the enormous grey slabs of metal. I wanted to jump up, to tell them to stop, that she was too small for all this, they were going to hurt her, but some instinct deep within me told me to stay still. To let them work to save her because I was about to lose myself.

My fingernails dug into my palms, my gaze trained on her face, willing her to wake up, to look at me, tell me to make these noisy people leave her alone, she was trying to sleep. That there was no need for all this fuss.

I stayed sitting, hyper-aware that if anyone realised I was still here, they'd force me to leave. They were all so busy, too focused on their own tasks, nurses drawing up medication, injecting it into the cannula, Katie's skin pale, almost blue, beneath the fluorescent lights.

I was aware of the exact moment when the energy in the room changed. I felt it like a sledgehammer to the chest. There was a thick, uncomfortable silence, the man in the bottle-green shirt turning away from my daughter, defeated, beaten.

'Time of death, four forty-two a.m.,' he said gruffly. He turned his head, seeing me watching him. 'I'm so sorry,' he said, meeting my eyes. 'I did everything I could.'

I just stared back. I couldn't say a word. Katie was gone, and with her she'd taken my final scrap of hope. My only reason to live.

FORTY

CARRIE

Now

'Oh my God!' I whispered, clutching Ava closer, my gaze flitting between Shannon and the gun in her hand. The dark barrel was all I could think of, waiting for the spark, the bullet to fly towards me. I didn't want to put Ava down, but I couldn't bear to have it pointing at her like that. I tried to sidestep, but Shannon tracked me.

'Don't move. You're not leaving with her,' she said, her words coming in a harsh bark. She was unrecognisable from the free-spirited woman I'd got chatting to in the staff room all those months before. I'd never seen this side to her, and it was terrifying.

Ava had fallen asleep in my arms as Shannon relayed her memory of the past, and prickling with awareness, careful to move slowly, I laid her in the cot behind me, shielding her with my body. It was clear that I needed to talk Shannon down before she did something reckless.

'You thought you got off scot-free, didn't you? That nobody

would blame you for what you did to my daughter. You got to carry on with your fancy job, a respected doctor, and she was just an inconsequential chapter along the way, isn't that right?'

'A nurse was fired for what happened to Catherine. *She* was to blame,' I said, determined to say whatever it took to get out of here with my daughter. 'And she faced the consequences.'

'You're a liar! I heard the two of you talking that night! I remember every word. Her trying to ask you a question and you snapping her head off. *You* were the doctor. You made the mistake!'

I stared at her, wondering if it was true that she'd heard the instructions I'd gone out of my way to brush under the carpet. I'd been so busy, so rushed that night. *Had* she heard the conversation with Sarah? And if she had, why hadn't she done anything about it before?

'I bet you forgot her within the week, didn't you? That she was barely a scratch on your life. I bet,' she added softly, 'you don't even remember her name.' She glared at me.

I set my jaw, trying not to let her words break me. The only part she was right about was that the consequences of my actions had gone unpaid. That the few people who knew the truth would never say a word. But the rest of her accusations... she couldn't have been more wrong. *Every* doctor made mistakes. It was the harsh reality of the job. And if I'd owned up at the time, admitted what I'd done, maybe I could have moved on. But I'd kept quiet... *no*, worse than that. In my panic, I'd pinned the blame on the first-year student nurse who'd adjusted the morphine pump to the deadly dose. She should never have even been touching it without a more senior nurse there to supervise. But she was in awe of me. Desperate to impress, to be remembered, and that had cost her.

I'd been through the night a million times in the years that had followed. I'd been rushed off my feet, distracted. Nick

Jameson, the surgical consultant who'd handed over that evening, had flashed me a knowing smile as the other doctors filtered out of the room, and I'd held back, waiting until the two of us were alone in his office.

He'd reached behind me, locking the door, heedless of the fact that we might be caught. That at this very moment, his wife, Barb, would be cooking his dinner at their expensive detached house overlooking the city. That my own marriage was the envy of all our friends.

After nearly a decade of medical school and training, I was now in my third year practising as a junior doctor specialising in emergency medicine. Jimmy was already ahead of me and climbing the ranks in a prestigious law firm, taking home a very generous salary. Our eldest child, Tommy, had just turned seven, and precocious little Maisy was just four and already so bright, so much more advanced than her peers.

To the outside world, we were the perfect family. And for the most part, it had been the truth. Jimmy had been everything to me since we met in college all those years ago. My dream man. I hadn't ever considered myself a woman who might have an affair. But the truth was, I'd worked so hard, so *fucking* hard to get to this position, and saying no to the man who held my prospects in the palm of his hand would have been career suicide. I told myself that was all it was. Pretended that the attraction between us wasn't the fuel that kept me coming back to him. And Jimmy could hardly complain. He'd been caught out too many times to play the victim. It was *my* turn to mess around for once.

So perhaps my mind hadn't been as focused as it should have been as I headed onto the paediatric surgical ward that night, my lips still swollen from being kissed, my underwear damp as I replayed the fast, intense sex we'd had over his desk, the photo of Barb staring at us as he came inside me. But that was why the nurses were so vital. They were as knowledgeable as us in some areas. They were there to point out our mistakes, ask questions, double-check the doses.

I hadn't even registered that Sarah was new on the ward. A student nurse, unauthorised to make adjustments to the medication rates. She'd been wearing a thick cardigan that obscured her light blue uniform, and I'd been distracted, weighing up the treatment options for another patient. She'd never said a word of protest. I'd told her what to do, and naïvely – stupidly, some might argue – she'd done it, without letting anyone know. I hadn't even got round to prescribing the new dose on the system. An emergency had come in moments later, and I'd been caught up with that. But Sarah had gone ahead anyway, later telling me she'd wanted to show how capable she was, how she could use her initiative – a trait that was always so valued in a hospital.

It *hadn't* been all my fault. I couldn't take the blame. I never touched the pump that night. That had been Sarah.

News travels fast in a hospital. I found her, after the morticians had come to take the little girl, hiding in the staff room, her face puffy from sobbing. I'd made her give me the piece of paper. Seen instantly what had happened. Instead of the hourly dose, I'd written down the total – the amount that should have been given over eight hours. Any experienced nurse would have realised that. But Sarah had given the lot in one fell swoop. And now a woman's child was dead.

'You said to change the rate to this!' she accused, looking at me as if she could pass the buck, save herself somehow.

I'd seen then what she meant to do. How she would take me down with her if she had the chance. So I'd lied. I'd destroyed the paper, told the panel at the inquiry that I'd made no changes to the pain relief prescription, that Sarah had taken it upon herself to change the rate. And Nick, in his desperation to protect me, had come to speak up for me, making a scathing speech about the irresponsible student nurse trying to pin the blame on me, embarrassing herself by making a nonsensical claim about a doctor who was impeccable in her role.

It was clear to everyone that it was Sarah who was in the wrong. Afterwards, when she'd been let go and I'd been thanked by the panel for my patience in this 'awkward' situation, he'd held me tight, telling me that I was too important to lose over such a 'silly thing'. That he wouldn't risk my prospects when the answer was simple. Let Sarah, the naïve young girl who had all the time in the world to start afresh, take the bullet. 'Nurses are ten a penny, Carrie,' he'd said. 'But you, my dear, are special.'

I had extricated myself from the relationship shortly after that, disgusted by his arrogance. But I'd found myself in the clear. Sarah had gone back up north to be with her family, disgraced, still ranting about how I'd set her up. She'd gone to the papers and it had backfired horribly, with them turning the spotlight on her, making it impossible to leave the house without a horde of reporters calling her a child killer, asking if she thought she should face jail time. Mercifully, I was viewed in a far different light. A hero, a victim, showered with sympathy for what Sarah had tried to do. Nobody would believe the disgraced nurse. And I was horrified to realise just how grateful I was for that.

I'd heard through the grapevine that the little girl's mother had gone off the rails. That losing her husband and child in the course of one day had been too much for her to cope with. She'd made an attempt on her own life but been found before it was too late. She'd been sectioned immediately afterwards, and despite myself, I had felt relieved that she wouldn't be in any fit state to ask questions.

I stared at Shannon now and realised that this was what I'd been waiting for all these years. I'd been unable to forgive myself. A little girl was dead, I'd stolen another woman's career out from under her, and, consumed by my guilt, I'd destroyed my marriage. It had taken years for me to admit the truth to Jimmy, though I never told him about my affair. He'd been shocked. Appalled. But he'd had no desire to blow up our lives by bringing my mess out in the open. It had been Jimmy who had told me to move on, forget the past, but even so, I could tell that it had changed the way he viewed me. He was never the same with me in the wake of my confession.

When he told me I should concentrate on the good I had done, I didn't believe him. I could see in his eyes that he didn't mean it. And I couldn't move forward. Couldn't forgive myself. I'd been consumed by the need to face the consequences of my actions. It had been all I could think of for years, throwing myself into my work, trying to make amends. I wanted to curtail my happiness to balance the scales.

But not by paying the price with my own child. I wouldn't let Ava suffer for my mistakes. She wasn't to blame for what I had done.

'Catherine Rose Briggs,' I said softly. 'I never forgot. I think of her every day.'

Shannon's eyes widened dangerously, the gun trembling in her hand.

'They said you were committed.'

'I was. For four years.'

I nodded. 'It didn't take you long to find me then – once you got out.'

She shook her head. 'Social media has come a long way. You post everything publicly – did you know that? So many photos of your children.' She gave a little laugh, her eyes twinkling nastily. 'All those pictures of Jimmy too. Even though we both know your marriage was dead long before he moved out. Even after he moved in with another woman, you were still posting happy snaps of the two of you, pretending everything was fine. I sometimes wonder if you believe your own lies. If it's more palatable for you that way.'

I frowned. I hadn't told her about Jimmy living with Leah, only that I'd caught him with someone else.

'Sitting next to you at work, going out to dinner and to yoga, knowing the truth, though you made out to the whole world that your life was so perfect... it was funny, really – if a little pathetic. Telling me that your husband was away on the oil rigs. How much you missed him. So many lies, Carrie. But it was remarkably easy to get you to open up, even if I did have to wade through the pile of shit you spewed out.'

I heard a noise from downstairs, as if a stack of books had clattered to the ground, but Shannon didn't seem to register it. 'When I first met your children, I thought it would be Maisy I'd take. She's the same age as Katie was when you killed her. There was something poetic in that, a like-for-like trade, if you want to be crass about it.'

'So why didn't you?' I asked. I had no desire to hear the answer, but I needed to keep her talking until I could figure out how to get away with Ava.

She twisted her mouth and shrugged. 'I suppose because she wasn't the same. Katie was bright and pretty and funny. She was my best friend. And Maisy... she couldn't live up to the memory. It wouldn't have felt like a fair swap.'

My eyebrows shot up, but I held my tongue, determined not to rise to her bait. How disgusting she was to suggest that Maisy wasn't good enough to fill her daughter's shoes. My blood was boiling, but I forced my face to remain blank as she went on.

'But Ava, she's still so little. She has the potential to be everything I hoped for.' She gave a bark of laughter. 'You haven't had time to ruin her yet... not like the other two.'

Her eyes burned into mine, challenging, and this time, I couldn't hold back. '*All* of my children are incredible people. You'd be lucky to have them in your life. But sadly for you, you'll never get near them again. I'll make sure of that.'

She stepped closer, the gun glinting in the light, and I felt myself shrink back, hyper-aware of how fragile the situation was, how stupid it was of me to goad her.

'How did you do it?' I blurted, grasping for a way to distract her. 'How did you sneak her away that day on the beach?'

Her eyes glazed over, staring past me to the cot, though my daughter was safely hidden behind my frame. 'Katie suits her so much better anyway. Ava was too soft for her. She needs a name that can live up to her adventurous spirit. Do you remember when her fringe grew long enough to fall in her eyes? How I showed you how to brush it into little pigtails?' she said, looking at me now.

I stared back at her, realising she was taking credit for that. Ava wasn't my first daughter. Did she think I didn't know how to put her hair up?

She smiled as if her words had stung me, rather than leaving me confused. 'Katie wore hers like that until she started school. She had the same curls back then, though they disappeared after she had her first haircut. The two of them could have been sisters.'

I shook my head. 'But they aren't. This is *my* daughter, Ava. You know that.'

She gave a sneer. 'Time can blur the memory, though, can't it? And it won't be long before she's calling *me* Mummy.' She gave a contented sigh. 'It was my mum, by the way.'

'What?' I asked, confused.

'At the beach that day. It's the first time she's been able to help me out in a long time. You saw her downstairs?' She tutted. 'She isn't the woman I need her to be, the mother I grew up with. Her memories are almost completely gone now. I missed the last good days while I was locked up against my will in that institution. That's something else you cost me. But she remembers her granddaughter. I didn't know if she'd be up to the task, if I'm honest. But when I told her to meet me at the beach and take Katie home for her dinner, she didn't let me down. You made it so easy to know where you'd be. You can never resist making a public announcement when you do something nice for your children, can you? What are you trying to prove?' she asked, laughing to herself. *'Taking my loves for a picnic tea on the beach,'* she parroted, and I remembered writing just that on social media last Friday lunchtime, excited at the thought of the first warm afternoon of spring, some much-needed time with my children.

'It was a bit tense when that detective came to show you the CCTV footage, I'll admit. But as you can see, we're pretty rural out here. I don't imagine the police bargained for a woman in her eighties taking a shortcut through the farmer's fields to get home. She's been walking that route since she was ten. Knows it like the back of her hand. And there are no cameras out there.' She shook her head and laughed again.

'Even with your child sitting right there on her lap, you couldn't be certain, could you? You let my doubt sway you, put a chink in your conviction. Any other mother would have seen right through me, known I was lying to you, and it would have all been solved in an instant. But not you. You don't even know Ava well enough to identify her when she's caught on camera, plain as day. *I* could have picked Katie out from a crowd of a thousand just by the way she turned her head, the little mannerisms that were uniquely her.'

She ran her thumb slowly down the grasp of the gun. 'Mum did me proud that day. She met me at the beach after I'd carried Ava away while your back was turned. I never imagined it would be so easy to get her alone, that even *you* would be so careless as to leave a toddler unsupervised next to open water, but it was almost too simple. And Mum was so happy. It was like going back in time, watching the way she was with her. I'd almost forgotten that side to her, but it's instinctive, isn't it?' She flashed me a look of disdain. 'Well, for most women. You seem to have missed out on the mothering gene.'

'Because I work? Because I can't be with them all the time? Is that it?' I retorted.

She laughed again. 'Oh, I know all your secrets, Carrie. Don't try and make out I've got you wrong. I know that you begged Jimmy to take time off from his job to take care of Tommy when he had measles so you could go and play God at work and avoid having to be a mother. You never even came home to check on him, did you? And I know that you missed Maisy's school nativity when she was six, even though you swore you'd be there. I know everything, Carrie!' Her words seeped through her lips with a hiss of smug satisfaction.

I stared at her, shocked. How could she possibly know any of that? Those were private issues I'd had with my family – none of them public knowledge. And she'd missed the most important parts out. Yes, I had chosen to stay at the hospital and work overtime when Tommy was ill. But that was because Jimmy had called me halfway through my shift to say he'd taken Tommy to the GP after he'd been sent home from school, and he'd been diagnosed with measles. I'd just found out that same week that I was pregnant with Maisy. Jimmy had *told* me to stay away. That it wasn't safe to risk catching it myself and harming the baby. It had been torture not being there for Tommy when he needed me, but I'd felt I had no other choice.

And the school nativity, well, I'd been putting my coat on, listening to the nurses talking about a concert some of them had been to at the weekend, when we got the emergency call that several ambulances were heading our way after a fire at a house party had got out of control. Eight patients, all with critical injuries and burns, had been rushed in, and we hadn't had the staff to handle them all. So I'd slipped off my coat and got to work. Sometimes in my job I had to make tough decisions. I had to put saving a life above my daughter's disappointment and my own desire to be there for her. I *had* to.

'How do you know about that?' I asked, my voice quiet as I watched her face closely.

'I wondered if Maisy might ruin it all,' she said, ignoring my question. 'If she'd tell you the truth. I had to frighten her, you see, when I took Ava. She knew me, of course. I snuck over and pressed my hand to her mouth and told her that whatever happened next, she needed to stay silent to protect Ava. That you were angry with them both and I had to keep Ava safe. She looked so confused, so frightened. Why would she be afraid of you, Carrie? Why did she believe me so easily?

'I saw her watching when I passed Ava to my mum, up on the path. I wasn't sure if she'd let me down. She had the power to spoil everything, and I was worried. But when you asked me to babysit that night, it gave me an opportunity to really drive my point home. I woke her up the minute you left, of course. And then once I'd made sure she understood, I left her in the house alone to digest everything. I got back in the early hours, not long before you, and I could see by then that she knew what she had to do.'

'No!' I cried, pressing my hands to my mouth. 'Oh God!'

She smiled. 'It wasn't something I enjoyed, you understand. I'm a mother, and it goes against my nature to scare a child like that. But I suppose there was a certain level of joy in knowing I was hurting your daughter the way you hurt mine. She was in quite a state when I came back, sitting there in the dark, her arms wrapped round her legs as if she could protect herself from the shadows lurking in the corners. The difference is, Maisy will survive this. My Katie didn't.'

'I can't believe you left her alone! What did you say to her?' I asked, my throat hoarse.

She shrugged. 'I simply explained that if anything were to happen to Ava, the whole world would find out it was because Maisy couldn't keep a secret. Couldn't keep her sister safe. I thought that was clever of me, really.' She gave a little smile, as if replaying the moment in her mind. 'Oh, and of course I made sure to tell her that you blamed her for not taking care of her sister. That if she'd been better behaved, none of this would have happened.'

'Better behaved? Maisy is an angel! What are you talking about?'

She grinned. 'Kids worry about the silliest things. A few weeks ago, when I met you at that café in town, Ava left half her biscuit. When you went up to order another coffee, I saw Maisy pick it up from the plate and eat it. I told her she was a very naughty girl. That she should have asked permission, and that she'd stolen from a baby. I warned her how angry you'd be if you found out. Katie would have laughed her head off, but not Maisy. She was so pale... so easy to convince. Maybe you should work on that. She's really too gullible for words.'

I felt sick, thinking of how Maisy must have tortured herself over this past week, too scared to speak up, knowing her sister was alive but not daring to tell a soul in case it caused Ava pain, risked her life. That she felt like she couldn't confide in me because of a stupid biscuit! How dare Shannon put the weight of that on her shoulders?

She ran a hand through her usually perfect blonde hair. Today it looked neglected, tangled, and I wondered if taking my daughter and trying to convince herself she could fix the hole left by her own child's death had formed cracks in her mind that wouldn't be easily mended. She had to have realised that it couldn't be as simple as swapping one for the other.

'My Katie would never have fallen for it, but then, like I said, she was in a different league. Too clever, too brave.'

'You bitch!' I spat. 'You fucking bitch! I did everything I could to save your daughter. She died because of a mistake. An awful mistake! I never meant for anything bad to happen to her. But you... you're pure evil. You think you're a better mother than me? You don't deserve to have that name! You're not safe to be anywhere near a child!'

She launched herself at me before I could register her moving. I felt my feet fly out from beneath me, my back smacking into the ground. Her hands wrapped around my neck, squeezing tight. Panic coursed through my veins as I tried to suck in a lungful of air, only to be met with nothing but resistance. I scraped at her hands with my fingernails, her eyes wide and manic as she glared down at me, all reason evaporated.

I caught a glint of silver and saw that in her urgency she'd dropped the gun on the carpet. My hand reached out towards it, the tips of my fingers touching the very edge. My vision filled with stars, fear pulsing through me, roaring in my ears. All I could think of was getting her off me before it was too late. If I passed out, she would be gone when I came round. And she would take my daughter with her. I couldn't let that happen.

With a final push of energy, I stretched out my arm, my fingers wrapping round the warm grip, still damp with Shannon's sweat. In one smooth motion, I raised it to her temple, pressing the metal hard into her skin, then swung my arm back and, with the final reserves of my strength, smacked the barrel hard into her head. There was a satisfying crack, and she gasped, falling off me to the carpet. The air burned as it rushed into my lungs, and I rolled to my knees, gasping painfully, my hand still tight around the weapon. Shannon scrambled to her feet, and with the power now in my hands, I pointed the gun up at her face.

'What the *hell* is going on here?'

My head snapped round at the sound of the familiar voice, relief flooding through me as I saw my husband standing in the doorway, taking in the scene. 'Jimmy!' I gasped, my throat raspy and aching.

Shannon pressed her hand to her temple, looking bewildered as she wiped away a trickle of blood that was trailing down her face, then she broke into a wide smile. 'Hello, darling,' she said, untucking her hair from behind her ear to cover her swollen cheek.

She walked past me, and before I could say a word, she reached for the back of my husband's head and kissed him hard on the mouth.

'Welcome home, Jimmy,' she said. 'I've been looking forward to showing you around.'

FORTY-ONE

I stared up at Jimmy, watching the way his hand instinctively moved to Shannon's back, a protective, unconscious action that was born of habit. He used to do that with me. And in the past months, I'd seen him do the same with Leah. The cogs whirred fast in my head as I tried to piece together what I was seeing.

'I don't understand,' he said. 'What are you doing here, Shannon? Do you live here?' He looked past her, his hand dropping like he'd been burned as he saw me kneeling on the carpet, my eyes trained on Shannon's back.

'Carrie, what the hell! Is that a gun? Did you bring a fucking gun here?'

'No, Jimmy, I didn't bring a bloody gun! She just pulled it on me! She's crazy!'

'What are you on about? For God's sake, put it down, will you, and explain what on earth is going on! I got your voicemail and I've called the police. What were you thinking, coming here alone? Did you really think you'd find—'

He broke off with a gasp as his gaze landed on the cot, the sleeping baby within it. 'Is that... is it really her?' He gave an animal groan, pressing his hands to his face. 'Oh my God, Carrie! You found her! You were right!'

He rushed forward, grabbing me by the wrist, heedless of the weapon in my hand, and pulled me up, hugging me so tight it felt as though my ribs might crack. He stepped back, then rushed to the cot, peering in. 'Is she okay?' he asked softly, his voice boyishly afraid as he watched Ava breathing peacefully.

I was grateful that she'd always been a deep sleeper. That she hadn't had to witness the scene that had unfolded moments before.

'Yes,' I said, coming to stand beside him. 'She's okay. No thanks to your friend here. Do you want to tell me what's going on? How you two know each other? And why the woman who abducted our child is calling you *darling*?'

'She did *what*?' he exclaimed.

Shannon smiled. 'I knew you'd be happy, Jimmy,' she said, her voice syrupy sweet, the smile too practised to feel genuine. 'I wish I could have told you sooner what I meant to do. But it doesn't matter now. You're here. And our little Katie is going to be so loved.'

'Katie?' Jimmy repeated, his brow puckering in confusion.

'Oh, you'll get used to it in time. The name isn't important, is it? Only that we're all together. You, me, Mum, our baby. We're going to be so happy, darling.'

I watched the interaction between the two of them, growing increasingly aware of how unhinged Shannon was. I couldn't help feeling relieved that Jimmy hadn't played a part in abducting our daughter though. I didn't think I'd ever seen him look more shocked, more confused than he appeared right now.

'You... you took my daughter?' he said softly. 'You let me think she was dead? All this time?'

'I didn't *want* to. But it wasn't the right time to tell you. I had to wait until the police had given up hope, until they couldn't pin anything on you. I couldn't risk them seeing us all together and making the wrong assumption about you. I was trying to *protect* you, Jimmy. So that we could move on safely.'

She walked over to the dresser, and I felt my stomach tense as I watched her. I wanted to point the gun again, tell her not to move, but it felt overdramatic somehow, now that Jimmy was here. I glanced at him, still trying to work out how this had come about.

Shannon opened the drawers one by one, pulling out handfuls of baby clothes, none of which were Ava's. Had she saved all of these from Catherine? 'We'll leave tonight. We can drive far away somewhere and start afresh. I always thought I'd like to live in a really busy city.' She grinned. 'We can lose ourselves in the crowds. Just another anonymous family. Nobody notices you in a place like that, do they? We'll be okay.'

'I was with you this afternoon,' he said softly. 'I've spent every day this week with you, at what I thought was your flat. I was with you the night Ava went missing, for God's sake!' he accused, and I realised that was where Shannon must have gone when she left Maisy all alone. 'I told you I didn't think I could cope with the pain of losing my daughter. That I was on the verge of a breakdown. You *know* what I've been going through, Shannon. More than Leah, more than Carrie! It's *you* I've been confiding in! Do you remember what you said? That no matter what, whatever came to light about Ava, you'd be there for me. And all this time, you knew exactly where she was because *you* fucking took her!' He launched himself forward, grabbing the bundle of tiny lacy dresses from her hand and tossing them aside. 'I loved you! I really fucking loved you!'

I shook my head. 'How have you had time to fall in love with yet another woman, Jimmy? I'm sure Leah will be delighted to hear that.'

He glared at me, and through his anger, I saw that he was breaking inside. Somehow, Shannon had managed to worm her way into his heart in a way no woman, not even me, had done before. And now that he was experiencing the other side of the coin, how it felt to discover you'd been betrayed by the person you trusted most, I was too sad and scared to feel any sort of vindication over his despair. All that mattered now was leaving with my daughter. I didn't care how or why they'd found each other. They were welcome to their lies and cheating.

I fiddled with the gun, trying to figure out how to disarm it. The hammer part didn't move when I tested it cautiously with my thumb, and I was afraid of setting it off. I had never held a gun before. I had no idea what I was doing, aside from the limited information I'd picked up from movies. All I knew was that it was dangerous, and that I didn't want to be holding it when I picked up my daughter. *And* that I couldn't let Shannon get her hands on it again. I glanced around, then, coming up with no solution, tucked the pistol slowly and carefully behind me, into my belt. Then I turned to the cot and lifted Ava gently into my arms.

Shannon's head snapped towards me, her expression feral. 'Put her down,' she demanded.

I ignored her, looking to Jimmy. 'I'm taking her home. Are you coming, or do you want to stay and finish your little lovers' tiff with our daughter's kidnapper?' I asked pointedly.

'I... I'm not staying here.'

'You're not leaving!' Shannon grabbed his wrist, her face panicked. 'You have to stay with me, Martin! You're supposed to protect us! Don't let her take our child – not again!'

'Who's Martin?' he asked, yanking his arm from her grasp. 'Some other guy you've been conning? Pretending to care about?'

'No, no, no, no! You've got it wrong! It's going to be okay; you just need to trust me. Take Katie and I'll get the car. We have to go!' she cried, her hair wild across her face, her eyes wide and unfocused.

I stepped past them, holding Ava tighter, making for the door. 'I'm not waiting for you, Jim. I'm leaving now.'

'No you're not!' Shannon let out a mighty scream, then rushed at me, grabbing for my daughter. Ava woke with a start, wailing as Shannon tugged at her leg, determined to take her from me.

'Enough, Shannon!' Jimmy yelled. 'You're going to hurt her!'

Ava was sobbing now, and I saw that Shannon had lost all sense of reason. She would stop at nothing to get my daughter. Jimmy tried to prise her hand from Ava's leg, but she held firm.

The bang was deafening. Shannon dropped like a sack of potatoes to the pale pink carpet. The smell of smoke and something metallic filled the small room as I watched blood spread across her blue jeans from the bullet wound in her thigh.

I stood over her as she gasped. 'You're lucky I didn't shoot you in the head,' I said breathlessly, adrenaline making me grip the gun tighter. 'That's what you really deserve.'

Jimmy stepped over the puddle of claret trickling onto the carpet and slid his thumb into the loop of my fingers, forcing them open and prising the gun from my hand. 'Let's go,' he said, meeting my eyes with his.

He reached for Ava, but I shook my head, unwilling to let her go again. He nodded, understanding, then pressed a kiss to her cheek and smiled. 'It's okay, sweetheart. Everything is going to be okay now.'

Deep male voices rose from the hall below, footsteps coming up the stairs – in no rush, by the sound of it. I heard the unmistakable voice of DCI Farrows. 'If she broke into the old lady's house, she's in for a whole world of trouble. She can't go taking the law into her own hands. Bloody woman can't admit that she might have got it wrong...'

He and two other officers, one male, one female, appeared in the doorway, taking in the scene before them. 'What the hell...?' whispered the female officer – not Mayville this time – her hand going to her mouth.

Jimmy placed the gun down carefully on the dresser. 'I think you owe the mother of my child an apology actually, Farrows,' he said, looking at the stunned detective. 'If you'd listened to her and done your job properly, you'd have discovered that this woman' – he gestured to Shannon, who was sobbing on the carpet – 'abducted Ava. Oh, and you might want to call an ambulance. She has a bullet wound from the gun she pulled on my wife. Self-defence, you understand.'

'I don't want a fucking ambulance!' Shannon screamed, the tears evaporating in an instant. 'Give me my baby! Give her to me now, you bastards! She's mine!'

I clutched my crying daughter, shaking my head wordlessly.

DCI Farrows looked at me, his usually smug smile conspicuously absent. 'Why don't you both go and wait downstairs,' he said, his voice quiet. 'I have some questions I'll need you to answer. Matthew, call an ambulance. And, Joyce, wrap the gun for evidence.'

I nodded, wanting nothing more than to get Ava out of there.

'*Carrie!*' Shannon screamed after me. 'If you take her from me again, I swear I will not stop until you pay. I'll take all of your children, one by one, until you know how it feels to have nothing left! I'll make you feel the pain of losing them until you can't stand to be in your own body, until all you can hear are their voices screaming for help, until it feels like bugs are scrambling around inside your brain.'

'I hope you're paying attention to this,' Jimmy muttered to Farrows. He put a hand on the small of my back, guiding me from the room, and I let him.

I held my breath, my lungs swollen and burning, hardly daring to believe I was walking out of there with my daughter safe in my arms.

FORTY-TWO

'I should explain.'

Jimmy was leaning back on the bonnet of my car, holding Ava, after my arms had begun to feel like jelly from the dead weight of her sleeping body. The ambulance had taken Shannon nearly an hour before, though we'd stayed tucked in the clearing across the lane, unwilling to have to look at the woman again. The police had taken statements from both of us, and, to my surprise, had left without arresting us.

I had been expecting the worst. Wondering what would happen to Ava when they took me away in cuffs. But DCI Farrows had been subdued and apologetic as he'd told us we were free to go and that he'd be in touch in the morning.

The moon had disappeared behind the thick clouds over-head, and I couldn't help but wonder what would happen to Shannon's mother. She'd been checked over by the paramedics and taken to hospital with a suspected urine infection and dehy-dration. Would she be found guilty for her part in Ava's abduc-tion? I hoped not. It was Shannon who had manipulated and orchestrated the whole thing. Her poor mother was just a pawn.

I stroked Ava's hair, unable to keep myself from touching

her, reminding myself that she was real, alive. 'I don't think an explanation is necessary, Jimmy. I think it's fairly obvious what happened.'

'And what's that?'

'Shannon knew who you were before she met you. She thought we were still married, and she wanted to take from me everything she'd lost herself. My daughter, my husband. She sought you out with the sole intention of causing me the most pain. And you, being the fickle man you are, fell for her. Just like you always do.' I smiled.

'Doesn't it upset you?'

I shrugged. 'You're not mine any more, Jimmy. I don't think you ever really were.'

He pressed his lips together. 'Don't think I don't have regrets, Carrie. For hurting you. Breaking up our family. These past few days, the fear of what might have happened...' He shook his head, pressing a kiss to the top of Ava's head, wrapping his jacket tighter around her little body. 'It's put everything into perspective. What matters. What's important. What I'm willing to do to fix it.'

'Fix it?'

He nodded. 'Our family. I want to come home, Carrie. I want us to be together again. You, me, the kids.'

I smiled. It was funny to hear these words now, after everything. It had been what I'd dreamed of since the moment he left. I'd hated having to hand over the children to spend their weekends with him and Leah. Being alone in the big, empty house. Feeling as if I was missing out on raising them. I'd truly believed that I'd failed at my marriage, like there might have been something I could have done differently that would have made him stay, made him love me enough.

'Is that a yes?' he asked softly, seeing my smile, and I had to laugh at the expression on his face. I knew him well enough to see that he thought I would fall at his feet in gratitude.

I coughed. 'That is a resounding no. Not in a million years, Jimmy. I wouldn't trust you, and' – I took a deep breath, the weight of the last year falling from my shoulders as a realisation hit me, making me feel lighter than I could remember – 'I don't love you any more.' The words felt strong and brave on my lips.

He looked surprised, a frown puckering his forehead, as if he were waiting for me to tell him I was only joking, and of course I'd take him back. I held his gaze. Finally, he nodded. 'I respect you for saying it. And I get it.' He slid Ava onto his hip and held out a hand. 'Friends?' he asked hopefully.

'Friends.' I shook his hand.

'Let me give you a lift home,' I said, unlocking the car. He'd told me he'd got a taxi to the cottage, as he'd been over the limit to drive when he got my message. He'd admitted that he'd been relying heavily on alcohol to get through the pain this week. It had been a relief to know how deeply he'd been affected by everything. It made him more human, somehow. 'I want to pick up the kids. Let them know the good news.'

He put Ava in her car seat, pulling the straps tight, and climbed into the passenger seat. I drove through the dark, quiet lane, out onto the main road. 'Leah deserves someone who loves her, you know.'

He nodded.

'You can't keep repeating this pattern, Jimmy. It's not fair.'

'I know. I guess what happened with Shannon was the first time I ever experienced the other side.'

'Not fun, huh?'

'Not one bit. But it might turn out to be the making of me.'

I looked over at him, his face taking on an orange glow beneath the street light. 'We'll see,' I teased.

I pulled up outside his house, and he looked behind him at Ava's rear-facing car seat. 'I won't wake her now, but can I see her tomorrow? Can I come over and spend some time with her?'

'Of course.'

He squeezed my hand. 'I really thought we'd lost her, Carrie.' He bit his lip, and I felt my eyes fill with tears.

'Me too,' I whispered.

He swallowed, then looked at his watch. 'It's late. You sure you want me to get the kids up?'

'Please. I need them with me tonight. Besides, you and Leah need to have a conversation. She's going to take it hard. I know you think I was wrong, and I'll admit, I made a mistake over her involvement with Ava's disappearance, but she *was* at the clinic that day. She thinks she's their new mother, Jim. That she can take my place. You need to explain to her that I won't ever let that happen, whether she stays with you or not. You need to talk properly for once.'

He sighed, as if it was the last thing he wanted to do, then gave a resigned nod. 'Okay. I'll just be a minute.'

'Thanks, Jimmy.'

He climbed out, and I watched as he headed up the path, my heart racing as I waited for Tommy and Maisy, desperate for them to see that Ava was okay.

FORTY-THREE

I wanted to rush up the path, to hurry Jimmy along, but
instead, I waited, pacing back and forth on the pavement
beside the car, my gaze drifting every few seconds to my sweet
sleeping toddler tucked into her car seat in the back. Her
cheeks were rosy, her dummy lying on her chest having fallen
from her mouth, and I couldn't stop pinching myself, proving
to myself that she was real. A sudden flashback hit me: the
roar of the sea, the salt burning my eyes, stripping my throat
raw as I dived for the seabed, the blinding frustration and
panic as I reached into the darkness for a body that wasn't
there.

I gasped, shaking my head, reminding myself that she'd
never been there, never had to experience the terror of the
waves crashing over her tiny head, stealing the breath from her
lungs. But that memory, the fear I'd felt that day, would never
completely leave me. It would serve as a reminder of what
might have been. How lucky I was to have a second chance.

I looked up as I heard Jimmy's front door open, to see him
stepping onto the path. Maisy was fast asleep, her head lolling
on his shoulder, and Tommy appeared behind him, his hair

mussed, his dressing gown hanging loose, the belt dangling down by his ankle.

He stopped on the path, staring at the car, his face half hopeful, half disbelieving. I was sure Jimmy had told him his sister was okay, but he looked as if he was too afraid to let himself believe it. He met my eyes, questioning, and I nodded silently, stepping aside and pointing to the back window. 'Here she is,' I said quietly. 'Come and see.'

He broke into a run, his hand clasping tight around mine as he stared in at his little sister. 'Is she okay?' he asked, looking up at me with innocent hope.

I nodded. 'She seems to be absolutely fine.'

Jimmy walked round the other side of the car, and I was amazed to see Maisy still sleeping soundly as he strapped her in and put a blanket over her. He closed the door softly, then came over to where Tommy and I were waiting on the pavement.

'Leah said Maisy was quite upset tonight. Cried herself to sleep. I guess she's burned herself out. Do you want to wake her and tell her the good news?'

I shook my head. 'Let her sleep for now.'

He nodded, and again I marvelled at the lack of tension between us now.

He pulled Tommy into a bear hug, and I heard him whisper, 'I love you. Take good care of your mum and sisters, okay?'

Tommy nodded, standing up straight, his chin jutting out proudly, and I smiled, seeing a glimpse of the man he would someday become. He looked responsible and grown-up. He said goodbye to his dad, then climbed into the passenger seat as Jimmy headed back up the path, looking in no rush to get inside.

I didn't envy him the conversation he was about to have, nor Leah. I was surprised to realise I felt sorry for her, sad that she was about to have her world thrown into disarray. I waved goodbye, then turned the car around, heading through the dark, quiet streets, Tommy sitting silently beside me.

'Dad said *you* found her.' He looked at me. 'He said that you went against the police, that you put yourself in danger, and if it weren't for you, we wouldn't have got Ava back.'

I gripped the wheel, taking a deep breath. 'You *do* know I'd do the same for you too, Tommy? I would do anything to keep my children safe. I love you. Probably far more than you'll ever realise – at least until you become a parent yourself.'

He looked down at his lap, fiddling with the belt of his dressing gown. 'A little while after Dad moved out, he came to drop us home and I heard you having an argument in the kitchen. It scared me. I thought—' He broke off, looking out the window, and I felt the moment on the verge of evaporating. It had been a long time since he'd spoken to me in anything other than dismissive grunts.

'Tell me,' I pushed, my voice soft. 'I promise I won't be angry.'

He lifted a finger, tracing it along the dark window, still not looking at me. For a moment, there was silence, then at last he spoke. 'I couldn't hear everything. But you were talking about a little girl who had died at your work. And Dad said you should have spoken up when you killed her... and that you needed to live with the consequences since you hadn't had the guts to admit the truth.'

'Oh,' I whispered. I felt dizzy, shaken at the idea that my son had discovered the thing I most wanted to keep hidden from the world.

'I know it's bad of me, but after that, I started to get nightmares...'

'Nightmares?' I repeated gently.

'About you...' He glanced quickly at me, then down at his lap. 'You killing me. Or sometimes Maisy, or Ava. I became really scared. I wanted to live with Dad, but you made me stay, and I know I'm not supposed to think it, but I was frightened that if you'd killed a child once, you might do it again. That the nightmares would come true. That's why when I fell down the stairs and broke my arm, I told people you'd pushed me. I *wanted* to be taken away,' he admitted, tears streaming down his pale cheeks. 'I'm sorry,' he whispered. 'I know I hurt your feelings badly.'

'Oh, Tommy,' I whispered, my eyes blurring on the road ahead as I swallowed against the ball of emotion wedged in my throat. 'I wish you'd told me what you heard. I can't imagine how afraid and confused you would have been by it.'

He shrugged. 'Just now, Dad told me it was Shannon who took Ava... and that you were brave and fought her to get her back. I never wanted to say anything to you, but Shannon has been telling me bad things about you since you first introduced us.'

I listened, feeling stupid that I hadn't noticed these interactions. I'd introduced Shannon to Tommy and Maisy not long after I'd met her, but we'd mostly met up when they were at school and I just had Ava with me, or when all three of them were with their dad and I told Shannon they were at my parents'. I'd been conscious of the lie I'd told her about Jimmy working on the oil rigs, and though I knew now that she'd known all along that I'd been lying, I'd done my best to stay alert when we were all together, so that I could steer the conversation in a safer direction if it started heading towards my marriage or Jimmy's work. Obviously I hadn't been as on the ball as I'd thought, though, if she'd had time to speak to my son without my hearing.

Tommy continued. 'She makes comments when you're distracted with Ava about how you're not a good mum. She tells us we'd be happier living with our dad. And I was so scared of what I heard that I believed she was right. I feel embarrassed to say it, but I... I thought you were a murderer.'

I sucked in a breath, trying not to show how deeply his words cut. How could my own son have believed such an

awful thing about me? That I'd set out to hurt poor
Catherine.

'But,' he went on, 'if she was right, if you really were evil,
you wouldn't have bothered to save Ava. You wouldn't have put
yourself in danger for her, would you?' He looked up at me,
needing reassurance.

I pulled over to the side of the road, turning off the engine
and taking his hand. 'Darling, I wish you'd told me all this. I
wish you'd trusted me. I have never hurt you, have I?'

He shook his head, biting down on his bottom lip, unable to
meet my eyes.

I took a deep breath. 'I didn't mean for anything bad to
happen to the little girl in the hospital,' I said, still holding his
hand. 'But I did make a mistake. I was in a hurry and didn't
make the checks I was supposed to, and because of my rushing
around, the little girl was given too much medicine, and yes,
sadly, she did die. And,' I continued, feeling lighter for having
admitted the truth out loud, 'I was so afraid of getting in trouble,
losing the job I'd worked hard for, that I didn't admit my part in
it. I should have made sure the nurse understood the dose. I
should have checked she was cleared to give medication. That
was my responsibility.'

'But you didn't mean to kill her? You didn't... want to?'

'No, sweetheart! Of course not. It was a terrible mistake, a
regret I've carried ever since. My mistake cost a life; it can never
be undone. And it was made worse by my silence. Which is
why, first thing tomorrow, I'm going to write to the head of the
department and give a full account of what happened to that
little girl.'

'But won't you lose your job?'

I shrugged. 'I might. But I'd rather that than having to carry
the burden of the secret any longer. Keeping it in only made
everything so much worse. If I'd been honest, told my family the
truth, admitted that I'd made mistakes, then you wouldn't have

had to wonder what your father and I were arguing about. I'm so sorry that you ever felt you were in danger with me, darling. That I could hurt you. I'd do anything to protect you, and yet my secrets have caused you so much fear and pain.' I squeezed his hand. 'I hope you can learn to trust me again. And that I can make it up to you.'

He smiled. 'You already did. You brought Ava home.'

I sighed. 'I'm glad you told me how you've been feeling. I know I'm busy, that I'm not around as much as you deserve. But no matter what, I'll always have time for you. I always want to hear what's worrying you.'

'Okay. Sorry, Mum.'

'Oh, Tommy, you have nothing to apologise for.'

I pulled him into a hug, and for the first time in months, he melted into me like butter. I smiled into his hair, holding him tight. I had my little boy back at last.

Tommy stumbled exhausted into the house, kissing Ava on her pink little cheek with a contented smile. 'Night, sweetie,' I said, watching him climb the stairs. 'Straight to bed now, okay?'

He grunted, and I took Ava into my room, placing her in my bed, then headed straight back outside to get Maisy. She blinked as I unlocked the car door – I hadn't wanted to leave it open with her sleeping – and looked up at me confused.

'We're home, sweetie.' I reached over her, unbuckling her seat belt and helping her to climb out onto the drive. She gave a shiver and wrapped her arms around her body, and I squatted in front of her, rubbing her shoulders with my hands. 'Darling, Ava is back. She's asleep upstairs in my room. We found her because of you, Maisy. Because of what you told me about the old lady.'

Her eyes widened. 'What? Are you... do you really mean it?'

I nodded.

'Show me! I... I don't believe you.'

I smiled and took her by the hand, guiding her into the warmth of the house and up the stairs to my room. 'Let's not wake her,' I said softly. 'She's had a long day.'

Maisy nodded, and I pushed open the bedroom door.

In the moonlight, Ava's hair glittered like gold, her long black eyelashes spread out on her pink cheeks. Maisy dropped my hand and walked across the carpet, reaching out to place a hand on Ava's belly, just as I had done at Shannon's cottage, checking she was real, alive. She looked up at me with tears in her eyes. 'Did they hurt her? Shannon said if I told you anything, they'd hurt her.'

I shook my head. I'd already given her a thorough check back at the cottage, and there were no signs of injury or assault. Shannon had clearly taken her role as Ava's fake mother very seriously, and for that, at least, I was relieved. 'She's okay, sweetie. She's going to be fine.'

'Shannon said it was my fault.'

I fell to my knees, pulling her onto my lap like she was still a toddler herself. 'Shannon told me what she said to you... and that she left you all alone here. I can't imagine how terrified you must have been. I'm so sorry you've been carrying that worry all this time. If I'd known...' I shook my head. 'Darling, you did *nothing* wrong. You weren't wrong to take the biscuit from Ava's plate. And it wasn't your responsibility to look after her at the beach.'

She glanced at me, her eyes glistening in the moonlight streaming through the window. 'I thought I'd let you down... that you blamed me.'

'Darling, no. Never! I'm so sorry you thought that. But why did you think I'd be so angry? Have I done something to make you feel afraid of me? That you can't confide in me?' I was hurt that she didn't trust me, that Shannon had been able to convince her of something so far-fetched. Surely she knew I would never blame her?

She was silent for a moment, and I held her tight against my chest.

'Shannon... she tells me things... she whispers.'

'Whispers?'

She nodded. 'That you're cross with me. That you wish I was different. More clever. More pretty. At first I didn't believe her, but then she said that when Ava is having a tantrum and you lose your patience, it's because you're already so cross with me that Ava is just the final straw. And sometimes you *do* seem so angry. When Ava cries, it's like you don't know how to calm down. You get snappy with me. So I started to believe Shannon might be right. That it *was* my fault. That I just keep getting things wrong.'

'Oh, Maisy.' I closed my eyes, trying to see the world from her innocent perspective. 'Darling, I get cross sometimes because I'm tired. I work long hours, and toddlers, well, they can be a challenge. But when Ava has a meltdown and I'm getting flustered, it's not because I'm upset with *you*. It's because I'm exhausted and sometimes hungry and I had expectations of how the day was going to go, and I sometimes feel like I could do with a moment to gather my thoughts. It's not always easy being a single working mother. But I never want you to feel like I wish I could change you. I *love* you exactly as you are. Ava too, even when she's screaming like a banshee. Shannon told you those things because she wanted to break your trust in me, make you doubt yourself, so that when she took Ava, you wouldn't speak up. *She's* the one in the wrong. Not you. Never you, my love.'

Her shoulders seemed to relax, the tension in her spine slowly dissipating. Finally, she looked up at me. 'I'm sorry I didn't tell you the truth, Mum. I was so scared.'

'You have nothing to apologise for, Maisy. *You're* the reason we have Ava back.' I kissed her forehead, feeling furious with myself that I hadn't noticed Shannon dripping poison into my children's ears. 'I understand why you felt you couldn't talk to me. I get it now. But, darling, if anyone ever asks you to keep a secret from me again, you must tell me, okay? I can't protect you if you don't. I need to know the truth. Do you understand?'

She straightened, looking at me with a curious expression on her face.

'What is it?' I asked, my stomach turning suddenly cold.

'Someone else asked me to keep a secret,' she said, wringing her hands tightly together. 'She said it could hurt you if you knew.'

'Who?' I whispered, frozen to the spot as I waited for her to speak.

She bit her lip, looking unsure, and I was terrified she'd revert to her mute state again and I'd be left to wonder.

Finally, she took a deep breath. 'Leah,' she said, meeting my eyes. 'It was Leah.'

FORTY-FOUR

LEAH

I walked into the kitchen, ripping a piece of kitchen towel from the roll and blotting my wet eyes. Jimmy followed, slumping into a chair, looking utterly drained.

'I can't believe you found her,' I said, the emotion still threatening to overwhelm me. To hear that Ava was safe and yet be prevented from rushing outside to hold her in my arms had been torture. Jimmy had explained that Carrie wanted to keep things as calm as possible, the implication being that I would rock the boat and ruin the happy reunion between the siblings, and despite my own desperate desire to see her sweet face again, I'd agreed to stay inside.

I screwed the paper into a ball, shaking my head. 'I was so worried when you didn't come home tonight. You should have told me what you were doing,' I said, leaning back against the counter.

'Well, you've hardly been approachable lately. And I didn't have much time. I wasn't expecting Carrie to go rushing into a situation like that.'

I nodded, determined not to argue. Not tonight. 'I'm just happy that Ava's okay. You can relax now. I know how difficult this past week has been for you. I've felt it too. I do love her, you know. I love all of them.' I smiled. 'Now we can concentrate on being a family, being together. I wish they'd stayed tonight, but I do understand why Carrie wanted them at her place.'

'*Do* you?'

I frowned. 'Of course. Why wouldn't I?'

He looked down at his lap, silent.

'Look, I know she and I might not be the best of friends, but I'm not a robot. I can grasp the concept of a mother needing to be with her children after a traumatic event.'

'You could have fooled me, the way you've been acting the past few days. I don't know who you are lately, Leah. You've been erratic. Scarily so. The way you acted when the police wanted to search the house... it made me question what you might be—'

'*What?*' I interrupted angrily, daring him to finish the sentence, to accuse me of hiding something, though I hoped he wouldn't.

'Nothing.' He shook his head. It doesn't matter now. Ava's safe. Besides, there are things we need to discuss. Whatever's happened, it no longer matters.'

I folded my arms, suddenly frightened that I'd pushed him away. It wasn't my intention. Far from it. I didn't want to lose him.

'My dad's in prison.' The words seemed to stick in my throat, and I closed my eyes, wishing I didn't have to say them out loud.

'What?'

'We had the perfect life when I was growing up. My mum was there for every special event in my childhood. She never missed a thing. She was everything I wanted to be. Spontaneous. Free. She made her own rules. But it was all reliant on my dad paying the bills, supporting her.' I clicked my tongue nervously, struggling to keep talking, though I knew I had to if I wanted to make Jimmy understand my behaviour of late. Why I hadn't been there for him when he needed me most. 'For a long time,' I went on, 'it worked. We were happy.'

Jimmy sat forward, frowning. 'I don't understand...'

'I was twelve when they came. We were all playing a board game – Cluedo. I was the red piece, Miss Scarlet. I always chose that one. I was holding it in my hand when the door was rammed open with such force I thought a bomb must have gone off. I didn't realise until hours later that I was still holding it. My fingers had been curled so tight that the base of the piece had cut into my palm without my having felt a thing.' I swallowed, looking at my hand, the fear I'd felt that night still so visceral, so bright in my memory.

'They pinned him to the ground, my dad, the man who protected me and Mum, and then they dragged him out of his own house in handcuffs, before swarming through our personal things like a plague of locusts. We lost everything. In one moment, my life went from this bohemian, carefree existence to absolute hell.'

'What did he do?' Jimmy asked, his gaze trained on my face.

I chewed my lip. 'We had no idea. At least, Mum *swore* she never knew.'

'*Leah.*'

I sighed. 'It was an armed robbery. Well, several, as it turned out. But the one he got caught for was a warehouse full of technology – TVs, laptops, stereo systems. The security guard got into a tussle with him, and... well, he got shot.' I pressed my lips together, remembering the moment I'd heard what my father had done. The shock of trying to piece together the truth, understand how the man who made me feel most safe had turned out to be a complete stranger to me. 'He didn't make it,' I whispered. 'My dad got sent down for a whole reel of charges, and I haven't seen him for years.

'Mum went off the rails. She didn't know how to cope,

couldn't fathom how to keep going without him. She became someone completely different. Bitter. Unkind. The mother who had been my best friend in the world vanished in a matter of months. To be honest with you, it would have been kinder if she'd died. She turned up here a few months back. I know Carrie mentioned it to you. It was the first time I'd seen her in ten years. She heard from a relative that I was doing all right for myself and came to see if you might support her too. I never realised she was such a vulture. She still refuses to get a job. She's only in her fifties, but Carrie mistook her for that old lady on the bus because she's spent the last decade locked in her damp flat, chain-smoking and drinking herself into an early old age, thinking Prince Charming will come and fix all her problems and her life will go back to what it used to be. She hates that I've got what she wants. And her bitterness has clouded any love she might once have had for me.'

I wiped away a tear, feeling the swell of emotion burning my lungs, wanting more than anything to break down, but I couldn't give in. Jimmy needed to hear what I had to tell him, and I knew he'd leave if I lost control. He'd never coped well with what he called 'hormonal outbursts'.

I took a few steeling deep breaths, composing myself. 'You must have wondered why you've never met my parents,' I said. 'Why I never talk about them. Why I only have a couple of old photos of them.'

I stared at him, watching his face, and realised that perhaps the most obvious answer was the right one. That he hadn't asked not because he was respecting my privacy but for the simple fact that he didn't really care.

His phone beeped, and he took it from his pocket, looking at the message. He frowned, then looked over at me, his eyes suddenly cold, probing. 'Carrie says you're keeping a secret. And that you've made Maisy promise not to tell.'

I felt like a deer in headlights as he fixed me with a hard stare. 'I... It's not exactly like that. She's made it sound sinister.'

'You're right. It does sound fucking sinister. You'll forgive me for jumping to conclusions after the week we've just had.' He rose to his feet, striding across the room to me. 'What does she mean by this, Leah? What are you hiding?'

I wrapped my arms around myself, staring at him.

'Oh,' he added, 'and she told me about you turning up to the clinic when Maisy went for her first therapy session. I thought she must have been mistaken, but now I'm not so sure.'

I sighed, realising the time had finally arrived to come clean. I'd waited so long to be able to tell him the truth. I hadn't wanted to do it like this. But now Carrie had forced my hand. And perhaps that was a good thing. It hadn't been easy to keep Jimmy from discovering my secret. I reached for him, ignoring when he flinched angrily away, linking my fingers tightly through his, despite his obvious reluctance to touch me.

'I'll show you,' I said softly. 'I'll explain everything. Come with me.'

I led him up the narrow staircase, through the wooden door and across the thick cream carpet to the dresser on the far side of the cavernous loft. I let go of his hand, dropping to my knees and pulling the white wicker basket from the little cupboard. 'Here,' I said gesturing for him to sit beside me.

'Leah, what is this?' he asked impatiently. 'I've had a hell of a night. I'm tired. And quite frankly, I'm losing my patience with this drama. Can't you just spit it out?'

I stared at him, unwilling to dance to his tune. If I was going to be forced to reveal my secret, I was going to do it my way.

With a frustrated sigh, he sank down beside me and grabbed the basket, flipping it over and tipping the contents onto the carpet. I winced, wishing he'd act with more care, reverence, as I always did.

He looked at me with a frown. 'What is this?'

I smiled. 'Baby things.'

'I can see that. Why? Why are you collecting baby things?'

I smiled again, my hand going to my belly. 'I wanted to tell you, but it wasn't the right time. Not with Ava missing. I've been so sick,' I said, laughing as I thought of all the mornings I'd had to dash to the bathroom, the times I'd picked at my food, trying not to draw attention to the fact that I couldn't face a mouthful.

I picked up a black-and-white photograph, handing it to him. 'This is from the scan I had a few days ago. *That's* why I was at the clinic. I had no idea Maisy was at the same place – my GP booked me in there weeks ago.' I touched the photo with the tip of my finger. 'They don't know the sex yet, but they said everything looks healthy so far.'

He glanced at the photo, his eyes narrowing as he read the writing across the top of it. 'Thirteen weeks? You're thirteen weeks pregnant?'

I nodded. 'Yes.'

He handed it back to me, his mouth puckered, the joyful smile I'd imagined him breaking into conspicuously absent. I ran my finger nervously over the image of our baby, tracing a line down the little spine, the curve of the skull, picturing the life inside of me, tiny and perfect.

This white basket symbolised everything I'd ever hoped for. I'd lost my mother after my father was arrested, and never recovered from having the closeness we shared snatched away from me. It still hurt now to think of how different she'd become. But this baby would be my chance to have that again. To create a closeness that would never be broken. I wouldn't turn on my child the way my mother had turned on me. Not ever. I had come up here so often, adding toys or items of clothing to my collection, sitting on the carpet and daydreaming about the child who would make use of them. I couldn't wait.

'I thought you were on the pill. We were using condoms.' His tone was flat, accusing, and I felt my cheeks flush.

'Well, I guess they failed.'

He looked down at the pile of baby clothes, knitted blankets, the little fluffy duckling I'd kept from my own baby years to pass on to my firstborn. He swallowed but said nothing.

'I know it's a shock,' I said hurriedly, taking his hand again. 'But it's the best thing that could have happened to us. We're getting married. We already have three wonderful children, and this baby will just cement all of that love. We'll be one big happy family. It's everything we could have wished for, Jimmy.'

He continued to stare down at the pile, unspeaking.

'Jim!' I cried, trying to snap him out of his shock. 'Aren't you happy? You said you wanted a wife who enjoyed being at home with the children. That's what you've got. I love your kids so much, and now we have one more. This is a good thing!'

He took a deep, sharp breath, then dropped my hand, standing so suddenly I fell backward. He cleared his throat. 'You should get yourself tested for STDs. To protect the baby.'

'What?' I shook my head, feeling slow and stupid. Scrambling to my feet, I grabbed hold of his wrist. 'Are you trying to tell me you've been with another woman?'

He gave a short nod, and I felt my heart turn icy in my chest, my hands beginning to tremble.

'Is it Carrie? I knew you still had feelings for her! You told me she wasn't a good wife – that you hated her!'

'It's not Carrie. I bloody wish it *had* been. I never should have walked out on her.'

'But you said—'

'I said a lot of things. I was caught up in a fantasy. But I regretted leaving her the moment I moved in with you. I wanted to make you and me work, to show Carrie that I hadn't thrown away our marriage for something meaningless, so I stuck it out, proposed even. But do you *really* think a man like me could be happy with a woman like you? You have no drive, Leah. No ambition. It's fucking boring coming home to hear what new baked thing you've made, what cleaning product you're trying out. It hurts my brain. You're everything I thought I wanted, but the reality is, I'd pick Carrie a thousand times over before I chose you.'

I stepped back, stunned. 'Is that what you think of me?' I asked softly.

He looked me in the eye, sneering. 'You're a robot. A Stepford wife. And you're too young for me. You've not had time to develop into who you are yet. Maybe one day you'll become someone interesting. But now you've gone and got yourself pregnant, I doubt it.'

'You're disgusting.' The words came as a whisper, and I realised, despite the shock, there was no chance of me crying. I was too angry at hearing what the man I loved really thought of me. I *wasn't* that woman. I had dreams. Hopes. Yes, I wanted to raise children and take care of a home, but that didn't mean I was nothing. Jimmy had never in his life had to take care of himself, cook his own meals, do his own laundry. Did he think it happened magically? I'd love to see him cope with the hundreds of tasks I took off his plate day in, day out. He'd crumble without someone to take care of him.

I swallowed, straightening my spine, my hands resting protectively on my belly as if I could shield my child from his vitriol. 'If it wasn't Carrie, who was it?' I asked, needing to know everything now that the gates had opened. I wanted every detail. Something to hold on to if I ever felt myself getting nostalgic for what we might have had.

'It was a woman called Shannon. You don't know her.'

I sucked in a breath. 'Blonde hair. Petite. Pretty.'

He frowned, raising an eyebrow.

'She came here.' I laughed bitterly, replaying her visit in my head, the sweet innocence she'd presented herself with. She'd been so convincing. Asking to see Jimmy when she had to have known he wouldn't be here. How calculating she was. I shook my head in disbelief. 'She tried to warn me that Carrie was a danger to the children. That she might be hiding Ava.'

Jimmy's mouth dropped open. 'She was *here*?'

I nodded, feeling sick that I'd sat across the table from the woman who was sleeping with my husband. Offered her coffee and biscuits.

He sighed. 'It doesn't matter. It's over now.'

I closed my eyes, remembering. 'She mentioned something as she left,' I said softly. 'That she knew how hard it was to have a child missing. And that she and her husband had recently had a baby, so she knew what a mother's love felt like.'

He folded his arms, his eyes turning sad. For a moment, he was silent; then, as if to himself, he said, 'She was deranged. She let me think she was something quite different from the reality. Shannon was the one who took Ava. She thought she could replicate something she'd lost...' He looked up at me. 'And having heard your story about your dad, I get the feeling you're trying to do the very same thing with me and this baby.' He pointed to the scan photo on the floor.

'How long did you wait before you went looking for someone new?' I asked. 'We've only been living together six months, and we started seeing each other three months before that. It's still so new. How did you even have time?'

He looked at his feet, and I was relieved to see a flash of shame in his expression. 'She came up to me in a bar a few weeks after we moved in here.'

'A few weeks. Just after you asked me to marry you then,' I said flatly.

'I knew this was never going to last,' he said, gesturing

between the two of us. 'And I fell for her. Hard. Clearly, it was a mistake, given what happened.'

I stared at him, seeing the pain in his eyes, trying not to let it hurt that he was so obviously heartbroken over the end of his relationship with this other woman when he obviously felt nothing for me. How had I let myself fall for his lies? Hope that we might have something real, something that might stand the test of time?

He gave a sigh, looking exhausted and broken. 'Look, I'm sorry, Leah, but this isn't going to be the happy ending you hoped for. I think you should move out. And maybe you want to consider a termination. A fresh start.'

A smile spread across my face as I looked him dead in the eye. 'Oh, I'm not going anywhere,' I said, my voice firm and brave. 'I'm *not* my mother. I never let myself rely on you for my safety. You'll remember my name is on the lease right alongside yours? You don't have the power to kick me out. You think I'm some weak, pathetic little girl who needs your permission to have this baby? Well, guess what? *You're* going to be the one to leave. And don't think I won't come after you for the child support you owe me. And if you don't want contact, that's fine by me. This baby will do perfectly well without a man like you in their life.'

I folded my arms, feeling the adrenaline pumping through me, making me feel stronger than ever. I could have everything I wanted. The home, the children. I just wouldn't have Jimmy. I might not have agreed with what my father did, may have despised him for abandoning me and my mother, but he *had* given me something – the gift of making my own choices. He'd cut us off financially and emotionally from the moment he was sentenced, and that had unlocked a sense of grit and determination in me that my mother had never been capable of herself. And then, on my eighteenth birthday, a letter had arrived from him, accompanied by the details of a bank account he'd opened on the day I was born. A trust fund. Financial freedom that meant I would never become my mother. I didn't need Jimmy to fulfil my dreams. I could do whatever I wanted.

I hadn't questioned where the money had come from. I had accepted it as payment for the loss of the family I'd needed during my teen years. Compensation, if you will.

'I don't need your permission, Jimmy,' I repeated. 'And now I think it's time you got the fuck out of my house.'

He stared at me, shock wiping his expression clean; then, defeated, he nodded slowly and turned away.

As I watched him go, I realised there was only one person I needed to talk to now. And that was Carrie.

EPILOGUE

CARRIE

Six months later

'Let me carry that, Mum,' Tommy said, taking the heavy picnic basket from me and heaving it onto his shoulder. Over the past six months, since the terrifying week when we thought we'd lost Ava, my now thirteen-year-old son had changed from a sullen, sulky child into a responsible and helpful boy who talked to me daily about his hopes, his dreams, his fears even. We were closer now than we'd ever been, and the relationship we shared meant the world to me.

'Thanks, darling,' I said, smiling as he crossed the little car park, heading for the fields beyond. There was a ruin there of an old watchtower, and the children loved to play in it, pretending it was their castle and that this was their land. The weather was beautiful for October, and I planned to make the most of it. I hadn't been able to face going back to the beach since Ava had been found – couldn't stand them being close to the sea, despite the fact that she'd never been in danger of drowning. Too many traumatic memories.

I hitched Ava onto my hip now, kissing her for the

hundredth time that day. Maisy's hand slipped into mine now that Tommy had freed it up, and she smiled at me. Out of all the children, it had taken her the longest to let go of what had happened, and I couldn't blame her. For the first few months, she had awoken every night, screaming that Shannon was in the house, coming to hurt her and take her baby sister. It had broken my heart to see her so frightened and not know how to fix it.

Shannon had been sent straight back to the secure mental hospital she'd only recently been discharged from, and though she was still awaiting trial for the kidnapping of my daughter, I was relieved at the knowledge that she was locked up where she couldn't harm our family any more.

I'd weighed up whether I should share this bit of information with Maisy, and in the end, deciding it couldn't make the situation any worse, I'd laid out the newspapers on the kitchen table, the headlines declaring: *Baby-snatcher locked up!* and *Deranged friend who stole toddler behind bars*. They were sensationalist and didn't sum up the reality – that Shannon was severely mentally unwell and was being given a comprehensive regime of medication and therapy, though I doubted it would do much good after her previous treatment had clearly failed. But seeing it in print had helped Maisy to realise she wasn't coming back. The photographs of Shannon in handcuffs on the court steps, the descriptions of the unbreakable security system she was being kept behind had made a world of difference. And after reading the articles, the nightmares had finally stopped.

Maisy squeezed my fingers now, then gave a squeal. 'She's here! Look!' She dropped my hand and took off across the field towards the watchtower, where Tommy was laying out the picnic blanket with the help of the one woman I never thought I could allow into my life.

Leah heard Maisy coming and turned, rushing forward and scooping her up into a hug, holding her tight against her low, round belly. She looked radiant, and I couldn't help but smile. It was funny to remember how indignant I'd been when she'd called me the night after Ava came home. How furious I'd felt that she'd pushed Maisy to keep a secret – though at the time, I'd had no idea what it was.

She'd explained everything – that she was pregnant, that she'd kicked Jimmy out, that she knew she had been selfish in having an affair with a married man, and how sorry she was for hurting me. And how Jimmy had done the very same thing to her – their engagement had been nothing but a false promise to help him save face.

I, in turn, had been cold, telling her that it didn't matter now. That Jimmy was no longer anything other than the father of my children as far as I was concerned – I didn't love him, didn't want him back. I'd been winding down, ready to end the call and get back to the children, when she'd told me she couldn't stand the idea of never seeing them again. That she loved them, and she knew she had no rights, none whatsoever, but would I please let her keep in touch with them.

I'd wanted to say no. To punish her for what she'd done to my family, and to finally take the opportunity to have my children back to myself, never having to hand them over to her again. But something had seeped into my mind, making me feel, I don't know, pity for what Jimmy had put her through. Empathy maybe? Or could it have been gratitude for the fact that even though I'd hated it, my children had been taken care of, loved even, by her when their father had been too busy satisfying his own desires to be there for them.

In the end, I'd told her that I would ask the children and we would do whatever they wanted. I hadn't expected them to agree to it. Hadn't realised quite how close they'd grown to Leah. I'd pasted on a smile as we'd sat around the dinner table and they'd insisted that they wanted her in their lives. I tried not to be hurt by how emphatic they were about it. But despite my reservations, I didn't want to damage my fragile new beginning with Tommy, nor to refuse anything Maisy asked of me while she was still so broken by her ordeal.

I'd arranged meet-ups at the park, in the woods, the countryside, unwilling to have the children apart from me since Jimmy was still taking them on a weekly basis – I didn't want to lose out on any precious time with them. I'd endured her company for their sakes. But as the months had gone on, it had become easier, and to my surprise – and hers too – we'd formed a deep friendship, despite my misgivings.

She was incredible with the children, and they clearly adored her, and that made her hard to hate. And they were excited that they'd be having a new half-brother soon. She'd confided in me the things Jimmy had told her about me, the stories twisted to make me look like the bad guy, an unloving parent, and though I knew I had my faults, had made bad choices, he'd failed to balance it with any of the good parts of my character. She'd voiced surprise, having spent time with us, at how much I cared for the children, how good a mother I was, and I'd felt seen, appreciated – something Jimmy had never been able to do for me.

She lowered Maisy to the ground now, approaching me with her arms wide.

'Hi,' I said, hugging her.

'Hello.' She squeezed me tight, then kissed Ava on the cheek, stroking her hair affectionately, before stepping back and lowering herself with some difficulty onto the blanket.

'I should have brought a deckchair for you,' I said. 'I forgot how hard it is getting up and down at this stage.'

'Oh, it's good for me. The physio said I should try and maintain as much movement as possible so I don't get stiff joints. And in the next couple of weeks, I'll be able to tie my own shoes again.' She winked, nodding at her Crocs as she stretched out her legs.

'What luxury!' I teased, letting Ava down so she could run across the grass.

I saw Leah's eyes following her, and sighed, trying to breathe away the anxiety. I had to let her play, to be with her siblings, but it was hard not to panic about it. Leah was probably the one person, aside from Jimmy, who understood, and who watched her with the same level of supervision as me. It was nice to have someone to tag-team with.

'So, did you get things finalised with the finances?' I asked, taking a Tupperware container full of ripe peaches from the basket and opening the lid. She reached forward, taking one and biting into the juicy flesh.

'Yep.' She nodded. 'Thankfully Jimmy's over his tantrum about me keeping the baby, and he's not going to put me through the stress of going to court for child support. I don't think he fancied the hassle. He's set up a monthly payment, and the first one cleared yesterday. To cover his share of baby supplies and furniture, apparently,' she added, her mouth full.

'Well, that's one thing off the list.'

She nodded. 'His new girlfriend wasn't best pleased about it, I hear.'

'The paralegal?'

'No, didn't I tell you? *She's* long gone. This new one is a student. She's *eighteen*.'

I grimaced. 'Five years older than Tommy. Really?'

'Apparently she's very ambitious.'

We both broke into peals of laughter, remembering Jimmy's accusation that Leah had no dreams. I hoped the girl would soon see sense and walk away.

'He'll never change,' I said, watching Ava clamber up a tiny verge, shouting to Maisy that she was the lord of this castle, followed by something about knights and horses that I was sure she'd picked up from Tommy.

'Nope,' Leah agreed. 'Anyway, enough about your

scoundrel of an ex-husband.' She flashed me a grin, which I returned. 'Tell me about the disciplinary hearing. What happened? Did they reach a conclusion?'

I nodded, my tone turning serious as I replied. 'I'm going to be allowed to stay on. They said that obviously I did the wrong thing in not speaking up at the time, but that ultimately it was the nurse's fault for misunderstanding my instructions and for taking it upon herself to administer the medication, despite knowing that she wasn't signed off to do it.'

'Wow... so you're in the clear?'

I shrugged. It had been hard to hear that the guilt I'd carried for such a huge part of my life was seen by my supervisors as a minor blip. That if I'd told the truth initially, I might have saved myself years of self-hatred and guilt for my undeserved enjoyment of my own family. I might have been a more present mother, not always on the lookout for a way to punish myself and get away from the things I believed I didn't deserve. It was sickening to realise the destructive power of a few small lies. But I had cleared my conscience now. And though I could never bring Catherine back, never undo the hurt I'd caused Shannon, I had saved many lives in the years that followed that terrible mistake. I had done a lot of good. I hoped that counted for something. Balanced the scales a little.

Leah reached out, squeezing my hand. 'I'm relieved for you, Carrie. I know what it means to you to be able to keep helping your patients. Your colleagues obviously know how important you are to the hospital too.'

'Thanks,' I whispered, then pulled back my hand. 'Ugh! You're sticky!'

She laughed, tossing the peach stone into a nearby bush and wiping her palm on her skirt.

Maisy, spotting the food laid out on the blanket, shouted to her brother, and the two of them rushed back across the narrow stretch of grass, Ava toddling after them as fast as she could manage. The older two collapsed, laughing, as they talked back and forth about what to start with, and how many chocolate fingers they were each allowed, but Ava paused, smiled at me, then walked across the blanket and lowered herself into Leah's lap, leaning her head back against her chest and stroking her chubby hand up and down Leah's bump, almost absently, her gaze trained on her siblings.

Leah's eyes widened, staring across the blanket to me, and I could see how hard she was trying to keep her emotions in check. 'That's the first time she's done that,' she said softly. 'The first time she's ever come to me of her own volition.'

I smiled, realising I felt no jolt of jealousy, no desire to pluck my child from Leah's arms and have her all to myself. All my married life, I'd wanted the traditional happy family I never got to have growing up. The rich, handsome husband. The beautiful, well-mannered children. The picture-perfect life with the fancy house and enviable career. I'd wanted it all – the list we were supposed to start ticking off from the moment we left school to prove we were successful. To show I could do better than my parents. And I'd nearly killed myself trying to pretend I had it, to the world – to myself.

Now, I felt differently. I didn't care about working my way through a stream of rules I'd had no say in creating. I didn't have to prove I was worthy of existing. Didn't need the world to validate me, tell me I was good enough. I had something more important. I'd traded my cheating, selfish arse of a husband for the first real friend I'd ever known. And watching her with my children made me realise that in letting go of the life I thought I was supposed to have, I'd gained something so much more worthwhile. Someone who knew all my secrets and still liked me – despite my flaws. A person I could trust, and who loved my children like they were her own.

I'd never held on to a friend in my entire life. My mother had set me on a path of loneliness from the very start, telling me

I didn't deserve to be here, that I was selfish to try and form friendships when I'd ruined her life, her marriage. I'd shut myself off from other children growing up, accepted the meagre rations Jimmy had thrown my way because I was sure that, with the exception of my children, it was the best I was going to get in terms of another human connection. I'd compromised so much out of desperation for someone to accept me for who I was. And here, with the woman who'd stolen my dream life, that had finally happened.

And that, I smiled, picking up a chocolate finger and crunching it between my teeth, was better than anything I could have hoped for.

A LETTER FROM SAM

I want to say a huge thank you for choosing to read *One Big Happy Family*. If you enjoyed it, and want to keep up to date with all my latest releases, just sign up at the following link. Your email address will never be shared, and you can unsubscribe at any time.

www.bookouture.com/sam-vickery

I hope you enjoyed reading *One Big Happy Family* as much as I enjoyed writing it. If you did, I would be very grateful if you could leave a review. I'd love to hear what you think, and it makes such a difference in helping new readers to discover one of my books for the first time.

I always welcome hearing from my readers – you can get in touch at www.samvickery.com, or find me on my Facebook page.

Until the next time,

Sam

www.samvickery.com

facebook.com/SamVickeryWrites

ACKNOWLEDGEMENTS

Thank you so much to everyone who has had a hand in the creation of this book. The wonderful team at Bookouture are always so incredible to work with, and I'm so grateful for all that you do. To my editor, Jennifer Hunt, who helped me figure out the many issues I encountered whilst writing this story and gave me focus when I needed it, thank you. As always, I have loved working with you!

To my wonderful team of editors and proofreaders, Jane Selley, Lauren Finger and Laura Kincaid, thank you! Massive thanks to my publicist, Sarah Hardy, for everything you do in the run-up to publication, organising book tours and helping new readers discover my stories! And thanks to my cover designer, Aaron Munday, for creating the perfect cover for this story. It's gorgeous!

To my wonderful readers, I hope you've enjoyed this story. Thank you for all your support. I am truly grateful for you!

And finally, to my wonderful family, Jed, Viggo, Aurora and Caspian. You are my constant inspiration, and I love you beyond words.

PUBLISHING TEAM

Turning a manuscript into a book requires the
efforts of many people. The publishing team at
Bookouture would like to acknowledge everyone
who contributed to this publication.

Commercial
Lauren Morrissette
Hannah Richmond
Imogen Allport

Cover design
Aaron Munday

Data and analysis
Mark Alder
Mohamed Bussuri

Editorial
Jennifer Hunt
Lizzie Brien

Copyeditor
Jane Selley

Proofreader
Laura Kincaid

Marketing
Alex Crow
Melanie Price
Occy Carr
Ciara Rosney
Martyna Młynarska

Operations and distribution
Marina Valles
Stephanie Straub
Joe Morris

Production
Hannah Snetsinger
Mandy Kullar
Ria Clare
Nadia Michael

Publicity
Kim Nash
Noelle Holten
Jess Readett
Sarah Hardy

Rights and contracts
Peta Nightingale
Richard King
Saidah Graham